Unofficially Yours

Unofficially Yours

Saga of Friends Who Fell in Love

AYUSHI JAIN

PARTRIDGE

A Penguin Random House Company

To order additional copies of this book, contact
Partridge India
000 800 10062 62
orders.india@partridgepublishing.com

www.partridgepublishing.com/india

Table of Contents

Acknowledgement

This book is one of my biggest dreams. I never knew that I will be able to write it. Therefore to say that this is just my book will be untrue. There are few people who helped and encouraged me to make my dream come true.

First of all I would like to thank my senior, my best friend and my best advisor - Nikunj Saxena. As this saga of love and friendship is narrated by a boy called 'RV', Nikunj sir helped me to step in a boy's shoe, making me analyze how a boy thinks and reacts to different situations. His honest feedback, advises and criticism helped me to complete this book successfully.

Editing being a major challenge, he too had sleepless nights and worked along with me to bring out this product at its best.

Special thanks to Anurag Shekhar (bhaiya) for proof-reading.

I would like to thank my parents Mr. Arun Kumar Jain and Mrs. Suman Jain. They have always supported me whenever I tried to do anything out of the box.

My sister Arushi Jain, took good care of me when I got myself completely indulged in writing the book.

I would like to thank Saumy Nagayach Sir for clicking perfect pictures of my sketches.

Last but not the least- my friends, my college group. This was not possible without them. Unknowingly they created scenarios and made it easy for me to write.

My Extended thanks to Partridge India, my PSA – Mary Oxley for guiding throughout the publishing procedure.

Special thanks to MS-word for catching up my spelling mistakes and grammatical mistakes.

Recipe for a perfect love

Sky without sun is incomplete,

Google without search is incomplete,

Facebook without Display Picture is incomplete,

YouTube without video is incomplete,

Similarly Life without Friendship is incomplete.

Make friends, true friends for life

One of them is your best friend, in ocean of friendship go for a dive

Add a little tint of love in your friendship and then see the magic

Feel the love and its music.

Birds seems to sing, tree seems to talk

With your that friend partner go for a lifelong walk

Farewell

26th April 2011/ Tuesday/6:00 PM

Cognizance Institute of Engineering Bhopal,

All the upcoming engineers were seated in the closed auditorium, boys dressed in formal suits and girls in saree. Everyone was asked to sit according to their specialization; CS and IT occupied the front seats, followed by EC, EX and other branches. The auditorium was fully occupied with final year students and their clamor.

Entire College was decked up for the farewell of 2007-2011 Engineering Batch. The room was clattered with students discussion, their mischiefs to backlogs and placements. Selfie fever was all around, few girls were trying to manage their saree, couple of them giggling and making fun of others. All hullabaloo settled down as our Principal and management entered the Auditorium.

Dean of the college Mr. Mayank Badkul started with the formal speech and thanked us for being the most captivating and amusing batch, then came Mr. Dheeraj Rawal, Managing Director of the college. I eagerly waited for the Principal's speech "Mr. Venkateshwar Ramu". He is a nice and genuine man, short heighted with a belly, short curly hairs, chubby cheeks, beneath his nose were his small moustache, he looked like a perfect replica of Santa in winters when he wore his red sweater. He had worked on us to make us perfect engineers, he knew all his students by their names, he imbibed the mantra 'Run behind knowledge and success will run behind you' in all of us. All his punishments, bunking classes, teachings and lectures will be missed.

After management was done with their 'Thank you' notes, Mr. 'Venkateshwar Ramu' came on the dais. Before he could start with his speech, entire auditorium resonated with huge round of applause. He gave a warm smile and started: 'It's finally here' he said spreading his arms.

'It's finally here, the moment of truth.' He said and paused for a moment. There was pin drop silence in the auditorium. He continued 'the stepping stone to the real world. This is what we've been preparing you for, from last 4 years. Through the good, bad, silly, fun and change, learning was both ways, we taught you discipline, gave you knowledge and you taught us how to be enthusiastic and have fun. It's finally time for you to step out into the bright light and grab the ticket to freedom. Now on, you will be responsible citizens, making decisions on your own. The piece of paper- your degree would remind you forever that I've accomplished something. Most of all it is the time to pause and look back at the journey of your wonderful 4 years and spend time with all your classmates, teachers, and juniors who were the part of your beautiful journey. All the best for your future, may you all shine high in the sky. College is going to miss you all'.

His speech made us all emotional. All the students stood up and applauded. We too are going to miss our college days.

After the batch photograph, we were asked to move to the open auditorium. As we entered the gate, dhol started and we were welcomed in the perfect Indian traditional way. Few beautiful junior girls dressed in salwar kameez, holding decorated plates applied "kumkum teeka" on our forehead and few others showered rose petals on us. We were given mementos and titles. Entire arrangement made us all feel very special.

It was around 7:30 now, Sun sank lower in the sky, the light of day draining away, giving way to the velvety dark of night, and the event started. Stage was on fire with the tapping feet of juniors, dancing on Bollywood item numbers.

Atul, my school junior, who was now my college junior too, presented a video titled '4 year journey – Batch 2007-2011'. Glimpse of our engineering voyage made few of the girls cry, friends hugged each other and made promises to be in touch forever. We are so going to miss this life.

10:00 PM college party got over and our gang party started. My college gang included: Nikunj, Prateek, Tarun, Sid, Arpit, Priya, Aditi, Neha and Me(Rajveer). We together were called as Gyaanis, as each one of us had lots of gyaan (knowledge) to shower on others.

Tarun: *Nick name: Tiddi.* He was named as Tiddi because of his lean structure. One of the best dancers of college, short heighted, flexible body, dark complexion, and his talks easily attracts people towards him.

Prateek: *Nick name:* Pajju. Favorite sir among the junior girls, fair, heavy built, materialistic, always talks about brands, flaunts about his things, show off guy.

Nikunj: *Nick name:* NIK also known as call center as he is always on call. With whom? Nobody knows, secret keeper, tall, dark, footballer.

Saurabh: *Nick name:* SID, also known as Maggie because his hairs looks like it, topper of the batch, favorite of teachers and all companies wanted him but he opted for further studies in US.

Arpit: *Nick Name:* Choudha (14) as this is his surname; the rich one in our group, his father owned 4 petrol pumps and 3 Honda showrooms.

Priya: fair, short heighted, chubby, with dimple on her left cheek, bubbly, she used to cry after every exam, saying that she will fail but when results are out, at times, only she and Saurabh used to be in the passing list.

Aditi: Tall, little dark in complexion, lean, long hairs, Gossip Queen; she can talk for 12 hours non-stop.

Neha: short hairs, lean, height 5'2", loves dancing.

Our friendship made engineering life memorable. Girls did not join the after farewell party as Neha stayed in hostel where entry for girls was restricted till 11:00PM. Aditi and Priya stay with their family, they have their own terms and conditions of coming back home on time. So tonight it's just the boys, we picked our bikes and reached our destination.

Bhopal also called as the city of lakes, capital of MP and one of the most beautiful cities, especially new Bhopal, lots of green trees, dams, lakes, and wild life century. We decided to head towards the upper lake "our Adda" where we used to chill-out during our college days.

We reached at the top of the hill. It is quite here, the sounds of insects are almost loud, it is shady dark and cool even during April. As we look down to the end of the trees, it opens up into a lake, beautiful Lake of Bhopal. The lake seems like a black void, mirroring the dazzling assemblage of the glittering stars. The faint wind brushed against the water's surface, the ripples ruffled the stillness of the surface, and shattered the reflection of the harbor.

'What a beautiful place this is!' Sid said, spreading his arms, feeling the cold breeze.

Sid stood on the partition separating road and the valley, Arpit lay on his bike, Tiddi, Nik and me made our-selves comfortable sitting on the road. Best part of this place is 'It is isolated and no one visit it during late hours'

'Yes indeed it is beautiful' Tiddi said, taking a deep breath, resting his hands on the road and gazing stars

'You guys are so lucky, you will be staying together even after the final semester exams, you big asses got placed in the same firm' Sid grumbled.

He continued 'I will be the one away from all, doing my masters from US where nobody knows me and I don't know anyone'

Tiddi, Pajju, Aditi, Priya, Neha Nik and I got placed in ZT technologies, Pune

Lying on bike with hands folded, eyes closed Arpit said 'At least you have the opportunity to enjoy college life again, I will be stuck taking care of my family business, handling petrol pumps, calculating daily profit and loss'.

'Why don't you join any IT firm for the time being? When you are bored you can join your family business' Nik suggested

'I am forced to follow my family legacy. Dad wants me to join the next day Final semester exams get over' he replied

'Bhai har month thoda petrol hi bhijwa diya karna' Pajju said and laughed out loud, everyone joined in his laughter.

'Life is going to be so different from now on' Tiddi said

'Yes, no sessional, no need to ask for pocket money, no exams, no punishments, no results. We will be earning, we can buy whatever we want whenever we want. Life will be awesome' Pajju said. Pajju always hated exams; all he loved was buying shoes, watches and expensive clothes.

'Agreed! No sessional, No exams, no punishments, no results, we will not be asking for pocket money too, but now on there will be no bunks, no Aunty ki tapri ki chai. We will be responsible for our decisions; we will be away from our parents. To get a one day leave we will have to take approvals from managers' Nik said cracking his knuckles.

'Hmm' Pajju nodded

'Hey guys, Gyaanis will still be together. We all are placed in same firm' Tiddi said happily, clapping like a kid.

'Ahem ahem' Sid cleared his throat, indicating he will not be there

Tiddi winked and indicated not to respond on Sid's reaction.

He continued 'So what we will do is; we will take 2 flats on rent in the same society, one for girls and another for boys. We can have dinner together every day. Waooo it will be awesome'

'Ahem Ahem' this time it was Arpit to make clearing throat sound indicating he too is not included in this plan.

Tiddi, me and Pajju intentionally ignored him too

'Yes, you are actually right, we can do this. This will be awesome. We will be staying together. What could be better than this? Gyaanis, new city, exploring places, planning trips, Pubs, gaming, night rides. Sounds cool!' Nik said

'Ahem- Ahem- Ahem- Ahem' Arpit and Sid made the noise again, this time louder.

'Hey, we have lot many hill stations near Pune – Lonavala, khandala, Lavasa, Mahabaleshwar, panchgani, Matheran and many more. Monsoon we can plan trips to these places' I added

Frustrated from our talks Arpit threw empty bottle on me and Sid kicked Tiddi.

'Oye, what happed to these two? Why are they angry' Tiddi said to tease them more.

'Arey, we forgot, these two poor fellows will not be there with us na' Pajju said and burst into laughter

I stood up and patted Sid's back 'Koi na, hota hai hota hai'

'And by the way we are not going to miss you' Tiddi said in a British accent.

Arpit and Sid looked at each other, ran towards Tiddi and started kicking him, I and Pajju joined them.

Arpit emptied 2 water bottles on him, Tiddi stood up.

'You morons' he moaned touching his back.

'Mr. Arpit Choudha you are gone', he said and ran towards him, rest of us again joined.

I and Pajju held Arpit's hand; Tiddi and Sid got hold of his legs, raised him up and then down, kicked him.

We shouted on top of our voices and finally hugged. We will remain friends forever.

$\mathcal{P}une$

My train is about to reach Pune, million thoughts racing through my head. Moving to a new city made me feel homesick, I missed my parents, felt nostalgic, but I was excited too, excited because I love new beginnings, rush of unknown exploration, new apartment, new job, a handful of college friends with whom I will share an apartment.. Everything seems so fresh and new like every day is going to be a big adventure.

I awaited this adventure, as now I'll get to know the value of money and freedom; I never knew I would have mixed feelings while starting this new phase of life. My parents gave me lots of counselling before I boarded the train. My mom told me to stick to my values and principles and dad advised to live a simple satisfactory life.

While I was in my thoughts, Pune station arrived, I heard someone calling my name "Rajveer".

2 army jawans wearing a camouflage pattern dress were looking for me.

'Are you searching for Rajveer Singh?' I asked one of them.

He nodded

'Hi, I am Rajveer'

'Hello Sir, Lt General Ranjeet Singh has sent us to receive you' he said.

7

My mamaji has served Indian Army for 20 years. Lt General Ranjeet Singh, one of the senior members of Indian army. He appointed 2 Jawans to drop me home as the city was new to me, they helped me pick up the luggage, and we got down the train.

The station was crowded with all sorts of passengers. Everyone seems to be in a hurry. Some Passengers were waiting eagerly for the arrival of the train. Some were sitting on benches and smoking or reading newspaper. Few were pacing up and down the platform. Vendors were having a busy time. There was rush at tea-stalls. The coolies were running here and there shouting 'Pune chala, Pune chala'.

'We are in Pune right? I asked one of the jawans

'Yes Sir' he replied

'Call me Rajveer'

'Yes Rajveer'

'Then why people here are shouting, Pune chala, Pune chala?'

'Sir in Marathi 'Pune chala' means move ahead' He replied and laughed

Ohhh, I need to learn Marathi, pretty quickly then' I winked

'It's good if you learn sir' living will be easy in Maharashtra then'

Crossing the crowd, somehow we managed to come out of the station, army colored gypsy was waiting for us, I grabbed the front seat and both the jawans made themselves comfortable at the back ones. I inquired the driver- how much time it will take for us to reach Kharadi- Fortune Green Society

'It will take around half an hour sir, depends on traffic, Kharadi is 12kms from here' driver answered.

I got my joining date as 22 September 2011 whereas Pajju, Tiddi and Nik had already joined on 20th September; they had already searched for our accommodation near the office. I made a quick call to my mom confirming that I have reached safely and then another call to Pajju informing that I will be reaching in about 25 minutes. He asked me to come as soon as possible else they will be late to office.

As we entered the society's gate I saw 4 gentlemen dressed in formals, ironed shirts- trousers, tie, leather belts, polished shoes, company ID card hanging down the neck and all carrying a black bag with Company's logo on it. I told the driver to stop. Those were my buddies; I looked at them and had a great laugh.

'Hahaha so my kids are going to school?' I teased them

'Yes and you will be taking admission in same school tomorrow' NIK replied.

'We are 4 days senior to you, respect us' Tiddi said proudly

'Sir, 2 days senior, 1ˢᵗ go and learn nursery Mathematics' I replied making fun of Tiddi.

'Areee guys, save this dogfight for later today, as of now we are getting late to office' Pajju said

'Take the keys RV, big one is for opening the main door and shorter one is for balcony, flat number is B5-404' Nik said.

Pajju guided me the direction; Jawans helped me in unloading the luggage. We had to make the arduous climb via stairs till 4th floor as lifts were not working due to power outage. We placed luggage in the living room.

I thanked Jawans for all their help, and offered them refreshments. After relaxing for few minutes they left.

'Janab koi bhi dikkat ho to call kijiyega, hum aa jayenge' one of them said while waving good bye to me.

I walked into the apartment, exploring rooms and finding which one's the best. It's a 3BHK, spacious apartment, with all the rooms attached to a passage. I could see the half open bags of my flat mates, giving clear indication that they have decided who is going to stay in which room and with whom.

I took a bath, as there is nothing much to do, no TV, no newspapers, home alone, and all friends busy, My hunger pangs started making their own symphony in the stomach, I decided to go out for lunch and explore nearby places.

At 5 Nik called me 'Dude, where are you? We are home, standing outside, keys are with you'

'I will be back in few minutes, be there, was buying day-to-day things'.

On returning I saw the school boys were sitting on stairs, all tired. I pulled out the keys and opened the door. Everyone rushed in, pushing me back.

'How was the day at work? How's the office? How are people in there?' I inquired.

'It is difficult to figure out all these things in just 2 days, day 1 was induction, they told us about the company, their clients and things' Nik replied

'As fresher we will have to go through 2 months of training, and then they will randomly assign us our streams: Java, oracle, .Net, testing, etc.' Pajju added.

'I hope I get JAVA development'- NIK said.

'But how can they assign any stream like this without knowing our interests?' I asked

'This is IT world sweetheart, you have to be open for anything that comes your way, you won't be having an option of saying NO' - Tiddi replied

'I don't want to be a developer, I am scared of coding' - Pajju exclaimed.

'Same here' - Tiddi added.

'Let's see what's in our luck' I started unpacking my bag and took out homemade snacks, just the smell was enough and everybody came running to grab their bite, I tried saving few for me. Fighting, snatching, eating like hungry poor kids and within few minutes we were left with empty boxes.

Professional life started 5 days' work and 2 days of weekend fun, life is good here; Earning, spending, exploring. Best part is that I am with my old friends, my college besties who know me inside out; there was no place for loneliness.

As planned Neha, Aditi and Priya took an apartment in the same society, B5-404 Boy's place and B4-404 girls.

We can wave hands to each other through our windows.

Everyone in the group shared the status Single and to have fun blast and avoid groupings within a group we made a "RULE": "No Couples in the group"

Boys are allowed bird watching outside the group, but within the group no one is allowed to flirt with one another. It has to be pure friendship and everyone has to follow the RULE.

Starting few days of the new job made us feel like free birds, we earned for ourselves, we can do whatever we want, no one is here to raise a question, but then as days and months passed, we realized that we are not free birds. We are 'IT engineers' who are strapped with the ID card hanging down their neck, just like a pet strapped with a chain. I had heard people complaining, how life in IT sucks, we realized it today. Every day a new task is assigned which is to be completed anyhow by the end of the day, sometimes it takes half day to understand what exactly the task is, how is it possible to complete by EOD and if it is not complete, then stretch and work, drop a mail to senior management. Stringent time lines, work pressure, Instead of 8hr daily shift we do 11hrs, as work assigned is never completed on time and then they have late night meetings. The employee realizes, it's the most integral part of the company and the company cannot run without it a single day when they approach managers for leaves. At times managers say that sick leave should also be informed prior. I mean how can that be possible?

Here we are expected to make a space shuttle with just a card-board sheet and glue (bare minimum resources). Timesheets, time lines, tasks, billing hours, work pressure, issues in production, client expectations, appraisals, running behind on-site opportunities, extra working hours, struggle for leaves, hike tensions, competition.....

Aaaahhhhhhhhhhh and being away from home adds ghee to frustration. Employees keep counting Monday to Friday and then again Monday to Friday. They keep complaining about something or the other. No one here is satisfied.

The only reason for me to live happily in this corporate world is "Gyaanis", my small family, my friends. Every day we used to have our meals together no matter what. Our meal times are fixed. 5 days of rigorous work and then fun filled weekends- movies, trips, planning, talking, chatting, beating, laughing and what not. We too, like other IT employees kept counting Monday to Friday. We counted 52 Mondays till Friday and a year passed.

New Arrivals

22nd September 2012/ Saturday/ 11:00 AM.

Priya came running to our place. 'Guys, what's up with you all? Still sleeping?? It's 11 in the morning. Wake up you all lazy buggers' she shouted

Me, Tiddi and Pajju lay on the floor, sleeping like Kumbhkaran who had blessing of sleeping for 6 months continuously and no noise, drums anything can wake him up. Priya kicked us, we hardly moved.

'Can someone please accompany me? Arohi is about to reach Pune, she is new to the city and carrying lots of luggage with her. She will not be able to pick it up all alone. Also, she is not acquainted with the places here' She said and tried to bring us in senses.

AROHI: Our college junior, Priya' s younger sister, artist, topper of 2012 batch, pretty, fair, straight hairs, sweet voice, Chinese beautiful eyes, she anchored almost all our college events. 1st time I noticed her was when she won around 7 awards in our college tech Fest - Erudition.

AROHI got placed in one of the firms in Pune. I considered her MISS ATTITUDE, as she had lots of it, according to me. Though I never got chance to interact with her in college.

Pajju and Tiddi were amongst her favorite Sirs.

Pajju **"Sir"** and Tiddi **"Sir"**.

"SIR", this was our college legacy. All the juniors have to greet their seniors by calling them SIR/ Ma'am.

Though the college was over, but legacy continued.

I admired her beauty, she was one of the most beautiful juniors in college and many seniors and her batch mates followed her, but she being sister of Priya, no one had the guts to approach her. One of the most talented girls in college who was known for her speaking skills, head of various student chapters, design head of the college and the topper of her batch. This amalgamation of all her talents and beauty made her the perfect one.

Listening about Arohi's arrival Pajju got up. Priya's kick bought Tiddi in senses too, they brushed their teeth and were all set to go, boys generally take less time to get ready when in hurry.

2 bikes and 3 people left to receive the new arrival. Nik and I got ready and reached B4 404- Girl's place for breakfast.

Aditi prepared Poha, Nik had bought samosas. Hungry stomachs waited for Priya, Pajju, Tiddi and Arohi to join us for breakfast, it was 1 PM, ideally it was time for lunch but then its weekend. Who cares?

I switched on the television. The girls were quite lucky as their owner provided them with 3 almirahs, 3 beds, fridge, sofa, and a television. All the almirah and beds were placed in their respective bedrooms, living room had a TV hung on the TV unit, mattress lay on the floor and a sofa set besides the balcony entrance. We all prefer sitting together on the mattress. NIK as usual, was on call. Talking to? God and he only know. World war 3 was 'ON' between Aditi, Neha and Me for the remote, I wanted to watch 'Football highlights', Neha wanted to watch 'Dil wale dulhaniya le jayenge' and Aditi was interested in watching 'Big Boss'.

Pushing and pulling each other's hair.

'RV, you dog. Leave the remote' Neha shouted and bit my hand.

Aditi scratched my other hand with her nails.

'Ahhh, you cats, biting and scratching' I shouted loosing grip of remote and Neha almost snatched it, pulling her hair I got the grip again and football highlights were on TV.

'If done with your cat-dog fight, let us arrange plates for breakfast?' Nik said disconnecting his call

Girls not interested in football gave me a nasty look, stood and placed breakfast plates on the floor beside mattress; Nik helped them in arranging the plates.

Doorbell rang!!

'RV can you please take a break from football and open the door?' Aditi shouted.

Bang bang!!

'Will someone open the door?' We could hear Priya shouting and banging the door

I switched off the TV and went to open the door.

Arohi

There, she was- AROHI, wearing black jeans, red top with a picture of Minnie mouse giving flying kisses. For a moment I thought those kisses were for me. She was carrying a laptop bag on her back, fossil watch on her hand and a sling bag (crossed way), her hair was straight on top and had cute wavy curls starting from her shoulder, she looked pretty as always like a delicate doll. Looking at her I got this strong desire to keep her protected, but then I remembered her attitude.

'Will you move on now? Can't you see we have luggage with us?' Priya roared and pushed me inside.

I came out of my thought process and smiled at myself. What the hell was I thinking? We have a "rule" to follow.

'Hi RV sir, how are you?' She asked me in her innocent voice

'I am good. How are you?'

'I am good too.' She replied

'So when is your joining?'

Heyyyyy AROHI is here. All came and hugged her and greeted her and obviously my question was ignored.

AROHI had a quick bath, changed her clothes and made herself comfortable in cyan blue pajamas and white color T-shirt.

She also joined us for breakfast.

I opened green and red chutneys, emptied them in 2 different glass bowls, passed on 1 Samosa to each, everybody helped themselves to fill their own Poha plates, All got their tummies full and the breakfast can be considered as lunch now, everyone adjusted and created space for themselves to lay down, watching "Jurassic park 1" on set Max.

'Most probably we will be staying in Baner' Priya announced

'What????' Neha questioned

'Mom had called in the morning; they have decided the place where we will reside now on, it's one BHK, sufficient for me and AROHI. She provided us with the broker's number, he will show us our new accommodation' Priya answered

'What do you mean by that? You are not going to stay here with us?' Aditi grumbled

'Arohi's office will be too far from here. She will have to travel approx. 3 hours daily' Priya answered

'What about your bus facilities Arohi?' Tiddi inquired

'They do provide bus facilities, but the distance is too much from here, Baner will be little close' AROHI explained

'I thought we are going to stay together' Neha murmured

'Every day travel, will be hectic for her' Priya explained

'This is not done yaar' Pajju complained.

'OK so here is a deal: weekdays you girls are allowed to stay there, but Friday you both will be coming directly to Kharadi from office and will be leaving back on Monday, so that we will have our group time together?' Nik suggested

'Yeahh that will be cool, as it is everyone will be busy on weekdays with their own daily tasks and shifts' Priya replied

'AROHI will you be getting office bus from Kharadi Monday morning?' I inquired

'Yes, but I will have to leave by around 7:30 in the morning to catch my bus, well that is all manageable' she answered.

Within few days of AROHI's arrival, her best friends, her batch mates and our juniors: Atul and Mini also joined. Atul shifted with us and Mini shifted with girls in Priya's room as she decided to shift Baner.

AROHI shared a good relationship with everyone in the group. She had something in common with everyone.

Priya obviously being her elder sister, they share everything.

Tiddi and she had their art in common, Prateek and she shared their career and business plans, Nik and she had their own college tech Fest or annual function talks.

Maybe I am a stranger to her because we do not have much in common, she doesn't like football. Maybe that's the reason we did not interact much during college days. Maybe that's the reason she is not open in front of me and might be this is the reason I considered her Miss attitude.

*   *   *

Arohi got involved in the group really well and I don't know why, but I got this strong desire to talk to her, to spend time with her and to know her better, maybe it's her charm I am attracted to or maybe I admire her as a human or because of the talent she possesses.

She gets along with anyone she speaks to, so innocent and down to earth. She doesn't talk much to strangers but once comfortable, she is a chatterbox.

Gyaanis gave a warm welcome to the new members of the group.

Weekend

26th October 2012/Friday/ 8:15 PM

My phone rang, number flashed, AROHI CALLING.....

'Hi RV sir, where are you?'

She sounded tensed

'I am at my place, tell me what happened?'

'Is Pajju sir home? I had been trying to call him, he said he will pick me up from the Pune fitness club, my bus dropped me here, he has not yet reached and not picking up my call too, I am new to the place, I am not sure about directions, could you please check with him once?'

'AROHI, Pajju left his phone at home today, that's the reason he is not answering your call' I replied

'Ohhh no, he is going to get lots of beating from me today, RV sir, can you please come to pick me up?'

'Sure I will be there in 7 mins'

'Ok, I am waiting'

I picked up my bike and reached Pune fitness in exact 7 mins. She was there waiting, a little irritated on Pajju of course.

She looked pretty in pink sleeveless shirt and black trouser; her pink bunny earrings looked cute.

'Waoo RV sir, you are quick, right on time'

Her compliment made me feel good and I patted myself for being punctual for the 1st time in my life.

'Well you know I am punctual, I do what I say, not like your Prateek sir' I winked

'Hehehe, good to know that, next time onwards, please you come to pick me up from my bus stop and let Prateek sir come back today, he is gone'

I am happy that I was able to make her laugh on my silly statement.

She sat behind me and I took a 'U' turn.

'RV sir, we never had much interaction during college na, you were like Mr. gayab kya?'

'May be because I considered you MISS ATTITUDE and that is the reason I never spoke to you' I tried to tease her

'OMG!! Are you Serious?' her mouth wide open

'You considered me MISS ATTITUDE?' She repeated

'Yes' I replied

'No, I am not' she tried to convince

'It's just that I do not talk to strangers, I am not comfortable and you were always busy with your football matches, so didn't got the chance to interact' she explained

I was happy that I am no more a stranger to her!

'Arey no need for this much explanation sweetie, I was just kidding'

She pinched me and smiled.

*　　*　　*

27th Oct 2012/ Saturday/ 10:30 PM

After dinner we decided to play our college time favorite game – Dumb Charades (guessing the movie)

Boy's Place:

Everyone tried to be comfortable in the living room, on 2 mattresses lying on the floor, both at a distance of around 1.5 feet from each other, providing passage for people to pass. 10 people, 2 single bed mattress. Nik, Arohi, Tiddi, Pajju and mini sat on one. Me, Aditi, Priya, Neha and Atul sat on another.

Mini stood up and explained the rules

Explaining the rules was our ritual ceremony for the game. We might have played this game for like 1000 times, but every time we play rules have to be repeated, it's like every time you visit a temple, you have to join your hands.

'Everyone listen carefully,

Thumbs up means Hollywood

Thumbs down means Bollywood

Cutting the word in half and then acting is allowed but No one is allowed to murmur… No lip movement. Any acting member found murmuring will be disqualified' Mini said

'Let's divide the teams' Neha screamed.

'Juniors in one team and seniors in other' Arohi decided

'But seniors are more, that won't be equal' Mini added

'Let's divide team according to our seating positions' Nik suggested Everyone agreed and teams were divided

Arohi announced:

Team 1:

RV, Aditi, Priya, Atul and Mini

Team 2:

Arohi, Nik, Pajju, Tiddi and Neha

'Team-1 Who will be the 1st to act?' Nik asked

'I am 1st, I am 1st.' Mini jumped out.

Neha murmured something into her ears,

Mini gave her a dirty look, asking 'how I am going to act this?'

'It's going to be vulgar :/'

Neha shrugged

Mini stood in front, taking her position and figuring out how to act counting something on her fingers. Her neck tilted onto left. This was the way she generally used to speak. Her face is never straight while speaking always tilted on one side.

She started

'Okay guys, here it goes' Mini said

'No speaking allowed' Arohi shouted

Okay, back to actions

Thumbs down

Priya – Bollywood

Mini showed her 1st finger

RV – 1 word

Mini paused for a while thinking how to act, she figured it out soon.

She looked up, pointed towards the ceiling.

People started guessing:

Priya – FAN?

Atul - terrace?

Mini showed a wrong sign by crossing her fingers

RV- Anything beyond that....

Mini- nodded

Priya- aasman...?

Mini – nodded

She moved her hands, suggesting something similar to this, try more

Tiddi – Aakash

AROHI hit Tiddi on his head and scolded 'you are on our team, don't help them'

Mini – go on, she gestured to come with more synonyms.

Me – AMBAR...?

MINI – thumbs up

Then she pointed out the iron rod lying in the corner of the room.

Me- rod...?

Mini – showed, thumbs down, suggesting a Hindi word for it

Me – sariya...?

Mini – Thumbs up. Guess

Priya – ambar sariya...?

Is the movie fukrey? You were acting the song, 'ambar sariya'?

Mini – BINGO!!

Priya – 'crazy girl instead of doing all that, you must have showed phook 'fook', by blowing air, that would had been easier.'

Mini- Ohhh!! That didn't strike me,

Previously I thought if I will break the word and act FUCK but that would be vulgar, so chose this way, she murmured to Priya, and they giggled.

'Anyways, we got that right' Priya said

BINGO! Team 1 gave hi5 to each other.

Team 2- Tiddi stood up to act

ADITI whispered something in his ears

Tiddi – oh! Such an easy one

TIDDI stood up confidently facing everyone

Thumbs down

Pajju – Bollywood

Tiddi showed his 1st finger

AROHI – 1 word movie

Tiddi pointed veins in his hands

Pajju – veins

Tiddi showed, thumbs down, asking them to convert in Hindi

Neha – 'NAS'

Tiddi – nodded

Tiddi acted this was the 1st half of the 1 word movie, he gestured to identify the second half.

AROHI on top of her volume shouted

'It's NASBANDI'

5 seconds of silence in the room and then the laughter rolled into the room, it moved around the people in its chaotic way. It came in fits and bursts - loud to soft to nothing at all and back to loud again.

Tiddi and Prateek rolled on the floor holding their stomachs, all the girls giggling. Nik laughs out loud clapping his hands.

Priya scolds her little sister controlling her laughter.

'If you don't know the meaning of the word then why do you speak?' she started to laugh again.

I saw the AROHI's face, for a moment she was clueless about what she spoke, why is everyone laughing like this?

Mini whispered in her ears, maybe she told the exact meaning of the word she just shouted.

AROHI felt embarrassed.

'I am sorry guys, I was not aware about the meaning, I just heard that word on TV, so I spoke, I am so sorry'

Laughter does not seem to stop, people rolled on the floor holding their stomachs.

'You are crazy, Arohi' Mini said and laughed

'Yaar hota hai kabhi kabhi, its ok, itna bhi kuch nai hua. I don't want to play anymore, I am going home' – she warned

Moments of laughter, the temperature in the house raised a couple of degrees.

I looked at her, she was shy, embarrassed, everyone teasing her, pinching her, giggling, laughing.

I loved her innocence; she is such a cute baby. I felt like pulling her cheeks and letting her know that it's okay, things happen at times.

I love it when she is around me; her cute little things make me smile.

$\mathcal{B}irthday$

18th Dec 2012/ Tuesday/ 11:00PM

I am waiting for the clock hands to meet @ 12, and the date changes from 18th Dec to 19th Dec- My birth date, I am sure Gyaanis would have planned something for me. I can imagine everyone coming up jumping, laughing and singing birthday songs. As of now they must be busy planning something weird.

I remember Tiddi's last birthday - Our group being creative, we celebrate theme birthdays, picking up hobbies of the individual we decide the theme and decoration is done accordingly. Mostly it is funny but Tiddi's birthday celebration was little different, he is fascinated by vampires, big fan of vampire diaries and black magic tutorials and what not when it comes to the subject black.

To surprise him, the theme of his b'day was black vamps; all of us were dressed in black with red color flowing from our heads, hands and different parts of our bodies. I swear to God that was the scariest b'day we would have ever celebrated. Midnight 12, Lights off, horror music, red spread everywhere, white candles, walls were decorated with 'Witches and flying bats' cut out of black sheet. For a moment I felt like we were shooting for some horror series. Everyone was taking their characters way too seriously. I have no idea what would be my birthday surprise.

My phone rang, Maa calling. It's 12:00AM. She and papa wished me 'happy birthday' and gave their blessings, series of call started, while attending the call I had this anxiety why no one from the group has wished me yet? Have they forgotten my Birthday? No one is home yet- Pajju, Nik, tiddi, Atul. Even none of the girls called to wish me.

Its 2:00 A.M now, I am done with all my calls and little frustrated too.

This is strange, it never happened; we used to give surprise at exact 12 followed by a cake cutting ceremony. I am not able to believe how can they forget my birthday? Where the hell is everyone? Well, this is surprising for me.

I tried sleeping in conversation with myself,

'I should call someone and confirm, where are they'

'Why should I call? It's my birthday, they should call me'

'It's them who forgot' I behaved like a high school birthday girl

Trin trin... Pajju calling... its 3:00 A.M

'Dude, where have you been? You at home?' he enquired

'Of course I am; where will I go?' I answered grudgingly

'Are you aware, Neha met with an accident this evening? We all are here at girl's place; she is not doing well, X-ray reports showing fracture in her left leg. All are here except you. Where have you been?' he asked suspiciously

'I am at home, nobody informed me about the situation. I was completely unaware, is she okay now? Wait I will come there' I replied

'It's 3:00 AM RV, we are not home yet and you didn't even call us once?' he grumbled

'I am sorry, I was not aware. I will be there in few minutes' I replied in guilt.

'She is okay now. If you want, you can visit her tomorrow. We too are leaving for our place' he said

'No No I will be there in 2 minutes' I requested him to wait there.

'I felt guilt-ridden. I was blaming them for forgetting my birthday, they were in a bad situation, and I should have at least called them once to confirm where they are' I thought while walking from my building to girl's building. I reached B4-404, I rang the bell.

The door was open, I entered, lights were off and nothing was visible. For a moment I thought there is no one at home. I switched on the lights and there they were:

Dressed in Manchester jersey's and shorts, they have converted the living room into football playground, net on both the sides, green grass carpet with the end lines, side lines, goal lines drawn out of white paint, a football cake was placed in between, walls were well decorated with football posters, my pictures, sketches, balloons and ribbons.

Everyone came to me and hugged, singing 'Happy birthday to you' I was completely astonished.

I scolded them for playing the bad trick of Neha's accident, I cut the oval football cake, took a slice and luckily AROHI stood beside me, I offered her the 1st piece but before she could eat, whole of the football cake was on my face. I could barely see anything.

Boys taking the advantage of the situation gave me birthday bombs by kicking my back.

Arohi and Priya tried to stop the kick rains and helped me to get my face clean.

NIK told 'AROHI is the master mind behind the plan. Design head of the college has done the decoration'

I was flattered and I looked at her.

My girl looked attractive in white jersey with "MANCHISTER UNITED" printed on it and blue shorts, those shorts were way too short. I can see her smiling, enjoying, dancing, with her hair open. I kept looking at her for a while, thinking she is the architect behind this plan, she planned everything for me. WOW!! Is this a sign?

I recollected my thoughts when I saw her dancing with Tiddi holding red color pomp- pomp in her hands, Tiddi teaching her cheer girl steps. Looking at them I realized she would have done this for anyone else too in the group; I am just a group mate for her, her senior. She is creative; she would have done this for anyone whose birthday was today or tomorrow or day after!!

I was entangled in my thoughts when Mini pushed me to join the dancing group.

Everyone was going to go crazy. The music was so loud that it made my skin tingle and my lungs feel like mush. The bass thumped in time with my heart beat as though they were one, filling me from head to toe with music.

Over the roar of music, a distant, hazy chatter could be heard. I couldn't make out any words, but laughter rang in my ears and wouldn't seem to stop. The song that was playing got louder, pulling me in and wouldn't let go. I had no choice but to join the group, jumping into a huddled group like Tic-Tacs being shaken in a box.

I could hear sound of the bell; someone standing outside the door.

I asked NIK to slow down the music.

It was society watchman standing out 'sahib raat k 4 baje, itna tez music, society se complain aaya hai'

'Bhaiya, sorry... Will slow down the music' Priya apologized

'Society is already against bachelors, if you all will do such things, they will ask you to leave' watchman warned

'We will keep in mind bhaiya, now onwards you will not get any complaints' I tried handling the situation.

Watchman gave a bizarre look, seeking inside the room and trying to count number of people inside, staring at girls wearing shorts and left murmuring something.

Bike Ride

The more I get to know her; more I crave to be with her. She is crazy, cute, adventurous, nature lover, strange, scared of street dogs but loves to play with puppies, scared of lizards and cockroaches, but can climb highest mountains, loves travelling, doesn't know swimming but can float in water. She has the sweetest voice anyone would have ever heard.

She is active all the time, roaming, running, playing, everyone in the group loves to tease her, she is a sweetheart but careless too, at times she forgets to take care of herself when in the mood of having fun.

She is very expressive and can make all kinds of expressions. I think WhatsApp copied her expressions and named them with different smileys. Her cute expressions have the power to melt anyone who is angry on her.

In spite of all these cute childish behaviours she is mature enough to understand feelings and relations, she is passionate about her career and she manages to follow her dreams, her art and never compromises on family and friends.

Because of her 'careless' attitude, everybody keeps a watch on her to ensure she is safe. It's New Year;

Gyaanis went for a drive till EON (our favorite hangout place) where madam came up with a new demand.

'I want to ride BIKE with gear' she said

'I am comfortable with all types of non-gear bikes, I want to learn gear ones, I will be able to manage handle but not sure about gears and weight of the bike'

'Pajju sir, chalo na, I will ride your bike' She requested Pajju

'Are you crazy, I have not yet insured my bike' Pajju replied

'Moreover I do not have any medical insurance' Pajju said giving high five to Tiddi and teasing Arohi

She gave a sad expression by rolling her lower lip out.

'Arohi come, I will make you learn' I said

Arohi clapped and jumped in excitement.

'Are you crazy, RV, why are you fulfilling such demands? No need, she might end up hurting herself and you too' Priya said grimly

'Don't worry, we will be able to manage, Come AROHI' I said

Arohi came to me showing tongue to her elder sister, I enjoyed the moment.

Sit, I will sit behind you, I explained her gear and clutch system,

There are 5 gears, 1st in down direction, press the clutch, push to gear one, slowly leave the clutch and raise accelerator.

'Got it?' I asked doubtfully.

'Yes kind of, but I am little scared, I don't want to fall down, your pulsar is heavy' she said

'Don't worry, you will learn and nothing will happen, just follow what I say' I assured

Okay!! Let's go.

She tried -clutch, gear and accelerator. The bike took a jerk and did not start.

'RV SIR, not happening' she complained

'It will happen, just coordination is what you need in between the 3 things, let's try once more.

Press clutch, push gear down, leave clutch slowly and simultaneously accelerate'

Okay 1, 2, and 3 let's go....

Again a bad jerk....

'Let it be, something happening to your bike, we will try later' she said

'Nothing is happening, it's just you are leaving the clutch in one go and accelerating, let's try one more time'

Follow the rules - Press clutch, push gear down, leave clutch slowly and simultaneously accelerate

Okay!! 1, 2, 3 Gooooo

'Bingoooo!!! I picked up' she shouted

The roads were empty as EON was in the outskirts of the city and generally weekend evening there is not much of moving vehicles.

Raise accelerator, press clutch and lift up for 2nd gear!! I explained her relation between gears and speed.

'WOW you able to handle, you are a good learner' I appreciated her.

'Let's go back, I want to show them all' she demanded.

I helped her taking a 'U' turn and other lefts and rights. She drove in front of all, pressing horn and celebrating her victory.

Shouting 'look I can drive'

After 2 kilo meters of drive, we came back to the place where we started. Others went to get some stuff to eat. Only Nik stood there and waited for us.

I helped Arohi stopping the bike and explained her, mechanism behind it, she heard like an obedient student.

I got down the bike, she tried balancing it alone.

'Are you sure you will be able to stand? Or should I put it on to main stand?'

'I will manage RV sir' she said confidently

I walked 5 steps from her towards NIK, when she shouted 'RV sir come back, I am loosing balance'

I turned towards her, she tried gaining her equilibrium.

'Ahhh its ok... I am ok now, continue your talks' she said

'Are you sure?' I enquired

'YES' she replied

I again turned back and then BANG, she was on floor with bike on her, one leg stuck beneath the bike and with the other she was trying to move it.

Ohhh Ohhh ohh ! I and NIK ran towards her, Nik picked up the bike.

'Are you okay?'

'My leg is hurt' she replied, trying to get up, a small tear rolling down her eyes.

'Thankfully only you two saw, please do not tell this to others, else I will get lots of scolding' she requested

I saw the beautiful excited face turn into a sad one, trying to bear pain, her leg was hurt badly. She is the delicate one, I took her responsibility and it's my fault. I scolded myself silently

---

Finally She Learnt
drving a bike
:)

*   *   *

Sometimes she demands to eat ice-cream at 2:00 AM or go for a long drive in chilling winters. At times to dance like crazy or start water war by pouring water on everyone and making them wet. Many of the times, she is the pillow fight initiator. I liked Arohi for being the most active and khurapati member of the group. She adds life to everyone and everything. Her weird and crazy demands are beyond imagination.

Once she came up with the demand of going to Lonavala at 1:00 AM because she wanted to eat Maggie there. We covered 75 kms to have Maggie and fulfil her demand. I started supporting all her mischiefs and promised to fulfil all her crazy demands as I love to do it.

*   *   *

Matheran

30th August 2013/ Friday/ 11:45 PM

As monsoon looms closer there are unlikely destinations near Pune which don their rain-soaked avatars with effortless charm and will seduce you to do the same.

We- The adventure freaks and nature lovers decided not to waste the rainy months ducking indoors. Exploration of nature when mud is wet is to be carried out, target was touching all the amazing places where nature is playing active role and where we can enjoy every breath with nature within the weekend time.

Its Friday night, we all are at girls place, B4 404, agenda was to decide and plan trips for this monsoon.

It's raining cats and dogs; we could hear the big fat rain drops falling on the tin sheets hung above the windows, avoiding rain water coming in.

Cool breeze flowing, making the rain dance along with it, it's pitch black outside as the rains have led to long and frequent power cuts across the city.

We lit 4 candles in 4 corners of the living room, balcony's slider pane was kept open for the cool breeze to flow in, little fire on the candle struggled hard to stay alive and face cool watery winds but alas it failed. Darkness surrounded us.

We all lay down on the mattress, talking what all places we could visit, also chit-chatting, and remembering old college days.

Tiddi continuously was searching something in his mobile, Arohi asked him to join the talks when he insisted everyone to sit in a circle, he had read few stories he wanted to share with all.

We all adjusted ourselves and formed a circle, luck by chance my AROHI sat beside me, she is scared of darkness and ghosts.

As in-house was full, AROHI too enjoyed the darkness and tickling talks.

Arohi in excitement asked Tiddi, 'what's the agenda? Why are we sitting in a circle? Are we going to play something? Truth and dare types...?'

'No sweetie, we gonna talk, we gonna talk about ghosts, evils, vampires and watch them live' he said in a petrifying tone, coming near AROHI, without blinking his eyes.

Arohi moved back and pushed Tiddi, saying 'we are not going to do any such things, please'.

Arey why not...? Neha jumped in, I too have many such stories, everybody agreed on sharing horror stories they have experienced or have heard or read.

I could see fear on Arohi' s face, no one was listening to her, Tiddi asked her to believe that ghosts do exist in real world. She needs to grow up and accept the fact.

I wanted to hold her hand that moment and tell her, sweetheart I am there with you, I won't let anything happen to you.

Tiddi began with his story that he has read online just before he asked us to sit in a circle.

With his eyes wide open he started:

'*This is a true story of a young girl named Lisa,*

37

Lisa often had to spend time alone at home at night, as her parents worked late. They bought her a dog to keep her company and protect her

One night Lisa was awakened by a dripping sound. She got up and went to the kitchen to turn off the tap properly. As she was getting back into the bed she stuck her hand under the bed, and the dog licked it.

The dripping sound continued, so she went to the bathroom and made sure the tap was turned off there, too.

She went back to her bedroom and stuck her hand under the bed, and the dog licked it again.

But the dripping continued, so she went outside and turned off all the faucets out there. She came back to bed, stuck her hand under it, and the dog licked it again'

Everybody listening to the story without blinking their eyes, Tiddi made all kind of gesture and postures with proper voice modulation, creating suspense he continued

'The dripping did not stop: drip, drip, drip. This time she listened and located the source of the dripping – it was coming from her closet! She opened the closet door'

Dead silence in the room, it was all dark by now, all the candles failed to survive cool winds.

He repeated again creating more suspense

'she opened the closet door and there found her poor dog hanging upside down with its neck cut and her favorite doll placed on the shelf with mouth full of blood. Written on the window on the inside of the cupboard was, 'Humans can lick, too!!!''

Stories made night more thrilling and to add more spices, Prateek came up with a new idea 'Let's watch a horror movie'.

'My laptop is 98% charged and will last long for 3 hrs. Let's watch conjuring' Pajju suggested flaunting about his new Apple laptop.

AROHI tried to protest, she insisted everyone to change the topic and talk about something positive, Negative talks disturbed her. My cutie pie was scared; I could make it out from her face.

I tried diverting her mind asking her questions about her Office, bike ride experience and her paintings, while everyone was busy setting things up for the movie, placing laptop at appropriate position, connecting speaker, voice check and stuff.

It was 2:00 @night.

Movie started, seating positions were not much interchanged. All adjusted themselves and formed a distorted semicircle in front of the laptop placed on a 1 feet high wooden table. AROHI, not changing her position kept sitting beside me, not willing to watch the movie but she had no other option.

She whispered in my ears, 'RV sir darr lag rha hai, please ask them to stop this please, can we watch any comedy movie? Please.'

'All in mood AROHI, nobody will listen, you just hold your pillow tight and do not worry we all are here, nothing will happen to you' I assured her.

'1ˢᵗ *scene began when Carolyn Perron and her daughter playing hide and seek, mom stumbles around and asks for a hint, little girl clap once, she goes in a next room speaks softly to find her daughter. Unbeknownst to her, an armoire begin to open by itself*'

Dead silence in the room, everyone's eyes was glued to the laptop screen, no one moved an inch, Arohi's eyes wide open; she held my arm, I held her by her shoulder comforting her and assuring that it's just a movie. She kept staring at laptop without blinking her eyes.

'*Mom asked for another hint when 2 strange arms come out of armoire and clapped twice*'

I jerked my arm away from Arohi's grip, she also realized that she scratched my arm with her nails and she looked upset at having done so.

She found out a different way to escape from the movie, with her earplugs on, listening songs at full volume. These made her little comfortable and soon 1hr 50 mins were over.

AROHI stood up and shouted,

'We were here to plan our trips and now it's 4 in the morning, I do not want to waste my weekend, so will anyone let me know where are we going?'

'I am sleepy, I will sleep now, you guys go where ever you want to' Tiddi replied

'No, no body is going to sleep now, we are going on a trip, it's raining beautifully outside and what are we doing here? Watching ghosts on screen and talking about them? I agreed on what you all told, now you all will have to do what I am saying' AROHI grumbled

'Raise hands who all are in' she ordered

Everybody raised their hands without speaking a word, I was looking at my angry AROHI, she looked beautiful in moon light, hair strands coming out of her bun, shouting at all, pointing fingers, making all kind of angry postures and expressions, I wish I could pull her cheeks and say, 'will do whatever you demand MY princess'.

Nik suggested planning a day trip to Matheran

'We can start around 5:30AM. Matheran is around 3 and half hour journey from our place. Let's book a traveler' he said

I counted number of people on my finger - Arohi, Neha, Mini, Priya, aditi, Pajju, Nik, Tiddi, Atul and RV, so total 10 people.

We can go for a 12 seater; I took the responsibility for booking the traveler. Nik guided everyone what all belongings to be kept.

We had just one hour and traveler will be here, I warned everyone not to be late.

Electricity board finally responded to thousands of complaints by providing electricity after 9 hours of darkness.

*   *   *

We made our way to Matheran, Setting off towards Mumbai on the Pune-Mumbai expressway, even after having sleepless night everyone was charged, singing loud, playing, taking selfies, group pictures, teasing, pulling legs, fighting, hardly any one sat on their places.

After getting off the Pune-Mumbai Expressway at the Khopoli exit and passing Lonavala we got onto the old Pune-Mumbai road. Approximately 18 km later, we turned right as per a big green sign, in Chowk town. Following the signs from then on we reached Dasturi Naka.

As no vehicles were allowed beyond this point, we had no other option but to walk. Matheran center is a 40-minute walk from Dasturi Car Park.

Everyone was damn hungry by now; we ordered 10 vada-pavs and Poha from the small shop at Dasturi Naka.

Before we entered the limits of Matheran, Matheran Municipal council charged us fees of Rs.25/- per adult.

Matheran is relaxing, and rejuvenating, one can really feel this effect in it's atmosphere; it is a crown placed in Sahyadri hill Ranges, at 2400 feet above sea level. Deep forest and Red mud road at Matheran are its trademarks and for transportation one can walk, hire a horse or rickshaw pullers. We decided to trek.

Once we entered, red dusty pathways welcomed us to the nature. We saw all kind of horses were being used for transportation purpose - Black, Brown, White, Tall and Short. There were monkeys too leaping from tree to tree or climbing the housetops.

All of us kept walking, talking with each other, laughing and taking group pictures, selfies and Facebook DP's. We were not aware of any sight-seeing points, we headed without any defined destinations, as it was drizzling, we wrapped up our mobile phones in a plastic bag and kept it in Pajju' s waterproof Fastrack red colored bag. Lusting greeneries, serene environments and unpolluted ambience made us relaxed and bought us more close to nature.

Everyone was enjoying themselves, Arohi and Mini trying to make foot prints on red sand, Pajju pulling Aditi's hair, Priya, Neha, Tiddi and Atul talking on a very serious topic 'how Indian government is handling tourism.'

We (Me, Nik and Pajju) were looking for more difficult/challenging treks.

I called everyone for a quick group meeting.

'Listen guys, nobody will roam alone, we all will walk in groups, in case if few members are interested in watching or exploring different destinations, they should inform others before leaving. Everyone will be at least in a group of 3' I ordered

'By chance if we depart then we will be meeting at Dasturi snacks center anyhow by 8 PM, as there is no network we will not be able to contact each other using cell phones' I continued

'Any doubts?'

'No' everyone replied

OKAYYY then let's go!!!

We have entered the Matheran Jungle, no roads, just a narrow path created by footsteps crushing grass guided us, on our way to unknown destination, and we found silent white stream cascading over the rocky outcrops. Pajju, Nik and me decided to trek till the top on those rocks.

I called out for a quick meeting again

'Listen everyone; Me, Nik and Pajju are taking a different path for a while. You guys go straight and wait at the point you find next, we will catch up with you all soon. Tiddi and Atul, please take care of the girls, be together. We will be back soon'

While I was talking to group, Nik and Pajju started with trek, expecting me to cover the distance and catch up with them.

'Okay but take care guys, trek is difficult' Priya said.

'Sure' I replied

as I started. I heard a voice.

'RV sir wait, I am also coming' AROHI shouted

'No, AROHI trek is risky, it's very slippery, you will end up hurting yourself' I warned

'I want to come, please take me with you' she insisted

'No dear, you will not be able to walk, its long route, we will have to cover this fast. In order to catch up with the group' I said

'I will do that, I will not trouble you, promise' she said, in a convincing tone.

'No need AROHI you are coming with us' Priya ordered her

'But Didi please, I want to go' AROHI replied

'AROHI I do not want any arguments, RV is also against it, right? Do what I say, we are concerned about your safety' Priya said in a firm voice.

'But Didi....'

'Shut up and do what I say, it's not good to do khurapat every time' Priya roared

My sweetie pie became sad, she followed her sister. I felt bad. I want to fulfill all her wishes and we can go for a trek because we are boys but she cannot because she is a girl, something was going wrong here and I cannot tolerate her sad face. I stopped them.

'Come AROHI, we will go'

'No RV sir! It's ok. I will go with the group' she mumbled looking at her sister.

'Come come! We will trek together, Priya do not worry I will take care of her, we will be back soon' I assured and took AROHI with me.

Priya went and joined the group, Nik and Pajju were ahead of us, too many trees and continuous drizzling blocked our view.

AROHI held my hand and followed my steps, we reached a point where we could see several typical trees, little shrubs, wild vegetables, flowering plants, there was no defined path and we could not move without touching a plant on our skin.

'Where are we RV sir? Where are Nik sir and Pajju sir?'

'I am not sure AROHI, they must have not gone too far, let's try searching for them'

By now we have entered the jungles of Matheran, It's very difficult to measure how dense a forest is, it had thick trees growing very closely together. I think we were lost. We could not make out the way we came from; also we were not able to make out which way to go. I got nervous as AROHI was with me, I have no idea how will she react when she finds out that we are completely lost. Its 1:00 PM in my watch we still have 5 hours to explore and find our group before its dark.

'Where are we going RV sir? Do you have any idea?'

'No, AROHI I think we are lost in the forest' I gathered guts to tell her the truth

'OMG! Waoo RV sir, this is so exciting, it is like a movie na, 2 travelers, adventure freaks are lost in dense jungle, fighting back to survive, tackling situations' she said like a director of an adventure movie.

To my surprise her reaction was completely opposite, she was not scared, she was enjoying and for me it is not like an adventure movie where 2 travelers or adventure freaks are lost. To me it seems like a romantic movie where hero and heroine are lost in the jungle.

Everything was same as they show in romantic Bollywood masala: Rains, A guy, a girl, lots of trees, at an instance girl is hurt and a boy picks her in his arms and then they kiss....

'But one question' AROHI interrupted my romantic thoughts

'Do we have wild animals here in the jungle?'

'Yes and they may attack us' I answered

'Oh, seriously RV sir, I heard we do not have any wild animals here' she replied in a low tone, looking 360 degrees round.

'No, there are no wild animals, I was just teasing you' I laughed

She pinched me and smiled.

I had her responsibility on me, I wanted her to be safe and return to group as soon as possible but I was enjoying these moments with her, we kept walking, she kept talking. She is a chatter box, I admire her so very much, her each word was music to my ears.

It started raining heavily, we could hardly open our eyes, I held her by her right arm, and we tried to walk. Rains made our path even more difficult. She was wearing knee length black cotton shorts and a pink sleeve less top with black horizontal stripes on it, her Adidas shoes made it comfortable to walk on rough and slippery areas of jungle, we were completely drenched in the rains, she looked erotically beautiful, her wet hairs attracted me towards her.

Shrubs, branches scratched her soft skin. Heavy rains, lost way, insects, shrubs now bothered her, my girl was silent now, wondering if we will be able to get back before sunset.

Passing through the dense, suffocating undergrowth, fighting through the very air, our trail opened up at the top of the waterfall. Fast moving water descends vertically, losing complete contact with the bedrock surface.

'RV sir I am tired, I cannot walk anymore and this place is so beautiful, please let's take a halt' she requested

We sat in a thick shade of a tree near waterfall, hiding ourselves from rains, we could hear notes of the cuckoo and the Bulbul and various other birds providing heavenly music. The thicknesses of the trees hide the musicians from our view. The view of the deep valley down from the point was breathtaking.

'This place is so beautiful' she spoke softly, lost in her own thoughts, not bothering about going back home.

'I wish I could stay here forever' she continued staring at the valley.

'Are you ok AROHI? You seem lost' I asked bringing her back from her inner thoughts.

'Yes I am fine' she replied

'Look what have you done yesterday', I showed her my arm that she scratched last night

'Oh, I am so so sorry RV sir, I did that by mistake, I really got scared, this was unintentional' she apologized

'It's okay dear'

'RV sir, you know what, you are good, I am really comfortable with you, you fulfill all my demands, at the same time you take good care of me and everyone in the group, thank you for all this' she complimented

'Thanks for the compliment ma'am, I have to take care of you, as your didi says that you are too khurapati, always ends up hurting yourself, everyone is always bothered about you' I replied.

She smiled

'I wish things to remain same as they are now, especially between all of us, I feel so proud to be part of a group like this, all college friends, connected by heart, it's too much fun'

She continued

'People often meet their friends after they start with their jobs and look at us, we still do everything together, we are so lucky that we all are still connected, the only thing which makes me survive in a new city, and away from parents is our group, for me it is like a big family'.

'Everything will remain same na, we all will be together always na?' She asked with lots of innocence in her eyes.

'I wish Gyaanis stay together always, but dear within a year people will start switching their jobs in order to get good hike, girls will start getting married, then it all depends on their husbands if they are comfortable, with them being a part of the group' I answered practically.

'I never want things to change, I like it this way' she replied

'Then there is a solution, you can marry somebody within the group. You will never be away then' I suggested

She laughed

'You know what the best thing about our group is?' she asked

'What?' I questioned back

'The best thing is we do not have couples in the group, no body sits in a group of 2 or 3, no secret talks, we stay together all the time and the best one is our policy –"no couples in the group".'

She shattered all my dreams in a single moment and made me recall our rule "No couples in the group"

'What if there are couples within the group? What if you fall for someone?' I asked

'I will never fall for anyone in the group and no couples in group please, it will disturb everything. They will need their own separate time, space and things will change' she replied

I got answer to my question; I tried changing the topic before she makes any other new rule.

'Hey, you like traveling right?' I enquired

'Yes, I love exploring new places, close to nature, only condition is 'no sun', weather should be good, also I like adventure sports, I want to do bungee jumping, parasailing, river rafting, sky diving, underwater diving, ice skating and the list goes on and on' she answered

'Waoo, you are adventurous, by the way all these things are in my to do list as well'

'Let's do one thing, we will make a WhatsApp group, and call it as 'wish list', we will write all our wishes, it can be anything- possible, impossible, practical, dreamy' I suggested

'Waoo that would be great!' she clapped in excitement.

'Shall I share one of my fantasy with you' she asked

'Yes, please go ahead' I replied

'No, its little funny for this practical world, promise me 1st that you will not share with any one and you will not laugh at it' she demanded

'I promise, I will keep it to just myself'

She sat turning my side, facing me, crossed her legs and started.

'At times I feel like my life to be a fairy tale and I am the princes of that fairy world with the magic wand, with lots of colors in it, too many people, all my close ones, no negative feelings, birds singing, close to nature, I want to fly high in the sky, fulfilling all my dreams, playing with colors, making new paintings, helping poor, conducting exhibitions, wearing princess dress, cute castles. I don't know how to put my feelings in words but I just want everything around me very beautiful just like they show in a fairy tale' she explained her fantasy world wish with her hands moving, and eyes wide open.

Cuddling herself she concluded-

'I know it's a dream world, not possible in today's scenario but I wish if I could visit this fairy land once.'

I smiled looking at her, her pure innocence attracted me more towards her; she is a kid who still believes in stories that our grandmothers used to tell us.

Watching me smile, she said 'look I knew, you will smile and think what rubbish I am talking all about'

'No dear, I'm not making fun of you, we will add this to our wish list and try to make what so ever is possible in this practical world' I replied

She smiled back.

'RV sir, I am feeling sleepy now, we haven't slept a single minute last night, I am not feeling well, How to get out of this jungle?' she said closing her eyes and resting her back on tree's thick trunk behind us.

'Please, try to be awake Arohi, we will find some way out'

'RV sir, it is getting dark, I am scared, please take me out of here' she said holding my hand

'Don't worry, we will be out of this jungle soon' I assured her making her calm.

I did not know what to do, I could see no path leading us out of this jungle and it's getting dark, I had assured her that I will take care but I am also clueless, which way to go. Rains, not ready to take a breath.

While I was entangled in my own thoughts I heard sound of footsteps, it could be an animal or human, I asked Arohi not to move from her place and I will be back in few minutes.

'No, RV sir, please don't go. I will come along' She said holding my hand stopping me to go.

Her touch and pretty nervous eyes did not allow me to leave her alone. I took her along with me.

We saw a villager sorting leaves.

I went to him and told that we are lost, it would be great if he could guide us till Dasturi Naka, he agreed, we followed him.

I could see Arohi shivering, sneezing and coughing. She caught cold. Lack of sleep made her feel weak; she gathered all her courage to walk back till the Naka.

We reached, everyone was already there waiting for us, all bombarded us with lots of questions- 'where were you both?', 'What took so long?', 'We tried searching for you' and many more. I answered them all. We changed our wet clothes in a cottage at Dasturi.

Everyone was hungry and sleepy, we stopped at a dhabha on our way back, after dinner everyone entered traveler silently, deprived of sleep and tired, all got hold of their respective seats and slept, Arohi sat beside me on window seat, last second seat of the traveler, she being sleepy rested her head on window. Sudden jerks were hurting her, I kept her head on my shoulder, I touched her forehead, and she had fever. I took out the blanket from my bag, covered her, kept my right hand on her shoulder and rested her head on my chest. I wish I could keep her like this for rest of my life.

Parvati

2nd September 2013/ Monday/ 09:00AM

I am sitting on my desk with my laptop open, instead of looking at laptop screen and starting with office tasks I looked out the window. I observed 2 birds playing something similar to Hide and seek. I don't know what they call hide and seek in their bird language. I started observing nature, beautiful trees, rains, birds and back of mind had just one thought "Arohi". To take her out of my mind was not possible for me now. I kept thinking about the moments I had spent with her in Matheran. Flashback of our tickling talks, her wet face, she holding my hand, the way she slept on my shoulder made me miss her more. I thanked God for deviating us from our path and creating the situation where I could spend few hours just with her and no one else around, trip to Matheran was a memorable one. I missed her; I had the strong craving to be with her all the time. I thought of calling her but something inside stopped me, thrice I picked up my mobile to make a call and then kept it back on the table. She behaved as a distraction for me from my work. Unless I talk to her I will not be able to concentrate. I decided to message her.

'Hi Arohi, GM'

'VGM RV Sir' she replied

'Office?'

'Yes! You?'

'Yeah, me too, Still having fever?'

'I am okay now. No fever but little cold'

'Medicine?'

'I don't like them'

'Areee, take medicine you will be okay soon'

'I will be okay on my own. I am drinking hot water these days' she replied

It got difficult for me to convince her She being stubborn will not listen to me, I wanted to meet her and assure myself that she is okay, what if I go and pick her from office and I will get to spend some time with her.

'I will be coming near your office this evening. I have some work, so you don't take office bus, I will drop you at your place while returning' I said

'Are you sure? My office is in out skirts of Pune, it's far'

'Yes, I will manage, will call you once there'

'Okay' she replied

I plugged-in my ear phones and got back to my work, my distraction now worked as motivation for me to finish my tasks soon so that I can reach her office on time.

My favorite playlist played 'ek ladki ki tumhe kya sunaun daastan'

Song reminded me of her, I again messaged her-

'ek ladki ki tumhe kya sunaun daastan,

wo pagli hai sabse juda,

har pal nayi uski ada,

log tarsee phool barse jaye wo ladki jahan'

After 2 mins I got her reply –

'haaye haaye re haaye ye ladka haaye haaye re haaye

karta nadaniyan kyun pooch to haaye'

Along with a smiley ;) I liked her reply

'Hey, What about wish list?' I asked

'I just created a group, Let us punch in our wishes' she replied

Wish 1(Arohi) – Want to try adventure sports, scuba diving, river rafting, parasailing and bungee jumping

Wish 2 (RV) – To buy open jeep

Wish 3 (Arohi) – To be the princess of my fairy tale world

Wish 4 (RV) – Go on a voyage with my life partner.

'ohh hoo RV sir, kya baat hai, Life partner. huh huh...who is she?' Arohi enquired

'hehe, no one yet, search still on' I answered

'RV sir, I got to go for a meeting, will see you in evening, Bye'

*   *   *

I picked her up at 6:00PM from her office, she was looking pretty in formals, black trouser and red shirt, with a puff and top pony, my cute Arohi looked like a perfect professional confident lady. I enquired by what time she wants to be home and by what time Priya will reach home from office.

'Didi will come back home by 9 after gym, if you want to meet her you will have to stay here till 9' she answered

'Let's go to CCD then?'

'Yeah, ok as it is I wanted to talk to you about something' she replied

I wondered what that something is all about, I enquired if everything is fine, she told me to have patience she will let me know.

We reached Aundh CCD, a perfect place to talk, we acquired corner table for two, and I ordered a toastizza and cappuccino combo.

She kept silent for a while and stared the coffee without taking a sip; I asked her what she wanted to talk to me about?

'RV sir you are close to me, my best senior and my best friend who fulfils all my crazy demands, you should know what is going on in my life, also I wanted your advice on an issue I am facing since last few days, something really important' she said

'Tell me what is it Arohi; I will try my best to help you out'

I had observed quite a few times that something was bothering her; I wish I could take all her problems and see that beautiful smile on her face, always

'Not today RV sir, will let you know in our next meeting, I want some time'

Girls are sometimes weird, I mean we met today, she could have shared all her things in the same meeting but she wanted time or I should rather say she wanted time to give a second thought, whether she should share her personal things with me or not. She was silently sipping her coffee; I was staring at her thinking what could be the thing which is bothering her so much. I had no other option but to wait.

Looking at her tensed face I assured her that she can share whatever she wants to, whenever she wants to and I will make sure that I won't break her trust and will not let anyone else know about her secrets. My statements made her comfortable. She looked into my eyes and gave a smile. Back to our coffee I tried to initiate normal conversation.

Before leaving she cleaned toastizza plate with tissue and drew smiley ☺ with tomato ketchup on it and wrote todays date, I clicked the picture of her ketchup drawing.

*   *   *

Few weeks passed, she did not initiate the topic of having a discussion with me on her issues. I too didn't remind her of her problems, if and when she feels comfortable she will surely share her glitches, problems, complications or whatever it is, till then I didn't bother her by asking questions about her issues.

Weekend I observed she was lost in her own thoughts; she acted to be happy and participated in all the group fun activities. I tried to confirm if everything is alright. She said she will let me know things soon. I waited...

27th November 2013/ Wednesday/ 11:30 PM

Beep Beep : Arohi' s message:

'Hi RV SIR, please take me to some good place where we could sit and talk for a while without interruption, some peaceful place, may be some temple far from the city.'

'When do you want to go? Now?' I replied

'No not now, may be this Sunday'

'Ok as you say'

'Also I am starting with my weekend classes to keep in touch with my art; I will be free by 4:00 PM. Will you be able to pick me up from FC road?'

'Yes, why not and we can go to Parvati. It is a good place, there are three small temples at top of a hill, we can sit there for a while and chat'

'Okay, sounds good'

'What will you tell Priya? Where are you going and with whom' I enquired

'If didi asks I will let her know that I am going with you to visit a temple, she is also aware of the situations so will not put many questions. She also has her office party Sunday evening. We will try to be home before she is back'

*   *   *

1ˢᵗ December 2013/ Sunday/ 4:00PM

I waited below her art class, I saw her coming down the stairs, beautiful girl, dressed in white kurta and red dupatta, she looked like an angel, Indian attire suited her. Her red dupatta complimented her pink cheeks. If ever things are good between us I will take her in front of my parents in the same attire.

She gave me a heartwarming smile as she saw me, we started for our destination.

We reached Parvati; one of the favorite relaxation spots for the residents of Pune. One has to climb 103 steps to reach the hilltop. A special black quarry stone has been used for all these steps. It is weather-resistant and except for a few places, the stone has survived for over two hundred and fifty years even after being fully exposed to sun, wind and water. The steps are so wide that an elephant can easily walk with all pomp and gaiety towards the temple.

Arohi found it little difficult to climb the steps in her white colored pencil heels, she took off her heels, held them in her hands and climbed barefoot.

People of all age groups were doing different activities, all the elderly people were busy doing exercises, some love birds sitting and chitchatting, a group of young NCC boys and girls in perfect uniform were marching down the hill. It is an enjoyable sight to see children running up and down the hill. We climbed the hill in about 20 mins, after visiting all the 3 temples and joining hands in front of the almighty, we searched for a quiet place where we can sit and talk comfortably without offending anyone. After looking around we finally decided to sit at the backside of the Shiv Mandir. It offered us the beautiful panoramic view of the Pune city.

'This place is so beautiful, thanks for bringing me here' she said

'Yes, it is beautiful and you are always welcome my dear, Now tell me what is bothering you so much?' I asked

She hesitated a little 'I don't know where to start; RV sir, whatever I am sharing with you. You won't tell this to anyone right?'

I again assured her, her secrets are safe with me. She said I have 2 big secrets to tell you.

I was holding my breath and listening very carefully to whatever she was telling me,

'RV Sir, Atul broke our group's rule'

'Which rule?' I asked

'No couples in the group'

'So are you a couple with him?' I asked disconcertingly

'No no not that, he proposed me some time back' she said

'I used to consider him a very good friend of mine but I think I lost him, he knew that I will never agree for this relationship with him. Still he did! Everything has changed between us, our friendship, our masti, our sharing, college memories and everything else too. I never wanted to hurt him but whatever I said to convince him was hurting him, he is losing faith on life, I tried explaining him all situations but he is not ready to accept. I don't know why good friends do this and then they lose most important thing in life "FRIENDSHIP", I still miss him but he is not ready to accept me as a friend, what should I do? Friendship is such a pure beautiful relation; I wonder why people spoil bringing all these things in between' She said

Listening to her, I was confused whether she was asking me for help or was warning me not to try on her. Somewhere I knew about Atul's case, because not only Arohi but everyone in the group was aware of Atul's care, possessiveness and madness for AROHI. I advised her to let the things be the way they are and after sometime everything will be normal and their friendship will be same as it was.

'I don't know what to do, If I talk to him, he will be hurt, if I don't then also he will be hurt, I don't want to see him this way, it is getting difficult for me, I don't want to lose a good friend of mine, what should I do?' she asked

'Arohi, give him some time, feelings are natural, it's not his fault, don't talk to him much as of now, he will be stable as time passes, he will understand that he is spoiling his friendship with you and he will be normal again, time is the best healer' I explained

She nodded.

I was now more concerned about the second thing. I had butterflies flying in my stomach; I was left with no patience. Before she could say anything I asked her what the second thing is all about.

She took a deep breath and said 'I AM IN A RELATIONSHIP'. For a moment I felt like someone hammering my heart. My sudden reaction to her sentence was 'Whattttttt????' in a loud tone, I saw people worshiping on opposite side turned towards us.

She got scared for a moment, I recollected myself and then in soft voice, comforting her, I asked. Who is he? And since how long has she been in a relationship?

'His name is Akash, Akash Jain, when I joined my firm in Pune, 3 girls -Anamika, Seema and Heena became my good friends. Three of them shared the same flat near my society. We used to study together during our training days at their place; I met Akash at Heena's birthday celebration. He and his few friends share the apartment in the same society as of the girls just like our group. Their society is just 2 minutes' walk from mine.'

'As both of us are Jain, our friends started teasing us; I was made to stand beside him while taking the group pictures. He used to enjoy all the teasing. Anamika, Heena and Seema convinced me for him as he is good looking, have a good job with decent package and the major plus point was 'same caste'; they all thought we both will make a great couple. Akash got to know lot many things about me. He had visited my profile for more than 100 times on FB. He got attracted towards me.

As we had a common friend circle, we used to meet quite frequently, slowly became friends and got to know that our families are connected too, his father shared a good friendship with my father as they worked in same department. He is 3 years older than me. We possess good understanding. He tried convincing me that together we can make a great couple and can lead a happy successful life, earlier I resisted but my family also liked him, he proposed me and I said yes.

My family likes him, his family likes me' she said and paused.

I was dumbstruck, I was praying her next statement to be 'All this was a joke' but it was not. Collecting all my courage I asked her: 'He likes you, you like him, his family likes you, your family likes him, both have good jobs, both stay in same city, both are of same caste then where is the problem?'

I saw a little tear rolling down her cheeks. She continued 'Things seems perfect but they are not, his family believes in some Guruji and he says that if Guruji says NO after studying our kundli's it would be difficult for him to decide what to do'.

'What? Will he leave you??'

I am not sure...

'Are you crazy? Is he crazy? Some mad person on the earth might do that. He has no right to be with you or play with your emotions if this was the condition. If I would have been on his place, I would have never gone for such myths' I said not able to believe Akash's statement

'When did he tell you about this Guruji thing? Before he proposed you?'

'No after that. If he would have told me before I would have not fallen for such a person who keeps conditions in Love' she replied

I saw her beautiful face turning red and sad. I can never see her like this. Keeping all my feelings aside I genuinely wanted to help her and make things perfect for her beautiful fairy tale life.

Not only this there are few more things, she said in her soft sad innocent voice.

'What else?'

'Is it possible RV sir, to be so busy that you hardly get time to talk to the one you love?' she asked

'It all depends on priorities Arohi; you can always take out time, no matter how difficult it is'

I saw continuous trail of thick tears coming out of her eyes, wiping her tears with her hands she continued:

'The person I fell for has changed RV sir, I am not able to figure out things, please help me. At once when he wanted me badly, he made all possible efforts to bring me close to him. When he used to have night shifts, he used to come early from his office in order to get my glimpse before I go to sleep, we used to talk for hours while walking in his society, he used to plan things for me.

Now things are all changed, he hardly gets time to call me. It's just me who is trying to hold our relation, I can compromise on anything just to be with him but he is just way too busy. We can spend hours together as we live nearby but every time I call him I get the same reply 'I am busy, I will call you later'

He is not even there with me when I need him the most, if I am not well, when I need anything, when I am willing to go out or other situations. I compromised many of our group gatherings to spend time with him. Weekends when I come to Kharadi, he never stops me, previously I liked it that he is giving me space to be with my friends but then I realized it's not space, it's just that he hardly cares if I am around him or not. He never asks me to spend any of the weekends with him. For him life is – morning office till 3 in afternoon, sleep for a while, tennis class, gym with his roommate, dinner and then again sleeps. I find myself nowhere in his life.

I tried to have discussion about what all I am feeling, he has no time for discussion too, he says please understand I am under too much work pressure these days. Give me some time.

I gave him his time and space, it's been months now, we have not talked for more than 5 minutes a day, I am not allowed to touch his cellphone, he says he don't like anyone doing so, I accepted this condition too' She paused and wiped her tears with her dupatta.

'RV sir am I thinking way too much? Are these things normal?' She asked

'Since how long he is behaving like this?' I asked

'It's been more than 2 months now' she answered

Listening to what Arohi said, I got the strong feeling that Akash is cheating on her but I do not want to say this as this might hurt Arohi. I asked her to give him some more time, don't bother him much, if he is actually serious, he will come to her and with time we will get the clear picture.

I silently prayed God to give her what she wants; I wanted to help her genuinely. I wanted to see her happy, smiling, doing all kind of khurapat just like she always does.

*   *   *

My dream 'to be with Arohi' took an end after Parvati's meet as she feels for someone else, I tried concentrating more on work than on her, but her problems still bothered me and somewhere in back of my mind she was there all the time. I played truth and dare with myself, asking questions and then answering it back to me. Is she okay? Are things ok in her life? Is Akash still bothering her? Is she happy?

For a moment I thought it is her personal life I should not intervene, but another portion of my heart reluctantly answered me back, she is also a part of your life, she came to you and opened up her life in front of you, she trusted you and all her problems are yours but I hate this 'Akash' topic. I do not want to discuss anything about him and any discussion with Arohi will include him.

Somehow I convinced myself, all I feel for Arohi is infatuation and not love. I should accept her with the one she loves. I have not heard from her after our meeting at Parvati. I thought to give her a call

'Hi Arohi, where are you?'

'Just got down from my office bus, walking towards home, how are you RV sir?'

'I am good; you tell me how you are? How are things?'

'Things not too good RV sir, lot many problems, lot many issues, just few days back I used to think my life is perfect, shayad kisi ki nazar lag gai, everything is falling apart and I am not able to handle' she answered in a low tone

'What happened? You talked to Akash?'

'Yes, he said he cares for me a lot, he doesn't want me to be sad but he is not sure if he will stand by me or not at the time of final verdict by Guruji' she answered

'What the hell, what does he mean by this?'

'I don't know RV sir, Di told me if a guy is not able to take stand for me then I should leave and walk away but I am not able to do so, I am trying hard to convince him, I am holding on our relationship'

'Arohi, you are such a sweetheart, still holding on, if it would have been any other girl instead of you, she would have left that jerk by now' I replied

'I cannot do that, I am deeply attached' she spoke in a heavy voice. I could hear her crying

'RV sir, this is not the only thing bothering me, there are few more things. Life is getting hard for me. I need Akash to be with me, to stand by me and support me in these difficult situations but he is nowhere' she said

'Other things? What had happened Arohi? Tell me'

'I have reached home, will talk to you later'

'Wait, you have class this weekend right?' I enquired

'Yes'

"You are not going, I will pick you up, you are bunking'

'Bunking class?'

'Yes'

'But why?' she asked

'So that we can spend time and you can share your other problems too'

'RV sir, I have not bunked any lecture in my entire life, I am scared'

'Oh My God! Are you serious? You have never bunked a lecture in your entire life?'

'Hmm' she replied

'Ok we are doing it then. Will meet you on Saturday'

Bunk At CCD

15th February 2014/ Saturday/ 11:30AM

I picked her from class and took her too our place of discussion, CCD, her eyes were little swelled up, narrating behind the scenes, she had cried a lot, I felt like going to Akash and give him a good punch, how dare he? How inhuman, who could make a girl like Arohi cry.

To cheer up her mood I bought her flowers, she smiled when I gave those to her, her smile was just a formality, inside she was bearing lots of pain. FC road's CCD was quite a big one; we chose the corner seat for 2, near a big glass window. I ordered our usual meal, toastizza with extra cheese and a coffee. She loves cheese, in spite of being a cheese lover; I wondered how she managed to maintain a perfect figure.

We made ourselves comfortable in the sofa chair.

'Is this your 1st bunk ever, seriously?' I enquired

'Yes it is, I never bunked any lectures, not even in college' she replied

'How is that possible, I mean why?'

'There is something you know, if I do anything wrong na intentionally or unintentionally, which is against rules, I get punishment then and there so I avoid doing such things' she said

I laughed at her this statement

'RV Sir, why you laughing, I am serious I will give you an example. You remember our college tech fest? 'Erudition 2009'?'

I nodded

'We had those registration counters; I and Aishyy had taken responsibility for one of the counter' She said

(We used to have tech fests in college every year, tech fest is something where lots of technical quizzes, competitions, games and workshop are being organized for 3 days, all other college students are invited to participate in those and win prizes but to participate they have to do registration at registration desk counter, paying the entry fees for the particular event/workshop/games/competition they have opted for. Generally we used to have 6 registration counters handling the bulk crowd coming from other colleges, 2 people handling each one of them, one is cashier who collects money and another provides the ID card)

She continued – 'I was the cashier handling the money, our table did not had the drawer to keep the cash, so I was keeping it separately in my wallet and Aishyy was writing ID cards, my wallet was small incapable of keeping too much of cash, so we switched our jobs after approx. 10 registrations, he became the cashier and I was the one providing ID cards. After the registrations were done, we collected all the cash in his wallet and gave it to the respective authority. I had my event starting 'the tech quiz', I was the organizer for that, as all the registrations were over so I left to prepare for the quiz. After few minutes I realized that my new cell phone was missing, I searched for it everywhere but did not find it. I opened my wallet and I saw starting 10 registration's cash kept in it which we forgot to submit, I went back to the counter gave the cash back to authorized faculty and that moment Aishyy returned me my mobile and scolded me for being careless and forgetting my cell at registration desk.'

'This could be a coincidence Arohi, how could you relate that you lost your cell because you had not returned the money and you found it just because you returned' I questioned

'I know you will find it little crazy. I know I was irresponsible who left my cell at the counter and whatever happened was because of me being careless or may be this is a mere coincidence but this happens with me every time, this is just one example. I will give you another one - 1 day I went to restaurant with 3 of my friends, restaurant cashier returned us Rs100 extra, my friends considered this to be his mistake and did not return the money, next day I was the only one suffering from food poisoning' She explained and convinced me to believe in her.

I laughed out loud holding my stomach and she gave me nasty looks saying

'Ok! Don't believe me. I don't want to share anything with you'.

'Aacha baba! Ok. I believe you; we will never go against rules. Let's come to the main agenda of this meeting, tell me now what are the other things bothering you, do not start with Akash, we will come to him later' I said

Before she could start, a CCD guy bought us our order toastizza with extra cheese and coffee, toastizza cut in 2 pieces, one bigger than the other. He placed both the things on the small circular glass table.

She continued after he left 'you have heard about my company's layoff right? They have fired 3000 employees in this quarter, people are saying that our firm is being acquired by some other organization; many of my friends got fired. Senior Management are not providing any reasons, HR just call the employee, collect their ID cards and ask them to leave the office campus then and there. One of the employees got fired just because he was leaving for his home wearing gym track suit instead of formals that too after completing his work hours. Situations are getting worse every day. They are not considering performance, rating nothing. My project is going to get over by end of this week, job of my entire project members are at stake. I had word with my manager too, if he could tag me in any other project but his reply scared me even more. He said he is also fighting hard to stay in the company, situation is same for all bands, managers, associates everyone'

'I am scared RV sir, I don't know what is waiting for me next and March is about to start, worst month for me, and all bad things happen to me in March'

I listened to her carefully and then answered

'Arohi, this is IT World– private jobs, they do not offer job security, we are just resources working for them, layoffs are very common and 1ˢᵗ of all stop blaming the Month and why are you scared, just update your resume on job portals, soon you will get calls, sit for interviews and you will be able to switch soon. You have hands-on on your technology, good communication skills; you will get a nice job with a good hike. Why to worry. This is IT world yahan aisa hota rehta hai.'

She nodded

'But all things coming together RV sir, I am not able to understand what is going on with me' she added

I offered her toastizza; she grabbed the smaller piece, leaving the bigger one for me. I asked her to relax and list all the issues she is facing.

'One - Company layoffs: DONE discussing.

What is the second one?' I asked

'Priya Di's wedding' she said and paused for a minute

And then again continued – 'Mom Dad had finalized one boy, di also liked him and everything was set. Suddenly boy's family started demanding dowry - Car, Cash and Flat in Pune. Earlier mom & dad thought that they will provide whatever Groom's family is demanding but then with their increasing demands everyone is afraid, what if, after wedding they start troubling Priya didi for more? Didi told that she doesn't want to get married in such a greedy family, she is earning well and she has self-respect. This issue has created a sad environment in family and now they will get to hear about me and Akash.

Everything is messed up around me RV sir, personal and professional life both'

'Hmm' I responded

We both kept quiet for few minutes grabbing bite of our favorite dish.

'I had word with Akash too, I asked him all the questions, why is he behaving this way' she started without me questioning her.

'What did he answer?' I enquired

'He said he is way too busy, he has lots of work these days even on weekends he has to be on office calls. RV sir I think it's me who is thinking so negative, maybe he is trying to work hard to ensure our good future and a happy, wealthy life. I stopped bugging him to spend time with me as he asked me to support him'

'Ok, so summing up all your problems: Company layoffs, Priya's wedding issue and Akash. Let's tackle them one by one each'

1) Company layoffs – nothing in our hands, what we can do is to start studying and get placed in some other company with a good package. I know it's not that easy but you can make it, I know your capability.

2) Priya's Wedding: sad situation for all family members but think it this way- we got to know about the behavior and demands of the boy's family before wedding itself. What if she would have got married and then we would have got to know about all these situations? That would have been worse right?

She nodded looking down.

3) Akash : Now tell me one thing- 'Do you really believe in whatever he is saying, after watching and noticing his actions from last few months?' I asked

'I trust him blindly, I believe whatever he says but then doubt arises when I see him going for gym and always available to attend his friend's dinner parties. I want his time to just share my everyday things with him. He should know where I am, what am I doing and vice versa.' She answered.

'Look Arohi, this guy might be cheating on you or maybe not, I just want you to be prepared for everything. I know boys, most of them are like this, they are after girls and can do anything for her till she says yes and once she is convinced and gives commitment they take her for granted. You deserve happiness dear, you deserve a lot better' I tried to explain her and warned her to be prepared for the worst.

'Didi also says the same thing but he means a lot to me' she replied

'Ok too much of serious discussion, time to cheer up, we will face all the situations together, now it's time for some chocolate. C'mon this is your 1ˢᵗ bunk and we will make it memorable' I said trying to cheer her up.

We rolled our eyes through the menu and came up with the decision of ordering Chocolate fantasy with ice-cream. I called the waiter and asked him to bring 1 chocolate fantasy with vanilla ice-cream. Waiter enquired if we want it with extra chocolate sauce, before I could respond Arohi said yes and demanded to warm it before serving.

'Have you noticed one thing? There is something good happening apart from all odds' I asked

'What is it?' she questioned back

'We are getting closer, our friendship getting stronger day by day, isn't it?' I asked doubtfully if she agrees to my point

'Yes it is, I think this is the only thing which is good at this point of time, thanks for being there with me RV sir, I feel good with you'

'Well I am RV you know, baat hi alag hai, people die to be with me' I winked

She gave a laugh saying you are Crazy, her sad face now has curves of smile, I was happy looking at her sudden mood change. At least I am capable of making her smile.

She took the tissue paper and drew a smiley on it mentioning today's date, writing both of our names in calligraphy, describing her 1ˢᵗ bunk then she asked me to autograph it. While she was showing her creativity on tissue I messaged her:

'Adaayen badi funky, kare hai nautanki,

ye chori badi drama queen hai,

badi badi aakhen hain aasun ki tanki

ye chori badi drama queen hai'

She checked her messages, read it and gave me notorious look. She laughed out loud warning me 'RV sir you going to get lots of beating from me'

I winked

'OMG its 6', she shouted looking at her mobile, she counted hours on her fingers and said 'we are here since last 7 hours?'

I was amazed too; we have spent 7 hours that is almost equivalent to entire day, sitting in a coffee shop and chit-chatting. I feel good. I had not spent these many hours with anyone sitting at one place. We both laughed, she told me to drop her at her place as it was getting late. We ate our chocolate fantasy and left.

I dropped her; and I drove back home thinking of her, her problems, solutions to her problem and about to make her life perfect again.

As I reached I saw her message:

Tere jaisa yaar kahan

Kahan aisa yaarana

Yaad karegi duniya

Tera mera afsaana

I smiled and replied her back

Yaaro dosti badi hi haseen hai,

ye na ho to kya fir bolo ye zindagi hai

'Thank you RV sir for everything, GN TC'

Get A Job

I messaged her she did not respond, I called her she didn't answer, I left her voice messages, still no response. Her last seen on Whatsapp was 8:00AM. This is for the first time she is not on line for so long. I thought to call Priya and will ask her to transfer the call to Arohi

'Hello Madam. Kahan...?' I asked

'Hey RV, I am in Bhopal' She replied

'Bhopal?'

'Yes, Mom Dad called me to discuss some family issues' she explained

'When did you leave?' I enquired

'Yesterday night, it was a sudden plan so did not got the chance to tell anyone'

'Hmm'

'Arohi came along?' I questioned

'No, she is there in Pune'

'Ok, Cya. Let me know once you are back'

'Sure' she said and I disconnected the call

71

Why this girl is not answering my calls and messages? I hope she is alright. I tried calling her again 'Arohiiiiii, pick up the call please. I am getting anxious now'. I called her continuously still no response. I missed her badly; I had been trying to reach her since morning.

Finally 1:00 AM I got the call back.

'RV sir' she spoke

'Where have you been Arohi, I had been calling you since morning, why were you not picking up the damn call? No reply on WhatsApp too? How can you be so careless, I was so worried about you' I busted on her.

She did not speak a word, I could hear her weeping.

'I am sorry, Are you ok? I was just concerned. Please speak sweetie, you OK na?'

'What happened? Tell me please' I asked

She did not speak a word; rather she was not in condition to speak a word.

'I insisted her, Arohi please speak, I might be able to help you, tell me what happened please'

'RV Sir, I broke up with Akash and I lost my job too, It's 17th March. 'March' I told you na' she spoke. Her soft voice sounded heavy. I did not know what to say. I was silent, so was she, I could hear her sobbing.

'I am coming there Arohi, please wait for few minutes'

'No RV sir, I want to stay alone for a while, the one I trusted most cheated on me, I do not want to meet anyone, I just want to sleep' she spoke in a breaking voice.

'Do you have office tomorrow? Notice period? Anything...?' I enquired

'Yes, I have but I am not in the condition to go. I will take leave' she answered

I felt helpless, I didn't know what to do, how to cheer her up. I had to wait till morning. I kept talking till she slept, she sobbed and felt asleep.

72

I took leave from my office and Morning 9 I went to her. I rang the bell, she opened the door. She has swelling in her eyes and was still in her day before office dress – red shirt and trouser. Her tears did not seem to stop; I wiped her tears and hugged her tightly. She cried madly.

'He cheated on me RV sir; I am not able to believe. I lost my job too, what is happening with me? I am losing control on my life. It seems someone has done some black magic on me' she said

I knew she would have not eaten anything since yesterday. I took her to her room, made her sit on double bed that she and Priya share. I went to kitchen boiled milk and prepared toast, she refused to drink or eat anything, I tore bread into small crumbs and made her eat with my hands.

Comforting her I said 'We knew this is going to happen, Akash didn't deserve you sweetheart, you deserve lot more happiness. You deserve someone who will keep you like a princess'

You know what? Akash gave me the same reason. He said 'Arohi, you are a real nice girl; I do not want to spoil your life by being in it, you deserve lots of happiness and I will not be able to provide that, I care for you that's why I am doing all this'

'How is this possible RV sir, if he cares, then why is he doing all this?' She asked innocently.

'You still trust him?' I asked

She nodded

'No Arohi, please... He took the advantage of your trust. Why are you not accepting the truth?'

'Seema told me that before I met Akash, he was trying on her. She also told me that he was trying for Vineeti too, his office colleague. But when I came in his life he broke his contact with both of them. I am not able to figure out what is right, what is wrong. Whom to trust?' she said

'I lost my job, mom dad are concerned about di's wedding, everything happening together. I don't know what to do?' she continued

I held her hand 'Arohi listen to me, he cheated you, this is his biggest mistake. He is the one who should suffer not you, he does not deserve you and sweetie you deserve a lot better and seriously are you concerned about job? There are hell lot of jobs in market and a girl like you who got selected in maximum campus placements in college is worrying about it? I am sure you will make it to a better place. It's just the bad time, we will face it together. Something big is waiting for you. Please do not lose hope' I tried encouraging her.

'RV sir, I don't want to stay here. I want me and Priya di to shift to Kharadi, with Aditi di, Neha di and Mini. You will also be there in neighborhood; with so many friends around I will get less time to think about Akash and will have courage to face all the problems. I want to be away from him' she said

'That would be great, that would be so much fun, we will meet every day and this is something that you love "Our Group" right? God is doing all this to bring you close to all of us. Not only on weekends but we will meet on weekdays too. The only reason you were staying here was your office, now that issue will also be resolved, we will search job in some nearby location as we have lots of IT companies near Kharadi. Hai na...!' I pampered her like a small baby.

She nodded!

'So this weekend you are shifting to Kharadi, wow that would be so much fun, please smile...smile baby!!' I said tickling her; she smiled with tears in her eyes.

Her tears made me feel weak, I cannot see her like this anymore, I felt so helpless and I tried to make her laugh but each of my attempts failed. I held her right hand and asked her for a promise that she will not cry for someone who has hurt her so much, who was just playing around with her, someone who is not worth her tears. I made her realize that she is the princess of her parents, most loved one in the group, and she has so many good friends who can do anything to make her smile.. Inspite of knowing this, if she will cry then all her loved ones will lose in front of that person who cheated on her.

'Arohi, look into my eyes' I insisted

She looked at me with her watery eyes; those innocent eyes can compel anyone to do anything for her.

'Will you promise me? Please?' I urged

'It is difficult, RV sir'

'Indeed it is dear but you will have to do this, you want him to win over all of us?' I asked

'NO'

'I want my khurapati Arohi back' I insisted

She nodded

Great! So this weekend you will be SHIFTING, start packing your bags! I said in a loud KING tone

'We will need to give 1 month prior notice to the owner, so next weekend not possible'

'Ok! Well in that case also we will be meeting every evening after office. We will study together, make profile on Naukri.com and other job portals and will prepare for interviews' I suggested.

'It will be difficult for you to come here every day. Baner is far from Kharadi RV sir, I will manage myself' she said

'I am not going to leave you alone in any condition. If you will stay alone, instead of studying you will recall old memories and will cry again'

'I will try to concentrate' she said

'Madam while studying with you I will also get a chance to brush up my technical skills. We will sit and study common subjects like SQL together and domain subjects separately sitting in the same room. I also need to switch and boost my package. So no more arguments on this' I ordered

She agreed

*   *   *

We made the timetable as her domain was different from mine, I am into Oracle Apps and she is a Quality Analyst. We decided to study the common topic like "PL SQL" together 1 hour every day and rest of the time we will study our respective subjects sitting in the same room.

Everyday 7:30 PM, I used to be at her place. I enjoyed studying with her. It felt like college days were back. Exams, tension to succeed. Only one difference was here the syllabus was not defined. We had lot to study.

We made our study set up in her living room. A wooden table placed at the middle of the room with two chairs on opposite side of the table. Her dell laptop hides her beautiful face from my site, forcing me to concentrate on my studies, after few hours of studies she used to prepare Bournvita milk for both us. I pulled out few interview questions on automation, manual testing, ETL testing and on BIG data, to help her with her interviews.

I loved that 1 hour when she sits beside me while studying PL SQL, it was like meeting of 2 opposite corners of the river.

Every day we studied hard, she was confident on clearing the interviews, I used to ask her technical interview questions and she used to answer them with full confidence. I felt proud looking at her. The way she is handling situations, she is brave and definitely she deserves happiness. I prayed to God silently to give back her beautiful smile.

Time was not in her favor, she feared what if God does not want to put end to her problems.

'RV sir, no matter how confident I am, no matter how much I study, right now time is not favoring me, I am scared, what if things are not good? What if they reject me?' she asked doubtfully

'Sweetie, God was testing you, his testing is done and you passed; now everything will fall in place. Soon you will get a good job and your Priya di will be married to a good person who respects her and your family' I assured.

'U sure...? Please ask God na, to make everything perfect now. I know he is trying to make me strong but please tell him I have become strong. I will not be able to bear any more' she said in a low innocent voice looking at her SQL sheets.

I liked her faith in God; I liked her approach of taking things positively in spite of whatever was happening. She believed God is doing all this to make her strong, her thinking and innocence is adorable.

'You will not suffer any more dear, bad times are over and everything happens for a reason, God must have planned something great for you, let us just wait for it' I replied.

She picked up her mobile and added a wish in our wish list 'To get a good job soon'.

'RV sir, Am I too immature?' She asked

'Immature? Why are you asking this question?' I enquired

'Akash told me once that I am immature' she said. I could see pain in her eyes.

'He is immature to think like this. You are mature enough to understand relationships and other essential things and along with maturity you have innocence of a child. He is immature, who is not able to understand you' I replied

She nodded

I asked her about the calls she is getting from different firms, also about her office situations to bring her out of Akash.

'Almost all HR's are my friends in my organization, as I had anchored few of the Global technical events and annual functions for the company they are trying hard to hold me back. Arushi, one of my HR friend told me that almost all projects are gone from the company, still if I want she can tag me in any of the project for the time being and then I can switch to other projects later, She also told me that I was lucky to get 15 days of prior notice as I was well acquainted with the HR and PDAC team otherwise all other employees are called by HR and they were asked to leave same day. As of now I have told Arushi that I am trying for other firms as staying in this company is a big gamble, there is no job security' she answered

'Also I have got calls from few organizations, next week is lined up for interviews, and I hope I will be able to crack those' she said optimistically

'You will surely dear, All the best' I wished her all the luck!

*   *   *

4th April 2014/ Friday/ 7:00 PM

A big oval table placed in between of the room equipped with needed technology is occupied by 12 IT professionals of WFN team with ID cards hanging down their neck, eyes stuck on laptops screens and hands on keyboard. A fat guy at managerial position sitting at the head position of the table asked everyone about the status of migration objects, everyone looking at the screens replied him. I had 2 objects left to be migrated, I tried making it as soon as possible, and I knew I was already late for my meeting with Arohi. I wrapped up everything in an hour, sent the status mail to higher authorities, closed my laptop lid, plugged out my charger, packed my bag and came running to parking. I realized I forgot my bike keys and cell phone in the conference room, I scolded myself and ran back again, climbed stairs till second floor and collected my belongings. I could see some eyes still on screen struggling with the objects. I quickly returned back to the parking. I felt something tickling my right thigh. That's my mobile, Arohi calling me. Oh! I am late she might be angry; I was ready for the scolding and picked up the call.

'RVVVVVVVVVVVVVVVVV sirrrrrrrrrrrrrr, where have you been…? I called you 4 times and you did not pick up my call, I want to tell you something' She shouted in an excited tone. I was hearing her like this after a long time

'I am so sorry Arohi; I did not notice your call, tell me what happened?' I asked curiously.

'I have 2 good news but I am not going to tell you so easily. You missed my calls and you deserve punishment for that' she said and giggled, I could sense her running in round robin fashion and talking to me.

'Ok, I accept all your punishments, 1st let me know the news' I urged.

'Priya didi's wedding got fixed. Boy's name is Rahul. Family is good, they are our old acquaintance, dii knows the boy since childhood, I am soooooooooooo happy, I want to go shoppinggggggggggggggggg' she said in a singing tone

'ohhwaoooo!! Great news! Congratulationssssssssss! I am so happy. What is the second good news?' I enquired

'I got offer letters from 2 companies both with 60% hike' she shouted with joy

A whoop of delight ran through my body, I jumped with happiness;

'Yesssssssssss yessssssssss she made it' I congratulated myself.

Her shout of joy gave me such a relief. I would have hugged her if she would have been in front of me

'Congratulationssssssssssssssss!!The party time begins now'

I shouted at top of my voice.

'When is Priya coming back?' I enquired?

'She will be back tomorrow morning, we have to pack now and move to kharadiiiiiiiiiii this Sundayyyyyyy' she said shouting, giggling enjoying her good time.

'Ok cool! So now I am coming to your place, It's time for celebration, get ready girl' I announced and disconnected the call

I was so happy to hear her excited and happy voice after so long, it was like music to my ears, and they were deprived to hear her enchanting voice. Waooo finallyyy!! She is happy and I am happy because she is happy. I wanted to reach her place as soon as possible, I wanted to dance and sing with her.

I reached her place by 8:15 PM, door was open, music was loud, system played 'Maine hoto se lagai to hungama ho gaya.' I called out her name.

She came running dancing with a water bottle, wearing red colored frock pattern one piece with small black dots on it and black heels, she danced following Kangna Ranauat's steps from Queen. She behaved as if she is drunk, danced and sang loud 'Maine hoto se lagai to humgama ho gaya', she took my hand and pulled me on floor to dance, I laughed looking at my 'water' drunk girl. She was happy, so happy. I pulled her cheeks and congratulated her.

We went out for dinner; she suggested a good roof top restaurant nearby her area. She looked pretty, her face glowing again, she was laughing, giggling, singing. She placed the order for the evening. We waited for our cuisine to arrive, she showed me the offer letters of both the companies in her mobile and my chatter box started narrating the whole day's story.

'Today is such a good day RV sir, especially few hours of the evening, My interview for APD was scheduled for morning 9, they told me they will be taking 4 rounds, 2 technical, 1 managerial and 1 HR. I reached at the address they provided me by 8:30AM, 1st round of interview started at sharp 9, I got selected in round 1 and interviewer forwarded my profile for 2nd round that will be taken up by senior authorities of the project. While I was waiting for my 2nd round to start I checked my mails. It showed me a new mail and that was the offer letter from the company whose interview was conducted day before yesterday. They accepted my proposition and offered me 60% hike, I was so happy, around 10:30AM my second round started. 2 gentleman, around 40 years of age, started firing questions, I answered them all, they were impressed when they got to know I had worked on Automation QTP, ETL, Big Data, Micro-strategy, QC in such short duration of my career, they complimented me and said we need such resources in our project, HR and telephonic also went well. I told the HR about the offer I am holding. She assured that she will be sending me the best possible offer within 3 hours.

I went back to my office, gave my resignation and asked SS-HR team to initiate clearance process, I informed all my friends about the situation, we gathered for a small party, and I got soo soo soo many chocolates' She said making her eyes big and spreading her hands.

'And while the celebration was on, I got mumma's call saying date for didi's wedding is fixed, I was on cloud 9'

After narrating her entire day she took a breath, drank water and passed a smile of relief.

'Things are good now RV sir. I just wish I forgive and forget Akash too' she added

'You will baby, after shifting to Kharadi, we will not give you time to remember him and I am so so so so happy for you. So tell me which organization will you be joining? And what location...?'

'Not sure, I think I will join APD. It's a product based company, and glass door rating is too good, I have heard it is associate centric, also it is nearby Kharadi just 12 kms from our society' She said

We discussed about package, other incentives and facilities both the companies are providing, looking at all aspects we both voted for APD. While we were in conversation, her mom called her to give her more information about Priya's wedding and to know more about her new job. She got busy on her call. I quickly went and ordered a chocolate cake for her. I came back in 5 minutes giving all guidelines to the waiter. She was still busy with her call when waiter arrived with cake and flowers. She was surprised, her eyes wide open looking at the cake; she gave me an amazed expression mixed with happiness.

'Mom, I will call you back in sometime' she said and disconnected the call

'OMG RV sir, what is all this?'

'Something special, for someone special on a special occasion and on completion of 1 wish from our wish list- you got the job' I answered.

'Awwwww, thank you so very much, you are such a darling, I love it'

She blew the candles, cut the cake, I clapped and congratulated her. Waiter took our picture; she made me eat the slice of cake with her hands. What a perfect evening, perfect dinner with a perfect person. I realized something that night, I did not wanted her for myself because I knew that is not possible, I just want to be with her till the time it is possible for us to be together, I don't want to miss a single expression of her face, I wanted to keep her protected from all the worries. I just wanted her to be happy with me or without me.

12th April 2014 / Saturday

Sunday morning, a loading tempo was parked outside Fortune Green society, Kharadi. With all kind of stuff - clothes, Almirah, water purifier, various boxes labeled as utensils, shoes, books etc. Me, Pajju, Nik, Atul and Tiddi went down to help girls with their luggage. Arohi and Priya were too excited shifting to Kharadi, on the other hand they get bogged down with all the packing they have done in just one day.

Priya guided loading Auto to come inside the society, along with 2 workers who were going to help us to carry luggage till 4th floor. Workers started unloading the auto.

'Bhaiya naye logo ka society main shift hona mana hai, kiska samaan hai ye...?' Watchman shouted.

I and Nik went to watchman asking about his concern. He told us that new people are not allowed to shift in this society, especially bachelors. Builder of the society has made this new rule, shifting is allowed only if builder permits.

'We will lose our job if we will permit madam to shift' watchman grumbled.

We called Aditi, Mini and Neha downstairs and asked them to call the builder, seek for his permission to let Priya and Arohi shift. All the boys stood away from that area to avoid any more bachelors' trouble. Aditi and Neha went to builder's office and bought him along with them where the auto was parked.

He had a heavy personality, dark in color, big pot belly, bald, wore white kurta pajama and heavy gold chains and 8 gold rings in his 8 fingers, he looked like Bollywood movie's mafia don.

'We have restricted the entry of bachelors in the society; we cannot allow them to shift according to the new rules' builder said crossing his hands in a stiff tone.

'We already had word with our owner that 2 of our friends are going to shift with us, he was all okay with this, It had been 3 years we are staying here, and we have never created trouble to anyone in the society. Also it is a 3 BHK, too big for 3 girls. Sharing between 5 girls is manageable' Neha tried to convince.

'How can your owner permit you without asking me? Call him here' Builder ordered.

Aditi called owner and explained him the whole situation, she urged him to come as soon as possible. Priya and Arohi got tensed as they were left with no place to go.

'He is troubling them more because all girls are standing there, Moron' Nik said angrily.

'Maze le raha hai aur kuch nai, ladkiyon ko pareshan karne main maza aata hai' Tiddi replied

'I think we should go there, guys' Atul said

I stopped them all; as our intervention could go against the girls.

Everyone waited for the owner, till the time girls tried to convince the builder. Owner arrived along with his mother; they both seem to be well educated. Looking at them we thought they will be able to handle the situation. Owner, his mother and the builder went inside the office. They had some discussion for about an hour and came back.

'Just because you are girls, we are allowing you. We do not want to hear any complaints from your flat' builder warned looking at Priya and Arohi.

Some man out of the blue interrupted and said 'There were few vodka and wine bottles kept outside their flat. I had clicked the picture and sent to you Guptaji. Remember?'

Aditi reluctantly replied 'those were not ours, people staying in front have kept it near our door, we have already informed about the issue to owner'

Few other settlements and rent agreement discussions were done, auto wala was getting impatient as he had other order of shifting, and he had to leave early. Builder prohibited the use of society lift for carrying the luggage.

Finally girls got the permit to shift, workers helped in unloading the auto, they refused to take luggage till 4th floor as it was already late for them. Priya gave them their amount along with waiting charges and asked them to leave. Owner along with his mother and the builder left too.

We all gathered, looked at the luggage, Arohi started counting 1-2-3-4-----45 items including big Amirah and different size boxes, then she counted the people -Nik, me, Pajju, Tiddi, Aditi, Neha, Priya, Arohi, Mini and Atul. So total 9 and half people.

'9 and half...?' Aditi asked

'I counted Tiddi sir as half' she giggled looking at tiddi

Tiddi hit her with the ball he was holding, she giggled again

So the body builder type people – Pajju sir, RV sir and Nik sir, please take care of almirah. Place it in my room, after Almirah is placed you can pick other stuff one by one.

Everyone looked at each other giving confused look

Are you seriously expecting us to carry this luggage till 4th floor? Tiddi asked doubtfully.

'Yes you have no choice other than doing so' Priya answered rather ordered.

'I divided the tasks na, What's the issue?' Arohi asked keeping both her hands on her waist.

'Arohi, are you done or you want to speak anything else?' Nik asked teasing her

'I am done' she answered

'OK, guys so now the plan is : me, RV and Pajju will go and keep almirahs first, then we will divide the floors, 2 people at each floor, ground to 1st – Pajju and Neha, 1st to 2nd – aditi and Tiddi, 2nd to 3rd Neha and Nik, 3rd to 4th Atul and Priya. We will pass on the luggage floor wise, this will take less time and less efforts' I suggested

'What will I do?' Arohi enquired

'You will give us water, coz if you fall carrying luggage we will not carry you till 4th floor' Pajju teased her

'Nooo, I will also do something' she said and picked one box and her guitar and started marching towards stairs.

We all laughed and started with our work, I had no floor partner, and I took medium sized boxes till 4th floor. It took 2 hours for us to bring the entire luggage and place them at their respective places according to the labels on them.

Everyone was tired; we ordered pizza and had lunch.

Priya and Neha will share one room, Aditi and Mini another. Arohi demanded a single room; she took the small room so that she can carry out her painting activities without disturbing anyone. Again we divided ourselves in unpacking and arranging the stuff.

Pointing at luggage Tiddi said 'Itna samaan koi leta hai kya ye to 10 logo ka samaan lag ra hai'

Priya and Arohi gave her angry look and signaled him to get back to work.

Shifting was fun; all of us were together, working, unpacking, teasing each other, fighting, talking, and eating. Arohi put her paintings and creative stuff on the walls of her room. Beautiful paper lamps, colorful balls were hanging down the roof, she placed her table facing north with a bonsai plant and a statue of Radha Krishna on it.

My princess converted her room into a small palace. Beautiful blue colored curtains, complementing lamps and colorful paintings gave a new definition to the room. Big windows in the room showered sunlight in form of blessing.

'Hey Arohi, look that is our window; we can talk through windows' Nik showed her our room window, visible from her room.

'Waoo, yes Nik sir we can communicate through windows now' she answered Nik

And looked at me, I looked at her and we smiled.

12 Hours

3rd May 2014/ Saturday/ 8:30 AM

'Mere samne wali khidki main,

Ek Chand ka tukda rehta hai

Afsos ye hai, ki wo humse kuch ukhda ukhda rehta hai'

'Gm RV Sir, hehehe nice song by the way' she texted back

'Come on your window'

I could see a hand sliding the curtain and she was there at her window, looking so pure in the morning sunlight, hiding her night clothes with a blue colored dupatta. Cool morning breeze tickled her hairs. She just got up; I could make that out from her eyes.

'What are her plans for the day?' I asked her making appropriate gestures to make her understand my question. She understood it and shook her thumb indicating she had No plans, she tried saying something moving her hand round above her head and pointing ceiling. I failed to understand, it was like "dumb charades". I gestured her to repeat, she did the same action again, and I thought it is better to call for ear pleasures as eyes already got their treat.

I called her up, asking for her plans. 'No plans RV sir, all didi's and Mini are going Mumbai for shopping this weekend and I am not going because I have an important workshop today. You tell what's up with you boys?'

'Nik and Tiddi left for Bhopal yesterday evening, Pajju has weekend office, Atul is going on trip with his office group, and I have no plans as of now. How many hours workshop do you have and when are all your flat mates leaving?'

'It is for 3 hours 11 AM to 2 PM and everyone is leaving in an hour' she replied

'COOL! So I am meeting you after your class, by what time you will be home?' I asked.

'RV sir I am planning to stay at Heena's place in Baner, as everyone at home will be back by Sunday evening. So tonight I will have to stay alone if I stay in Kharadi. I am scared' she replied.

'Areyyy why you are scared…? I and Pajju will be there and Heena stays in the same society as Akash? Right…?' I asked

'yes, but…'

'No If's no but's, if you will go there, you will be again entangled in Akash's memories and I don't want that. You come back home, we will have fun here' I ordered.

I could see her nodding. She smiled and disconnected the call. She waved me goodbye and closed the curtain.

She was back home by 3, we met at her place. We had rats jumping in our stomach; we decided to order food online. Confused what to order, we provided options to each other:

'Pizza' I asked

'No, no Pizza today. Chinese?' she said

'NO' I replied

'Italian?' I asked

'NO' she replied

'I want to eat something good but what?' she said confused with many options

'RV sir, let's cook' she said making her eyes BIG.

'What do you mean by let's cook?' I asked

'okay I will cook, happy?'

'Very'

We went to kitchen, figuring what we can cook.

'OK so here is an idea, presenting before you, CHEF AROHI' she said wearing an apron

I laughed at her gestures

'So CHEF Arohi, what is the menu for the day?' I asked

'I will be making Butter Paneer Masala, parathas, Daal and Rice for you. Mr. RV please have a seat and wait for few minutes, your food will be ready soon' she greeted me as a guest of her small restaurant.

She took out onions, tomatoes, green chilies and started chopping them; She asked me to equally divide green chili, chopped onions and tomatoes in 2 parts as she will need it to make both daal fry and Butter Paneer Masala. I watched her making butter paneer and tried to learn the recipe.

She asked me to grind few cashew nuts and add little water to it, before switching on the grinder; she got busy washing daal and kept it on a burner to get it boiled. On another burner she kept a frying pan and heated cooking oil and butter, added chopped onion and bay leaf to it. By the time I was done with grinding of the cashews, she told me to stir onion till it gets brown and her guest @ restaurant was turned to her helper in kitchen. While I was busy stirring she took some flour out in a big plate, added water, pinch of salt and made soft solid paste, she made small roles out of it. I watched her and loved her multitasking skills.

Back to Butter Paneer Masala, she added green chilies, red chili powder, and cashew paste waited for a minute and added tomato. I was again given the task to stir it. She started making parathas on 3rd burner. After few minutes she returned to the 2nd burner, added coriander powder, few masalas, little milk, water, cream and salt. I was back to my position stirring it. Changing my task she told me to cut paneer into small pieces. I followed her order.

She was ready with her parathas, Butter Paneer Masala was done too, and 2 burners were empty and now its turn for the rice. All my tasks were also over and I was free to tickle and irritate her.

She made all the arrangements for making jeera rice and placed cooker on burner number 3, I played with her hair, she pushed me back, I tickled her, and she pushed me back. I opened her hair this time she put her spoon down, kept both her hands on her waist and gave me angry looks.

'RV Sir I am working na, can't you see? Go and sit on the dining table' she said pointing finger towards the dining table and tied her hair again. Disobeying her order I stood beside her. She ignored my presence and got back to her tasks, while rice was getting prepared, she put tadka to the boiled daal. I started to play with her hair again, she pushed me and I kept my hand on the cooker in order to balance myself.

'AAOUCHHHH' I screamed

'oh No...! I am so so sorry' she regretted her action and put my hand in the running water

'Look this is why I was telling you not to do any masti here' she scolded and applied antiseptic on my hand.

'I am so sorry RV sir' she kept on apologizing. I loved the way she was taking care of me.

'It is ok, sweetheart, I am not hurt that bad' I said making her calm.

She made me sit on the chair and prepared the dining table

'FOOD is ready' she said on 3rd whistle of cooker.

'Finally, I will get to eat' my hunger gave the reaction.

'Wait sir I will serve you the most delicious meal that you will not get in any restaurant' she said and served me Paratha, daal and Butter Paneer. I was again a guest of her small restaurant.

'I cannot eat this food' I said

'Why' she asked perplex

I showed her my burnt hand and said 'How will I eat with cream on, someone will have to make me eat'

She smiled, 'you are naughty RV sir' she said sitting next to me

She made me eat with her hands, I loved the food, I wish I could kiss her hands and let her know they are magical. Every bite she made me eat with her hands was like 'amrit' to me.

'kisi k haanth se khane ka maza hi kuch aur hai' I said and winked.

She smiled,

'Waise you are very rude, you did not even complimented me that food is good' she said crossing her hands.

'Ohh yes!! Food is ok ok, you need to improve a lot, I will teach you cooking, join my classes. 'how to be a perfect chef' and you will learn soon' I teased her.

She pinched my arm, kept the plate down and said 'you eat on your own.'

'Acha baba I am sorry, food is so tasty that I can eat your fingers too, I didn't knew that you cook so good, now make me eat please I am still hungry' I tried coaxing her

We finished our lunch, cleared the table and came in the living room, I switched on the Television and the advertisement on sports channel made me recall tonight is "Manchester vs Barcelona"

I called Pajju in excitement to bet on the teams, he chose Barcelona; mine was Manchester, bet 2000 bucks. Pajju informed that he will not be coming home tonight as he will be going sports bar with his team mates to watch the match, He invited me too. I did not accept the offer rather made an excuse that I will be out too. I did not tell him about Arohi being alone at home.

'Manchester will beat Barcelona for sure this time' I said to myself

'When is the match' she enquired, passing a water bottle to me.

'Tonight starting at 1:00AM' I answered

'Ohh!! I think I should go and stay at Heena's place, I do not want to stay alone' she murmured

'Why do you want to go there, I will stay here with you? Is there a problem with that?' I questioned

'Pajju sir also coming kya?' she questioned me back

'NO, he has plans' I replied

She looked confused.

'Are you scared of me?' I asked

'No, it's not that'

'Then what is it? we all have spent so many nights together, this is not the 1st time' I said

'Yes RV sir but there is a difference na, we 'ALL' had spent so many nights together but today....' She said stressing the word 'ALL'

'So you are worried because it's just you and me tonight' I said

'Yes, it will not look good na' she said

'Not look good? To whom? We will not tell this to anyone' I announced

She gave me a puzzled look

'Look dear 1st answer me few questions, are you scared of me? Do you think I will do something to you?'

'NO, it is not that, it's just what people will say. Didi also taunted me once saying that I have started talking to you a lot, when I was on call with you' she answered

'Listen, what matters right now is what you want, what you feel is right; if people will not understand we will not tell them. We will enjoy our time and there is nothing to be scared of. We are good friends and we are not doing anything wrong. We will just be talking and watching TV. Important thing is you should be comfortable. If you want to go to Heena's place I will drop you there' I said.

'RV sir, I wanted to talk to you about something' she said in her innocent and concerned voice

'Tell me dear'

'We are friends na, last few days you and I have come closer, everyone has noticed that. Please promise that we will not fall for each other' she said nervously

'What' I enquired

'RV sir, being best friends is the 1ˢᵗ step to fall in love, I do not want the same scenario that happened with Atul, he felt for me and our friendship got spoiled. I do not want the same situation between us. We have become really close and I feel myself very comfortable with you. I do not want to lose you and our friendship. So, to avoid any such situations let us make a rule – 'We both will not fall for each other'.' she said

'But feelings are feelings na, what if we start feeling for each other?'

'No, NO na, to avoid that only I am asking to make this rule' she insisted.

'Are but that will be awesome. You and I, same group, you will never have to leave your group even after marriage, one of your wish will be fulfilled. Things will be perfect and best friends make best couple' I convinced and winked at her.

'No na RV sir, you do not understand. It is not possible. Inter-caste marriage, no way, my parents will kill me. Please agree to my point' she pleaded me to accept her request.

'OK, if you want it this way, then we both will not fall for each other, RULE accepted'

Ahhh such a relief, she said and lay on the mattress.

'So you still want to go at Heena's place' I questioned making a demon expression with my one eyebrow up

She giggled and answered 'now I will stay'

'We are not going to tell this to anyone na, It's our little secret' She asked

'Yes dear, people do not have the capacity to understand our friendship, so this will be between you and me only' I assured

We had discussions on many things that night. I got to know her better; she got to know me better. We shared stuff we like, dislike, fav movies, fav food, common choices like bhindi ki sabzi, Butter paneer Masala, our passions, our career, our family, her ambition to be a great artist, she shared her business plans she had in her mind but to execute them she needed money and to earn that IT was the great option, she wants to achieve everything on her own without bothering her parents, I got to know a different side of her.

Sweet, little, innocent, khurapati Arohi is actually very ambitious, she is able to manage family, friends, career, and her passions very well. Her decision making ability and plans proved her to be a mature girl with a smart thought process. I told her about one of my dream 'to be a part of Indian army', I told her about my NDA interviews and how luck did not favour me in achieving my dream. I told her about my responsibilities towards my parents and home, how everything is dependent on me and bhaiya and it's us who has to take care of mom, dad and their health. I shared my plan of opening a small restaurant in Pune. She listened carefully.

We kept talking and changing places. Living room to balcony, again back to living room, then her room, back to balcony, finally in living room. Lunch was heavy so we adjusted our dinner with a glass full of chocolate milk. It was just two of us @ home yet nobody else's presence was missed. I felt so complete. We had so much to talk.

She told me about her childhood best friends Arti and Shaheen and all the khurapats they did together. Once she started with the topic 'Arti', 'Shaheen' it was difficult to stop her, she told me how different they are from each other yet best of besties, they both were Arohi's guru who taught her all kind of khurapats. She was so proud having them as their childhood besties.

She told - Arti and Shaheen were the bold ones and she was the silent one, I wondered 'Is she really the silent one? Girl who speaks without taking a pause' She told how different were their dreams, She wanted to be a great designer, Arti wanted to be a psychiatrist and Shaheen aspired to be a director. Shaheen's parents supported her and today she is in the industry making films with Shahid, Amir and other famous actors. She told me proudly about her achievements. Arti's and Arohi's parents wanted them to go for engineering as they were scared of sending their girls in a different field's altogether. Both followed what their parents wanted but never compromised on their dreams, with engineering and jobs they continued their passion.

I told her about my experience of being in a boy's school, about our urge of talking to girls. I told her about my childhood friends, my football trophies, about my siblings, my elder brother and sister and about how they both did not liked milk. Every morning before going to school three of us used to get a glass of Bournvita milk. I being a milk lover used to finish my glass in one go, both my siblings waited for mom to go in kitchen for packing our lunch boxes, as she used to go in, I used to empty both of their glasses as well, so 3 glasses of milk every morning. She repeated my sentence making her eyes big '3 glasses of milk every morning, OMG! This is the reason of you being so strong' she said touching my biceps. We laughed, we got emotional, sharing old memories and it was around 12:50 AM when she reminded me about my football match.

1:00 AM Manchester and Barcelona were there on the field. I sat on the mattress lying on floor in front of the television, supported my back on the wall, she also lay down on mattress, reading her novel. She held my hand and felt asleep. I watched her sleeping.

She looked so innocent with her child like features; there was a part of her that was still a little girl. She looked so peaceful like an angel while sleeping. She curded herself and held my hand with both her hands, I bent down and smelled her hair, looked at her more closely, the shade of pink on her cheeks complimented her lips. Her eyelashes were perfectly curled up and looked longer, she moved a bit breaking my trail of thoughts.

I cannot look at her like this, I am not her boyfriend. I am just a friend to her, her senior. Her RULE echoed in my mind. 'We cannot fall for each other'. Plus it will be too awkward if she wakes up and found me gaping at her. I tried distracting myself, I concentrated on the football match, as the luck was mine, and she was with me. Manchester WON!

I tried waking her up, asking her to move to bedroom as there were too many mosquitoes in the living room. She did not respond to my request; she was deep in her sleep. I do not want to disturb her sound sleep. I wrapped her in my arms and picked her up, her face tilted towards my chest and rested there, I could feel her warmth. She whispered something that I could not understand; maybe she was talking to herself in her dreams. I could easily handle her, she is light weighted. I carefully took her inside the room and placed her on the bed, I covered her with the blanket. I wanted to sleep besides her, I wanted to keep looking at her all night but I did not want things to look wrong in her eyes. I didn't know how she will react when she will wake up and will find me next to her. I stood there for a while, staring at her, she curled herself again inside the blanket. Unwillingly I moved out of her room and slept in the living room thinking about my beautiful moments with her.

* * *

At sun up the next morning, she woke me up with a sweet smile; I could hear the most soothing sound reaching my ears, 'RV sir, wake up. Its 9 in the morning' I opened my eyes, 1ˢᵗ thing I saw was her holding a cup of coffee, her hair fell on my face as she adjusted herself to keep coffee mug on the side table besides me. Her fragrance was like a lovely natural perfume, so fresh. I wish I could hold her and smell her.

She shook me again; her vibrations bought me into senses, out from my beautiful thoughts.

'RV sir, here is your coffee, please wake up its 9' she said

I rubbed my eyes, held my cup of coffee and looked at her. She was ready with her questions and fired one by one when she saw me awake and back to my senses.

'RV sir, how did I go inside my room? On my bed?' she asked

'Don't you remember?' I enquired

'No, I don't. All what I remember is I was reading my novel here in the living room while you were watching your match'

'Yes that is correct' I said

'Aree, so how did I went in my room, on my bed?' she asked me impatiently jumping on floor

'I took you in your room' I answered

I saw her facial expression changing, form questioning to curious and nervous.

'You took me? How????????' she asked in a low tone, barely audible with her hands joined and fingers crossed

'You are not that heavy, you have maintained yourself very well' I replied keeping coffee mug back on side table and cracking my knuckles.

'You picked me up in your arms' she said in a concerned tone and sat beside me

'Yes, I did' I answered

'But why...? I was comfortable here na' she asked

'Mosquitoes were troubling you here, I tried waking you up but you were in your sound sleep and did not responded me back, so I had no other option' I answered

She looked down and then towards me and then again down, confused thinking something, I could sense her discomfort of knowing the fact I carried her in my arms.

'Is there a problem with that Arohi?' I asked

'Ummmm... RV sir' she paused.

There is nothing wrong in this Arohi

'Why are you so tensed? Don't you trust me? We have not done anything wrong' I convinced her

'RV sir, that day also, when you came home (Baner one), I hugged you' she said and then went silent... Her legs shivered in nervousness.

'So Arohi...? What happened? Why are you thinking so much sweetheart? You needed me that time, that is why we hugged and friends can hug, there is nothing to be worried about' I said.

'You sure...? Nothing is wrong na? RV sir?'

'Yes baby! Everything is fine. We are best friends right?'

She nodded

'Then? Stop thinking and lets enjoy our special time together' I said and raised my coffee mug

she raised it too...

CHEERS!!

Goa

There are too many things a person wants to do before his/her wedding, all the scenarios and elderly talks, upcoming responsibilities made Priya very sentient and anxious. She panicked, she wanted hers to be the best wedding as every girl would want but before that she wanted to enjoy her bachelorhood, her few days of freedom. Especially the posts on Facebook "20 things to do before you get married", "25 things to do before you die", "10 destinations you should visit with your friends before getting married" compelled her to plan something really awesome before her wedding.

She proposed an idea- What could be better than going on 'A TRIP TO GOA'. What's not in Goa! Beach, beauty, adventure, water sports, casino, partying, nightlife, biking – all these collectively define what Goa is. It is the dream of every youth. A thrill of excitement coursed through everybody's veins.

'wwoohooooo GOA is ON!!' Tiddi shouted

'Who all are in?' Priya jumped out of sofa and raised her hand

Every member in the room raised the right hand in unity.

'When are we leaving?' Arohi questioned

'Decide the dates' Pajju interrupted

'Ohh!! Will have to apply for leaves, I hope I get it this time' Neha said

'Aree haan! Leaves. How many days we need to apply for?' Aditi added

Too many spontaneous questions came up without any answers. To get the discussion easy and spread message across the group we chose the great invention "WhatsApp". Priya created a group called "GO GOA" with blue waves as its display picture. Group opened our channel of communication and simplified our business. First task was to decide the dates according to the leaves and availability of the people, second was to search accommodations and make reservations. There is a lot that needs to be done.

All the IT employees in "GO GOA" group excitedly participated and dates were decided. Electrifying excitement could be sensed in the messages. I could imagine everyone concentrating on their cell phones with their desktops open in front while on work.

Arpit too needed a holiday for some refreshment, hell lot of research and development for the business made him tired. He joined in too and luckily Sid's (Maggie) India trip was during the same dates.

Dates were decided as 20th June 2014/Friday

Almost all of us made it; Pajju told he will be joining us on Day 2 morning @GOA after completing his night shift for Friday. Final count till now was: Arohi, Aditi, Neha, Priya, Mini, Pajju, Arpit, Sid, RV, Nik, Tiddi and Atul. Total 12, my God that's a big group and ultimate fun was waiting for us.

Arpit will be coming all the way from Jabalpur and Sid from Bhopal, both assured they will be reaching by Friday afternoon and evening all of us will leave for our destination.

Reservations in "Neeta Volvo Multi XL sleeper bus" were being done for 11 people, as Pajju was joining a day after. 2 BHK's in M N Resort near Baga beach was booked. All set for the place. Everybody shopped swimming costume, light shirt/top, shorts, thin trousers, skirts, sarongs and what not.

* * *

20th June 2014

Finally the day arrived, there was some different *hulchul* in the air and everything seems so exciting. Everyone was charged with the electrifying energy. Arpit reached Pune on time. Sid's train was running late, he told he will be joining us directly at Bus stop. We started from Kharadi at 7:30 PM to avoid traffic delays and be at stop on time.

We reached Swar Gate Neeta's Office at around 8:30PM. It was dark, street lights illuminating the road, different tours and travel shops lined up opposite to the bus stop. Travelers waiting for bus were looking at their watches every now and then. Few spent their time reading newspapers or magazines. Others discussed political matters. Few regale themselves with some refreshment or cold drink at the nearest tuck-shop. Beggars avail such opportunity. They just beg or sing to beg.

We enquired about our bus from Neeta's office. Receptionist told bus is on time and will arrive exactly at 9. Group indulged themselves in GOA talks and made plans according to days. Excitement took a break when Sid called and informed his train has taken halt due to some technical issues at around half an hour away from Pune and was not sure when it will start from there. It was already 8:30. No clue what to do? We assured; we will not go leaving him.

8:45 Sid updated, his train has started from the place and he will reach Pune by around 9:20. Our major task here was to convince the driver to wait for a while till Sid arrives.

'9 baje GOA, 9 baje GOA' one bus arrived and conductor started shouting

I quickly ran towards him to confirm if it was our bus, damn it is our bus, exactly on time as receptionist advised.

We requested driver to please wait for some time as one of our group member is on his way. Girls did a bit of melo drama 'Bhaiya, please ruk jao, group main jaana hai, one member is left behind.' Their drama worked and driver agreed to wait for a while. Driver asked us to load our luggage in bus and be seated inside, we did that. Everybody being tensed came out and stood in front of the bus. Sid was on call with Tiddi providing updates; his train has not yet reached Pune. Damn!!!

Driver became impatient and enquired about Sid, we told him he is about to reach and requested him to wait. He murmured something in his mouth and again agreed on our request. He shouted again to come and sit in the bus, we followed him. Sid informed he is about to reach Pune.

Driver enquired, how much more time does Sid needs to reach bus stop?

'He is about to reach bhaiya bas 5 minutes aur' Arohi replied. We all looked out the window, sitting at lower berths. Pajju went to pick Sid from Pune station.

After waiting for 5 minutes driver started the bus. 'We will not wait anymore, already it is 9:30' He shouted on top of his voice. All the boys got down the bus.

'bhau, kaye zhala? Bus k andar betho?' He said

'Just 5 minutes more Bhaiya and then we will leave' Nik requested

Listening to this driver got very angry, he started shouting in his regional language, with his hands up and down, he refused to wait and started the bus, and all the members of the group came down and stood in front of the bus. Driver got annoyed and warned that he will accelerate and will run bus over us if we do not move. Girls got scared; Arpit tried talking to him, trying to handle the situation. Driver got too furious to listen anything. Arpit came down and joined us. Passengers inside the bus got impatient too but as we were the majority in bus, No 1 said anything. Diver accelerated and changed the gear; we held each other's hand and stood in front of the bus. Looking at this driver's face turned red. Crowd gathered and enjoyed the scene. Driver angrily got down the bus.

We saw Pajju coming from a distance; I said Sorry to driver and asked everyone to get in the bus. I winked at Gyaanis and they understood my indication. I gestured Sid to quietly get inside the bus in crowd. Sid entered with us. We being 12 people driver was not able to recognize Sid. He in a confused state started the bus without asking or shouting anything. He kept murmuring for a while. We all occupied front 4 seats, 2 lower and 2 upper. Laughing at the scene that happened, telling Sid about what all we did for him. Our voices went loud. Conductor interrupted our discussions and advised us to go on our own respective berths and sleep. This time we obeyed.

GOA started with a different experience, no one would have ever thought about. Thinking about what all drama happened tonight I fell asleep.

While I was in my dreams I felt continuous jerks and vibrations, 1st I thought it to be my mobile but How can a mobile vibrate, shaking me up from top to bottom? I came into senses and realized bus taking jerks and it stopped. I looked at my watch; it was 2:00 AM.

To make our night more exciting conductor came inside the bus, walking through the narrow passage between the seats, waking up people and telling them to get down. Arpit enquired and informed us that it is a case of ABS breakdown. We half-awake waited for another bus to arrive.

Sid looked at driver bhaiya and said 'Pune main to bahut jaldi ho rahi thi, time ho gaya! Ab kya bhaiya? Goa kahan hai?'

Driver ignored his question, within an hour; we were shifted to other Neeta Semi sleeper Volvo. Being in a big group I did not get chance to sit with Arohi or talk to her, we exchanged looks but hardly spoke to each other. Even though she was in front of me I missed her.

We reached Goa around 11:00AM; two prepaid taxis dropped us to our Resort.

M N Resort is set in the foothills of Arpora, a little less than a kilometer from Baga Beach, Calangute Beach and a few 100 meters away from the well-known Saturday Night Market (Mackie's Night Bazaar). As we entered we saw in-house multi-cuisine restaurant-cum-bar on our right and swimming pool on our left. Receptionist told that our bookings were delayed for an hour as our rooms were still occupied, guests will leave in half an hour and half hour they need for cleaning activities. Another surprise Goa gave us.

We waited in front of the swimming pool, tired of journey. Everyone badly needed a bath. We sat near the pool on yellow-orange colored tiles along with our bag packs. Took group pictures and made plan for the day. We decided to go Baga beach first as it was near by our Resort and then Titos at night.

We were in our after travel photography session when house keeper handed us our keys. We asked him to click a group picture.

Nik, Atul and I, helped the girls in carrying their luggage to their rooms, everyone took a bath, and we decided to meet within an hour for lunch and then will leave for the beach.

Goa being the land of sun, surf and sand, everyone made themselves comfortable in 'GOA WEARS': Mingle of many colors, patterns and accessories. All boys and senior girls were ready and we waited for the junior girls- Arohi and Mini to join us on lunch table.

I saw Arohi along with Mini coming towards us. She looked pretty in her Chiffon floral one piece with mixture of many colors, blue and white were the prominent ones. It ended approx. 8 inches above her knees; her hairs were open, a tiny blue hair clip tied her few left sided hair strands. I kept staring at her. Chair besides me was vacant, I gestured her to sit beside me but before she could occupy Mini occupied it. She made her seating between her favorite Pajju and Tiddi sir. We completed our lunch and headed towards the beach, crossing most happening narrow streets of GOA leading to Baga beach, observing restaurants, pubs and bars that offered all kinds of cuisines, road side shops selling long beaded chains, bracelets, funky t-shirts, shorts, flip-flops and much more. We saw few daily soap celebrities on our way to the beach. Narrow Street opened up into a beautiful and a crowded Baga Beach.

Shacks were occupied by different races across the world, we ran directly in the water, half wet splashing water on each other.

'Parasailing'

'Hey look there, who all in for parasailing?' Arohi shouted

'Let's go for it' Nik said.

Arpit was our cashier for the trip, as being the rich businessmen and owner of many petrol pumps and showrooms, he had bought the cash and we had our cards. Deal was - He will be spending on sports, food, shacks and other stuffs and we will transfer him once we are back to Pune.

Arpit, Nik and I calculated the money- Rs. 13,200 for 11 people along with the dip in the sea. I signed on the clauses on behalf of everyone. We put on the life jackets according to our size and ran to grab our seats in 12 seater speed boat which was waiting for us at the shore. We felt the speed and grace of this highly responsive water racing machine.

Somewhere in middle of the sea, away from shore, 6 members were transferred to another speed boat connected with a big canvas balloon.

I held Arohi's hand and bought her in my batch of parasailing. 'Two people will go at a time', pilot advised. Luckily Priya was not in the same batch else she would have gone with Arohi.

'I might get the chance to go with her', I silently thought.

Our batch included Me, Nik, Pajju, Mini, Neha and Arohi. Pilot called out for the 1st pair – Mini and Pajju ran. I held Arohi by her hand and took her at the deck of the boat. Nik and Neha were busy watching Pajju and Mini getting tied and hooked up to a rope connecting big parabolic canvas of red color.

'So, finally! We are going to do something from our wish list together' I said holding her both arms and trying to make balance.

'Yes, RV sir! You remember this was in our wish list?' she said

'How can I forget, after all it is our wish' I said

She smiled

'Will you come with me?' I asked

She nodded. This was the 1st time in Goa I was talking to her, I felt so good. There was some magic in the moment. Instead of our lips our eyes spoke more. I think she too missed me.

Pajju and Neha were back, it was turn for the 2nd couple. Nik asked Arohi to come with him, Arohi looked at me and then him

'Nik sir, I am feeling little dizzy, you go with Neha di, I will go in next turn' she said

'What happened? Are you not okay?' Nik enquired

'I will be fine within 5 mins; it's because of continuous movement of boat. I am ok. You go!' she said

Nik and Neha went ahead. Arohi winked at me. I was shocked for a moment; she can cook up stories to be with me. I liked it, she made me feel special. It was our turn now.

'RV sir, I am scared' she said

'Yes, you should be. You are going with me' I said and winked

She smiled

'Aree sach main, ab darr lag ra hai' she said holding my hand, balancing herself while moving to platform from where we have to takeoff.

'I am there, I will not let anything happen to you' I assured.

Strapped on to a life jacket and a harness, Pilot tied her in front of me, her back body touching me, for the 1st time I am so close to her. We took off from the platform of the speedboat, parasail is connected to the speedboat through a wire; the harmony at which the boat and parasail worked together was just unparalleled to any synchronized act, pilot made us dip in the sea, Arohi held my hands instead of the ropes attached. After few dips, what I saw blew my mind. I was up there around 200 feet from sea level, with someone I admire a lot. The view is extraordinary. A bird's eye view, how they hunt for fish in the turquoise waters. It was breathtaking to see so many shades of blue beneath me. The freedom felt flying on the parasail is not comparable to an airplane. I felt like superman with my superwoman. I felt so complete. I looked up in the sky. Shades of blue, white mixed with orange, yellow and red made it extremely beautiful, sun was about to set. I asked Arohi to look up and then look down. We were in the middle of vast endless sky and deep Blue Ocean. I was up there with her. She spread her hands in the air and asked me to do the same, I followed her. 'It looks so beautiful here' she whispered. I held her palms stretched in air, she responded by tightening the grip. Current of happiness was flowing within me.

'It is so peaceful here, I do not want to go down' I said

'Even I', she replied

I wish I could keep holding her like this. I had a feeling of pure joy and ecstasy. It was incredible looking down from my seat, seeing us float above Earth, suspended by nothing but a canopy and a harness.

Being up in the air, flying in the glider made me feel tiny. It made the world feel tiny, given that everything and everyone was just beneath my feet. It also made my problems, concerns, and thoughts seem tiny. Up there in the sky, nothing matters. All I can experience is purity and serenity. I felt utter happiness within. With Arohi, I felt complete. This would have not been so good if it would have been someone else other than her.

But like all good things, everything has to come to an end, descending was the worst part, when you don't want to come down. Can I stay here for one minute more, my mind pleaded?

Parasailing with Arohi was an overwhelming experience for me.

*　　*　　*

Goa is considered to be the city with best night life in India. We decided to go for the Goa's most popular club and bar Tito's. I have heard, it offers the ambience of a trendy nightclub with the perfect mix of fun and music. It is often regarded as the partying hot spot of North Goa and is conveniently located along the Tito's road in Baga, Calangute. For the party-goers, this is the place to be. Shake a leg on its long terrace or simply watch the action and unwind over a drink. We flashed our ID's, the bouncer at the gate checked the stamps on our hands and let us into the club. The first thing that struck me was the loud, bass drowned music, followed by a wall of hot air and body odour, like a hundred of people cramped into a small dance floor. It was fairly dark with lights here and there, few multi colored flashy and spot lights. In there were a lot more scantily dressed ladies, lots of them wore what looks like straight dresses, more or less short, shorter than shorts. Our group ladies were included in same category.

On 1st floor was the bar. Some of the ladies were dancing in a seductive way all by themselves whilst others were closely 'marked 'by guys who were either dancing in front of them or behind them. DJ played all the hottest mixes that made us tap on our feet; we danced hard in front of the bar. Aditi got excited when she saw "Jagiya- daily soap actor" dancing; her excitement took a break when she realized he is not in his senses and is drunk.

While coming to Goa Sid had shared his US experiences, where everybody is alcoholic and he feels out of place because he has no idea about drinks and he cannot risk drinking in front of US folks for the 1st time, he wanted to try today as he was with his best buddies who can handle him.

Tiddi and Atul were the best advisors for him, He started with vodka shots. Mini, Aditi and Neha took the shots too. Everybody got interested. This was something new for the group and everyone wanted to go for it. Arohi refused. I liked her decision.

Tiddi forced Sid to have more drinks, Sid refused, Tiddi insisted.

Nik and I made sure that everyone should be drinking in limits. We allowed just 2 shots for girls.

Mini, Sid and Tiddi did not listen to us. Mini lost her control. She was now dancing like other drunken girls in the bar. Aditi and Priya took care of her. Music went loud. Tiddi too started dancing madly. He pulled Arohi and made her take two round turns; she tried to manage herself and him too.

Sid still on the bar, he kept on drinking.

He rested his both hands on bar table; with his head down, looking at him concerned Priya went to him, confirming if he was okay. She offered him a glass of water. He took the water and poured it on Priya. Priya got furious and went to Nik complaining about the scenario. Nik turned to have a look at Sid.

By the time Nik could reach to him, he had snatched drink from the lady standing beside him at bar and drank it. Pretty lady gave him an angry look. Nik went there and apologized on behalf of him.

He then snatched the bottle from bar tender and drank half of it down. Sid then came to the dance floor, he did the best dance he would have ever done in his entire life. Bottle of alcohol bought his talent in front. He went to each girl of the group and complimented 'you dance really well, I like you' girls giggled at him and tapped him saying 'Sid hosh main aa jaa'.

By now Tiddi, Atul, Mini, Sid and Neha were completely out. Others were trying to manage them. Sid again went back to the bar and had few more drinks. He went back to his same position with hands resting on the bar table and head hanging between the V shape formed by his hands. He asked for more drinks and puked on the bar table. Bar tender stepped back, shouted and called for his friends. Nik and I went there, tried to pull Sid but he refused and jerked, he puked all over the table. Bar tender irritably announced the bar to be closed.

Nik ordered everyone to come out of the club, he pulled Sid along with him, Sid wished 'happy new year and happy Diwali' to everyone he crossed by. Some laughed and some gave him disgusting looks. Aditi and Priya tried handling Mini and Neha. Tiddi hanged on Arohi, he being lean Arohi was trying to handle him. I stopped Arohi and took control over Tiddi. Atul gained his senses back and helped us balancing the situation. Nik booked a cab. Cab waited for us at the area outside the street, 11 people could not go in a single ride. We decided to send Neha and Mini first as Mini was dancing on the streets and repeatedly saying 'Why are we leaving? I want to dance'. Arohi, Priya, me, Tiddi and Sid stayed back. Nik went with others and asked us to wait; he will be bringing the same cab back. Sid crossed his legs and sat on the street in front of the club, Arohi tried talking to him.

'Hww, Sid sir, you are so drunk' she said

'You look beautiful Arohi, you dance well' Sid replied. Next time Priya tried

'Hww, Sid, you are so drunk' Priya said

'You look beautiful Priya, You dance well' Sid replied. Arohi and Priya laughed holding their stomach.

Tiddi gave a try with the same question

'Hww, Sid, you are so drunk' he said

'You a** h***, you bastard, I do not drink, you forced me to drink, F*** you man' he shouted in his US mixed accent that he has developed while his stay in US.

'You Bastard, You a** h***, you have no control' Tiddi replied

Both started arguing, situation was getting out of control, Girls stared and were not able to understand the situation, all this was new to them. To handle them I slapped Tiddi and Sid both. Tiddi became quite and sat on the floor besides Sid. Sid puked again and lost his consciousness, he laid down in front of the club. Bouncer came and asked me to take him home.

Nik was back, Arpit came along with him. Arpit and I put Sid's hands on our shoulders and made him walk; he could not stand on his legs. We had to drag him or pick him; Nik supported us and pulled him up a little by holding his jeans. Slap worked in bringing Tiddi to his senses. He followed us along with Girls.

We reached the Resort, It was 3 at night. Sid slept in 1 room; Tiddi being normal did not created any scene. Girls went in their room. Everyone slept where ever they found place. I was lying out on sofa in the living room. It was a memorable day, too many things in a single day. I missed Arohi. I messaged and wished her good Night.

She replied back 'you awake RV sir?'

'Yes, I am, what are you doing?' I answered and questioned

'Nothing much, just lying in living room. All beds are occupied, so I am lying here' she said

'Waooo, same pinch' I replied

'Thank God you messaged, I was feeling fearful alone in the living room, everyone else slept' Arohi texted

'I knew you'll need me and that is the reason I messaged you ;)' I actually winked to myself when I texted her

'Hahah, aacha so Mr. Rajveer Singh, what is your moment of the day?' she asked

'Moment of the day...? What do you mean by that?' I asked

'Your best moment of the day, which brings smile on your face. The moment, that will be enticed in your memories forever' she explained

'hmmm'

'Kya hmm...reply, think about the whole day and pick one moment' she demanded

'Parasailing, it was the best moment for me in the entire day. Yours?' I replied and asked for her best moment.

'Same pinch parasailing it was just Waoo... I felt like a free bird in the sky, it was like I had wings and I am flying' she answered.

'Could you please call me? My eyes are getting close, too tired, will not be able to type. Please make me sleep on call. You can disconnect after I sleep' she insisted.

I called her up to fulfill her innocent demand, she spoke 'hello' in her half sleepy sweet voice. She sounded like a 5 year old. We talked for a while about our day 1 at Goa, about our experience of parasailing, she stopped speaking and fell asleep within few minutes, and I could hear her breathing. I did not disconnect the call, I did not want too. I heard her breathing till I fell asleep.

Next day everyone woke up at 9 AM, we gathered to have breakfast arranged by the resort. Sid took what all was required to get rid of his hangover. Arpit and Nik told him stories of the previous night. He felt embarrassed and said sorry to all the girls. Everyone giggled and teased Sid in every possible way. Repeated his sentences 'you look beautiful, you dance well'. Sid took a pledge that he will never ever drink. Tiddi and Mini too got to hear their last night 'kaarnaame'. All non-drinkers had a nice time teasing the Tito's drunkards. Prateek arrived by 9:30AM. He got to hear what all he missed.

We booked 6 bikes for 12 people, planned the day and started our 2nd day journey at 11AM, everyone chose their partners, Mini came and sat with me, and Arohi chose to sit with Pajju. She looked sweet and catholic in her blue colored one piece made up of denim; I noticed her anklet in her left leg as she sat on the bike. It complimented her bare legs.

6 bikes one after the other, it was a Waooo experience. No one could break our chain trail. We visited Basilica of Bom Jesus church, beaches nearby and made our way to Chapora fort. Narrow straight roads with splendid weather made bike ride more fantastic, I drove behind Arohi's bike. Our eyes did the talking and distracted us from our conversation with our bike partners. We reached Chapora around 5:30PM, trekking up to the fort was little difficult for girls in their foot wears.

As we reached we saw huge, irregular, red laterite stone walls, a gate, bastions with cylindrical turrets, a few vague barracks and weeded bushes. Pointing out to a place Neha shouted 'That is DIL CHAHTA HAI location'. Everybody ran there to get them clicked. Fort provided us the panoramic view of the sea. Magnificent views of Anjuna beach, Chapora beach and Vagator beach can be seen. It has steep slopes. We got the chance to see sunset sitting on the edge of the rocks. While returning we visited Anjuna and Chapora beach.

Plan now was to have dinner and change to comfortable clothes, take bedsheets and night out at Baga beach. A big group got divided into small small groups: people interested in Drinking (Pajju, Atul, Tiddi, Mini and Aditi) sat on the bedsheets and opened up their bottles. Priya got busy on the call with her to-be-husband 'Rahul'. Sid, Neha, Arpit, Arohi, Nik and I sat on sand, recalling our college memories.

It was a full moon night, water everywhere made the night cool. I wanted to spend some time with her alone. I got up and asked Arohi to come for a walk with me. She looked at me in shock; everyone else too looked at me. She stood up and followed me.

'RV sir, are you crazy? Why did you asked in front of everyone. I hope they will not think otherwise' She said

'I wanted some time with you. If I would have not asked then you would be sitting with them chit-chatting. They are our friends, don't worry they will not think anything bad' I said

'Hmmm' she replied

We silently walked bare foot on sand for a while; waves kept washing our feet's in interval of 30 seconds. She played with the wet sand, making structures while walking.

'RV sir, race lagate hain? What say' she turned towards me and said making her eyes big, her usual excited expression

'Race? You will lose' I said

'Ahhhaan in your dreams' she replied

OK SO 1 2 3 Gooooo

She ran in her full speed avoiding sand reluctance. I followed her, trying to catch her we both fell down. She laughed and clapped.

'Maza aye na' she said breathing heavily

'Yes' I replied

'Let's sit somewhere for a while' she said

We searched for a less crowded place, our group members were far from our sight. We lay down gazing stars. We lay silently there, her left arm touching my right hand. I could feel her. I got confused with my feeling for her. Earlier I just wanted her to be happy where ever she is, with who so ever she is, Now I want her to be just with me all the time, to talk with me, to eat with me, to laugh with me. I don't want anyone but just her. There was some energy in her that attracted me towards her. I held her left hand in mine and turned to her side, she lay still looking at the stars, I tuck her hair behind her ear, she closed her eyes in reflex, and I moved her chin towards me. Moon light falling on her face highlighted her fresh young face, her glowing face compelled me to kiss her, I tried controlling my senses but her beauty compelled me to be closer to her. I bought my lips near hers. I could breathe her and sense her increasing heartbeat. She opened her eyes and pushed me back.

'RV sir, we do not have to fall for each other' she said turning towards me and looking at me with her eyes full of mixed emotions.

I could sense her nervousness, she shivered. She held collar of my t-shirt, crumbled it in her palms and again said softly 'RV sir we are not allowed to fall for each other na.'

I asked her to look in my eyes, she refused.

'Arohi' I said

'No, RV sir, we are not allowed' she repeated.

'Nothing will happen against your will' I assured

She tightened her grip holding my collar. I took her in my arms.

'Friends can hug na' she enquired.

I rubbed my nose against hers and answered

'Yes, friends can hug'

She slides down in my arms with her hands on my chest, avoiding contact of my chest with hers. 'Keep hiding me please' she insisted. I tightened my grip in response. She slept in my arms.

While she was sleeping comfortably, trail of thoughts ran in my mind - This is not friendship; there was something between us which she is refusing to accept. May be she is scared as she got ditched in her relationship once but it had been months now. I wish someday I could make her mine, I wish someday I will be able to tell her my feelings. I want to make her realize that I will never ditch her, she can rely on me.

I just love the moment I am in. It feels like she fits perfectly in my arms, I wish the night never ends. I kept holding her thinking about how perfect my life would be with her when my mobile rang and bought me out of dream world to the real world.

Priya calling – 'where are you? Arohi with you?' she asked anxiously

'Yes she is with me. We are in front of some resto at Baga' I lied

'Come back, we are going back to resort in sometime' she said

'hmm we will be there in couple of minutes' I said and disconnected the call

Arohi panicked listening I was talking to her sister.

'RV sir, please let's go! Di will scold me. Please' she said and got up.

'It's Okay, no one will say anything to you. I am there to protect you' I said keeping my both hands on her face.

She nodded and we walked back to the group.

Night I called her, she disconnected and texted 'Priya di and Mini beside me. Can't Talk'

'Oh, sorry for the call' I replied

'Your moment of the day?' she asked

'When you were in my arms at beach' I replied

'Yours?' I asked

I waited for her reply, 15 mins....20mins................

I texted:' There? Awake?'

No reply. May be she was shy to reply or she slept. It was a mystery for me.

*   *   *

Next day we covered few more places and beaches of Goa, Arohi hadn't replied to my messages nor was she talking to me. I tried talking to her but big groups made her escape easy. Each time I tried talking to her she finds a way not to be indulged in the conversation by either moving to Nik or Pajju or Priya or her junior gang group. Atul and Arohi too started getting along well with each other again. I felt ignored.

Evening we had plan for club cabana. Her behavior was bothering me. I was not in mood of dancing, while everyone was enjoying the music and tapping their feet, I came out of the dancing area in fresh air. I found a quiet place for myself in isolation and sat there, I observed how smart lightning had turned a simple place to a happening pub. I stared at the neon pool visible from my location.

Arohi came searching for me

'RV sir why are you here?' She asked

'Does it bother you Arohi?' I said in an angry tone

'Yes it bothers me' she replied

'Go from here Arohi, nothing matters to you' I said pushing her shoulder to move back

'Excuse me' she said huffily

'What do you think? I had been ignoring you willingly?' She asked

I did not respond

'No I was not ignoring you willingly Mr. Rajveer, last night when we came back from beach, Priya di scolded me. She said what was the need of going alone with you, we both are coming close is visible to everyone. She told me to maintain some distance from you as she heard our friends talking about us. She warned me about our family situations. Also I heard Neha Di and Aditi Di talking about us in other room. They were discussing within themselves that I am hiding something from them, also according to them, I am spending most of the time with you' She said and paused for a while.

'So what is the problem? If 2 people in a group want to spend some time together? Can't they?' I asked

'No they cannot, because we are in a group. You know "no couples in group funda". This will spoil our group' she answered

'I am sick of your rules. What do you want me to do?' I asked

'Let's not be with each other at least in front of all, please' she said

'Arohi I like you' I said looking in her eyes.

I continued 'I ...' she stopped me by putting her index finger on my lips.

'No RV sir please, I cannot be yours. Please don't make it difficult for me. Please' she whispered in my ears coming close to me.

I grabbed her in my arms, she struggled to come out, feeling her discomfort I loosened my grip and let her go.

GOA trip ended, with lot many memories to cherish and lot many questions unanswered.

Priya's Wedding

Goa Party ended, everybody got busy with their normal day to day schedule. I tried for a personal meeting with Arohi but she was way too busy with her sister's wedding shopping. I didn't get chance to talk to her after Goa. I cannot express how badly I was missing her.

Gyaanis gathered to see Goa's pictures at girl's place. I gestured Arohi to sit besides me, but she did not. Either she did not understand my actions or willingly chose to sit somewhere else. I started feeling incomplete in my complete group. I stayed quiet without involving much or talking to anyone. Tiddi and Nik pinched me for being so silent. They asked me if something was wrong or if I need any help. I assured them that everything is fine.

Arohi behaved normally with me like she behaves with her other "Sir's" or like she used to behave with me earlier, as if nothing has happened. For her everything was normal. 'How can she be so casual?' I asked myself.

'May be all these things don't affect her much, it was just a moment - she came close to me and now she is away. I am just her RV sir, her senior, that's it'. I tried answering and convincing myself.

Arohi got herself busy in selecting Invitation cards, decorations for different events, dresses, flowers, where to get the makeup done, creative gifts for the groom's family, selection of venue, food items etc. She hardly got time to notice anything or anyone. She seems to be little changed because my

Arohi was best at managing her time, her tasks, her hobbies, job, family and friends. This was so not her.

She used shopping as her best weapon, it helped her to avoid being a part of group gatherings too. It is truly said that shopping for an Indian wedding is one of the most adventurous and fun filled part of the entire event. She enjoyed it with her sister. Priya and Arohi left for Bhopal 2 weeks before Priya's wedding. Busy with preparations Arohi did not access her phone much but long distance between us made her talk to me on messages, she used to message me at night, initiating formal conversation like, about Gyaanis arrival to Bhopal, wedding arrangements etc. She avoided the talks that included just me and her.

Priya and Arohi ordered us to stay at the venue for two days and attend all the events.

Wedding cards were sent to us by courier- 18 July 2014 Mehndi at 11:00 AM, 6:00PM Sangeet,

19 July 2014 Haldi at 9:00AM followed by evening reception and late night Kanyadaan.

*   *   *

18ᵗʰ July 2014 / Friday / 1:00PM

We reached the venue, Vrindavan Palace

'We are late, Mehndi would have been started by now' Neha said.

I called Arohi and informed her about our arrival.

She advised us to wait at Palace entrance and she will send someone, who will provide us with our room keys. We waited in the parking. Hotel care takers carried our luggage and asked us to follow them, as we entered the Main Gate; a group of people dressed in white with red dupatta tied on their waist welcomed us by playing dhol. Arohi's mom applied Tikka on

119

our forehead; she thanked each one of us for coming to her daughter's wedding.

We got ourselves ready and headed towards the function; a big hall in palace was decorated with vibrant purple and blue color scheme, topping it off with vibrant purple orchids and white roses. I saw Priya sitting at the center stage of the hall, she looked pretty in her blue-white salwar suit, and room's decoration complimented her dress. 2 ladies were applying mehndi on her hands, she sat straight concentrating on her mehndi and advising design makers the type of design she wants. Her mom informed her about our arrival, she waved her hand towards us and gestured us to sit beside her. Everyone in the family greeted us. A group of ladies of age group around 35 to 55 were singing and dancing forming a circle, her mom asked us to join the dancing group. We being fun lovers jumped in and started dancing, making all the aunties to sit back.

'Kaun hain ye log?' I heard one of the old aunties asking the other one

'Priya's friends' other one replied.

'Tell them it's not disc, this is mahila sangeet' 1st one said and laughed.

I asked Neha, Mini and Aditi to bring aunties back to the dance floor, they successfully completed the task. Everyone was happy, smiling and singing. I held Priya's mom's hand and bought her to the dance floor too. She refused saying 'Nai beta, you dance. I am too old for this'

'Aunty it's your daughter's wedding, you are the one who should enjoy the most' I replied

Everyone insisted her to dance.

Fulfilling her guest's demands she performed few traditional dance steps, we whistled. All the ladies and girls sat down to get mehndi designs on their hands; Boys captured pictures of beautiful, happy ladies.

I saw Arohi entering the room, 6 kids of different sizes followed her. 1st one holding Arohi's dupatta and others formed a chain by holding shoulders. I went and stood in front of her crossing my hands, she stopped and looked at me for a moment I felt everything near us stopped. We looked at each other without speaking.

One of the kids spoke 'didi train kyu ruk gai?'

'Bhaiya move, we are playing train train' another one said.

I looked at them removing my glance from Arohi. I sat on my knees to have conversation with kids.

Arohi's mom called her to apply Mehndi on her hands. She walked, leaving her train behind. One of the Kids shouted –'Didi our train??' She stopped, turned and said looking at me 'this bhaiya is your new engine'

She sat in between the group of girls, 2 design makers started making designs on her hands. We kept exchanging looks. I could make out from her behavior that she missed me too but will not accept it; as usual our eyes did the talking.

She gestured me not to stare at her as guests may notice it. I tried shifting my glance but my eyes did not found anything as beautiful as her. She whispered something in one of the design maker's ear and giggled.

Air through the window made her hairs unmanageable; her wet mehndi hands did not allowed her to settle them. I wish to arrange her hairs but I can't, in front of so many guests. I stood up and closed the window. She looked at me and whispered 'thank you', I read her lips. I gestured her saying she is looking beautiful in her yellow salwar kameez. She smiled and looked down. I loved her shyness.

*   *   *

Sometimes I feel weddings are all about changing clothes and jewels, different attire for different functions, Sangeet was about to start in few minutes. Everyone rushed in their rooms to get ready for the event. I opened my baggage wondering what to wear.

Arohi sent me pictures of 2 dresses. One purple and other red, she asked me to choose one. I choose the red evening gown- sleeveless, with red velvet on top, golden and black embroidery at waist and free fall of Satin along with net till feet.

'Thank you for making my choice easy' she replied

'Always welcome'

Her message made my selection easy too. I wore red kurta with white bottom.

We all reached the Venue, event was about to start. Decorations were on the theme '*A night in Shanghai*'. Red Chinese inspired lanterns overflowed above the dance floor ceiling setting the mood just right! Eight trees each covered with hundred lights making the night memorable, two custom designed dragons embellished with fresh floral, blue & white. Chinese vases with Japanese blossoms called for the perfect centerpieces! Decorations were beyond spectacular! I wondered how much Priya's dad must have spent on the wedding decorations.

I heard a sweet voice coming from speakers asking everyone to settle down as sangeet ceremony is about to start. Arohi came on stage holding a mic. She looked like a princess in red gown. She along with a boy from groom's family anchored the show. Somebody in the crowd told that he is Rahul's brother 'Raj'.

Rahul's parents seem to be big fan of Shahrukh Khan as they named both their kids on his on-screen role play. I hope he would have not said SRK dialogues to Arohi- 'Raj, naam to suna hoga'.

'He is handsome yaar' Aditi said

'Convince him to marry you, he owns a BMW' Tiddi said

'BMW? Seriously? How do you know?' Neha said making her eyes big while speaking the word 'BMW'.

'Contacts beta! I know everything' Tiddi flaunted

'Ohh, so you do fielding for boys too' Neha scoffed and high fived Mini.

'Stop it guys! Look there, Arohi is inviting Priya and Rahul on stage' Nik said.

Bride and groom were invited on stage, Priya looked beautiful in her peach lehanga, and Rahul looked handsome in his white sherwani. Both looked happy and complimented each other. Couple sat on sofa one level down the stage and others were seated one level down the couple.

All the bride and groom relatives have prepared dance performances for the event, few were really good and few were way too funny. Bride and groom's family challenged each other and stage got converted to dance wars. All chacha-chachi's, mama-mammi, siblings and kids showed their talent on stage.

Rahul and Priya performed on 'Tum Hi Ho' from Aashiqui 2.

Arohi invited her mom and dad for the performance. This was the 1st time I saw her dad. He looked like a gentle man; bald, seemed little tired with the preparations of wedding, her mother looked calm and beautiful. They did not perform anything instead spoke few words about their daughters and thanked all the guests for showering their blessing on the new couple. Their speech created an emotional milieu. I could not see Priya as she was in front row but I could see Arohi wiping her tears standing at corner of the stage.

Grooms parents joined them on stage and assured, they will take care of their daughter just like their own daughter. In-laws exchanged positive gestures. Raj saw Arohi crying and tried to console her. Feeling of jealousy ran through me looking at them, I hated him for this.

Last but not the least, was performance of the Bride's only sister and anchor of the show – Arohi. She performed on 'Manva Laage'. Her moves were feminine and beautiful.

After all the performances 'it was DJ time'. All the active members of both the families' came on the dance floor. Priya and Rahul joined too. Arohi saw me and came near me:

'Red kurta, haan...! Someone looking handsome' She said

'Thank you ma'am, well you are also looking ok ok in your outfit' I said

'Just ok ok?' she said making a sad expression by pouting out her lower lip.

'Just kidding, you look like a princess' I said pulling her cheeks

She smiled

'Can we meet at night? After everyone sleeps?' I asked

'No, not possible, not at all. All guests and friends are here. Also I have to make a papad file tonight so I will be busy' she said

'Papad file? What is that?' I enquired

'Arrrreee there is one file that bride's family make, we write messages and jokes about each member of groom's family' She answered

'So when can we....' I was in middle of my question when Raj came and asked Arohi for dance, she looked at me and went ahead to dance with him. A possessive voice within me provoked to hit Raj.

*   *   *

Mid night 1:00 AM I texted Arohi

'Slept?'

'Nahh'

'What are you doing?'

'Makin my file, almost complete' she replied

'Everyone in your room slept?' I enquired

'Yes, they slept'

'Can we meet please?' I asked

'Hmm, what if anyone wakes up? Where to meet?' she asked

'Nothing will happen, so many relatives are there. They will think you are in other room. Meet me at terrace' I said

'It must be too dark, I am scared coming there' She replied

'You call me once you leave, I will be on call with you. You will not feel scared' I suggested

'Ok, I will bring the file along. I want to show you my creations' she replied

I waited for her at terrace. She called me when she left her room.

'RV sir, I am scared. I hope no one finds out else it will be a big issue'

'Nothing will happen, trust me, it's too dark here, no one will be able to see us. Where have you reached?' I asked

'I almost reached, climbing last few stairs, please come out. Darkness bothering me' she said

I came out; she was there in her night wears, lower and a loose thin white t- shirt, cuddling her papad file tightly. We entered terrace and locked the gate, thankfully terrace had both side locking system. It was the dark night, hardly anything visible. She switched on flash light of her mobile and focused on the file. We stood near the pillar, leaning on one side wall of terrace. She was excited to show me the captions and various designs she made for the file.

Page one- about Bride and Groom, then his father, his mother and relatives........

I took file from her hand, switched off her mobile's flash light and placed both things on the pillar.

'I am here to talk to you, to express my feelings not to hear about Rahul's family' I whispered in her ears holding her hands.

I came in front of her bringing her closer to me, her back rested on the wall. I tried being very soft and gentle. I smelled her hands; I loved fresh fragrance of her Mehndi. She pulled her hands away from me; she looked down avoiding eye contact. I held her face in my hands, adjusted her hairs gently. She held my arm while I was playing with her hairs, slowly trying to push me back without applying much pressure

'Arohi' I whispered

'huh' She replied breathing heavily

I went closer, she held my t-shirt in her hands, and she crumbled it indicating my closeness has some effect on her.

'Did you miss me' I asked

She nodded innocently

'I too missed you a lot' I said

'Arohi' I said coming more close to her, she got sandwiched between me and the wall, this time she did not reply instead tightened the grip of my t-shirt.

'Look at me' I said. She shook her head

'Arohi "I Love...."' I was about to complete my sentence when she interrupted me

'RV sir our rule' she said in a low tone, crumbling my t-shirt as hard as she could.

'My heart does not know any rules, all it knows is that it has fallen for you and it beats for you' I replied

I continued 'I tried explaining everything to my heart, all your situations, all your rules everything but I lost my control on it, now you are the one who rules it'

'But RV sir' she whispered

I put my finger on her lips.

'I love you, Arohi' I whispered

I kissed her on forehead; she closed her eyes and fell in my arms. I hugged her tightly, she tightened her grip too.

'I am scared RV sir' she spoke, hardly audible

'Scared of what sweetheart' I asked rubbing her back slowly

'About the consequences' She said

'I will handle everything; just tell me your feelings. Do you love me?' I asked, holding her face in my hands.

She nodded and hid in my arms again.

'Please keep hiding me' she requested. Her shyness made me fall for her more.

'I want to hear, I love you' I said

She shook her head. 'I want to go back; else someone will come looking for me. Please' she said nervously trying to escape from the situation

'You are not going anywhere unless you speak?' I locked her between wall and myself. She tried moving, she applied all her pressure but failed in her attempt.

'Let me go na please' she requested again

'Not till you speak' I said

'I feel shy' she replied.

'I want to hear it now else I am not letting you go in your room tonight' I said

'No na will say when we will reach Pune' she said

'Pune, hahah, you will not have time for me there, always busy in the group with your Nik sir, Pajju sir and Tiddi sir' I replied

'I will find time na baba' she said in convincing tone.

'You are delaying it for so long; I thought we would marry in the same mandap as your di'

She laughed and punched me softly on my chest.

'Okay, so we are going on a trip to Kolad after returning Pune. Just you and me' I said

'Kolad?' she asked

'Yes, to fulfill one more thing from our wish list. River Rafting' I answered

'Just you and me? You think it will be possible?' she asked doubtfully

'Yes, I will make it possible. You need not worry about it' I said

'Ok. We will see, now let me go please' she said

'First, promise. Kolad is on' I asked

'Ok I promise, now please. Koi aa jayega' she pleaded

I released her from my grip and set her free to go; she walked away when I pulled her again towards me holding her hand.

'And what about this RAJ? Haan?' I asked

'What about Raj?' she repeated my sentence as if she did not understood anything

'Why is he always behind you?' I asked

'How would I know that?' she replied smartly

'Tell him that you are mine' I said

'Who said I am yours?' she questioned

'So you are not mine?' I asked in low volume, looking at her

'I am **unofficially yours**' she said smiling and looking at me, she released her hand from my grip, picked her file and mobile and ran towards her room.

'And yes, wear white at your own risk tomorrow' she warned while leaving.

I failed to understand why she said so. I followed her to ensure she reaches safely.

Few moments with her did not let me sleep; I just wanted to keep holding her, expressing my feelings. I love the way she hides in me. It makes me feel so complete. The moment I close my eyes I could see all the memories in flash back. I waited for dawn so that I could see her again.

Morning 9, Priya sat beneath a beautiful Mandap draped and hung Marigold garlands providing ethnic and traditional look. Decoration not only beautified the surroundings but also filled it with positive energy.

Priya looked beautiful in her yellow saree. All the married ladies applied turmeric on her face and gave her best wishes. After the main function was over, Priya's mom asked Gyaanis to apply turmeric on Priya's face.

We all went ahead and applied a yellow color paste on her face. To challenge Arohi I wore White shirt, now I understood why it was for. Each member of the group was done with the custom of applying Haldi to the bride.

Now it was our turn to play Haldi, all the aunties stared at us along with Arohi; they attacked us in union throwing turmeric mixed with water on us. Arpit, Tiddi along with Neha and Mini became the easy targets.

Me, Nik, Pajju, Atul and Arpit ran towards the lawn trying to save our new dresses. Everyone followed us. Priya's mom gave us a plate full of turmeric for our defense.

Yellow color was flying in air. It was like playing Holi with one color. Arohi applied turmeric on my face and shirt.

'Bola tha na, don't wear White' she said

I went close to her, she stepped back.

'RV sir no, too many people here' she murmured.

I applied Haldi on her cheeks

129

'Haldi laga di now just sindoor is remaining' I said and left.

She stood still for a moment like a statue in the lawn.

*   *   *

All the rituals were carried out, arrival of baarat, varmala, evening reception followed by fireworks. Priya had this wish to have lots of fireworks on the day of her reception, Rahul fulfilled it. Bride looked beautiful and her happiness added glowing charm to her face. Late night most important ceremonies were arranged, yag mandap, mantras, 7 vows, kanyadaan, sindoor rituals were carried out. Everyone was happy specially Priya and her family.

I had not slept since last 2 nights yet I had no sleep in my eyes, in front of me was Arohi sitting behind her sister, helping her with the rituals. I showered flower petals on her when everyone was showering those on bride and groom. She gave me an angry look mixed with love. I loved it.

I gestured her after few days we both will be sitting like this in a mandap, she smiled and indicated me not to make any more gestures.

Morning 6:30 AM groom's family was ready to take Priya their home. Priya hugged everyone and cried. I saw her mom and dad crying too. Her dad seemed to be very strict, he spoke very less to all of us but looking at her daughter leaving his place and going to someone else's home made a stiff father emotional. Daughters are deeply connected to their parents; I had a live example in front of me. Arohi and Priya hugged their father. He dropped Priya to the decorated Vintage car. Rahul was sitting inside. Priya's family helped her to sit comfortably managing her lehanga. Everyone waved goodbye as the couple moved to start a new journey of their life.

I saw Arohi's mother still crying looking at the gate. Arohi kept holding her. I went to the beautiful ladies

'Aunty, she will be very happy and nothing will change. Rahul lives in Pune. You can visit her anytime. Things will be just like the way they were.

Instead you should be happy as you have got a son who will take care of you and your daughter now on' I said

'haan Beta, I know, still it pains when a daughter moves from our home to someone else's. I wish her all the happiness in life' she said

'surely aunty, Rahul is a nice person. He will keep her happy' I assured

'Yes, Rahul is gem of a person. Now I am just tensed about our little daughter Arohi, she is also grown up. Need to find a perfect groom for her too. I do not know what happened between her and Akash. Everything was set between families. She never answers me whenever I ask her this question' she said looking at me and then at Arohi.

'Mummy why do u always bring this thing in between' Arohi grumbled, leaving the conversation she went inside.

'Look beta, this happens' she said.

'Aunty Arohi deserves someone very good and genuine; she is so sweet and delicate. She needs a person who can take good care of her and love her lots. She cannot stay with a person who played with her emotions. Don't you worry! You will find a very good groom for her too, who will keep her happy' I said holding her mother's hand

She nodded, gave me wishes and thanked for coming to her daughter's wedding.

Kolad

I enjoyed my night calls with Arohi, She sleeps in her room alone, so it's easier for her to talk without bothering anyone and without letting anyone know that she talks to me, I do not want my roommate Nik to have a disturbed sleep, so I chose talking to her in balcony. Our call starts with normal day to day routine discussion, about work, home, food we ate and new people we met. We discuss each and every minute detail; her voice modulation helps me to understand her lively or sleepy mode. Her sweet voice becomes sweeter when she is sleepy, she sounds like a little 5 year old.

With time our mood, and discussions shift to different topics, starting hour of the call is normal discussion then her everyday fear 'RV sir I am scared, I don't know what will happen in future.' I help to overcome her daily fear and assure that I will stand for our decision and her parents will say yes for our relationship. I could feel her being cozy in her bed which initiates sweet romantic talks. She sleeps on call while talking; I do not have to speak much after she sleeps, I too lay down on my bed without disconnecting the call, hearing her breathe. Thanks to telephone companies who disconnect the calls after every 2 hours avoiding too much of bill at the end of the month.

Being a part of big group, it was next to impossible for me and Arohi to spend time with each other. We thought for a workaround and I started picking her up from office so that we can spend our precious personal time while returning home.

Everyday meetings, discussions, little fights, sweet smiles bought us closer.

* * *

24th September 2014 / Wednesday

Weeks passed by, our schedule continued. I reached her office at 7, today she took long to come out. She was not speaking anything. I enquired if everything was alright, she just replied 'huh'.

We reached CCD nearby her office and occupied the corner table at the roof top.

'Is everything ok Arohi? Something happened in office?' I inquired

'What does he think of himself? I told you about that manager na, he is after me, trying hard to tag me in his project. I have already told him that I am happy with my present team and not interested in his project. He is a stalker, follows me wherever I go. He irritates me a lot. I am not complaining to HR just because I do not want him to lose his job. I have informed everything to my Manager. He said he will take action against him but GOD knows when. I am way too irritated' she busted.

'My Baby, you have complained to your manager na, he will take care of him, you don't worry. Give me a smile now' I tickled her to cool her down and make her smile.

'Is there anything else bothering you' I asked

'Hmm, our group' she answered

'What about our group?' I asked

'Everyone seems to be have changed, earlier we all used to sit and talk, we used to play games, we all enjoyed each other's company but today nothing looks same like before.

Starting with Prateek sir – no one knows where he is, for any plans he simply says NO, Tiddi sir always busy with his TV. Nik sir in his matches,

Atul is in different world all together, Aditi di and Neha di have become way too moody if I go and ask them about any plans they say : 'you plan we will let you know we are in or not'.

People here living in same society behaving so differently, it seems nobody is bothered about anyone else, now a days when we meet on weekends, instead of talking or spending time with each other everyone is busy watching television, there is silence between friends because that idiot box speaks and what all they watch is, those repetitive reality shows. I do not know how to bring my old happening group back. I miss old times' she said

She continued 'new habit of few of the group members- "Alcohol". Fun for them these days is to booze and dance like crazy, what about the people who do not drink? They get bored. It's just music, tapping drunk feet and no communication, no sharing within the members. Once or twice these things are good but not always. I want those talks back, that fun back, where no one needed alcohol to set the mood, our talks were enough. Please do something na RV sir. Please make them all understand'

'hmm, GROUP'

'Baby, with time priority changes, earlier group was the priority, now a days all the members of the group are taking it for granted. We all are together since last 7 years. So to everyone it is like "group to hamesha rahega hi" now they are more concerned about their own life, it is just you who is talking about the group and is concerned about it. We all meet on birthdays and on weekends, to watch television together is enough for everyone. Do not expect much. Please' I replied

'We all are so connected, why everyone has stopped showing that. We all used to feel so proud being a part of "Gyaanis"' she said in a disappointing tone

'Yes everyone is connected through heart, whenever any member will need help, all will be standing there to help him/her. Little changes with time are expected and you are a darling to everyone, they all care for you, this truth will remain same always' I said

'It's not about care. I wish, everything to be same as it was' she said joining her hands and looking up in the sky.

It started drizzling slowly and then the drizzle got converted into rains, we ran in from roof top, to grab a table with roof on top.

'Was my prayer so unreal that it started to rain in winters' she asked

'Wow I love unseasonal rains' I said looking up towards the sky. Rains are always best for romance and I got the chance.

'Soooo.... Miss Arohi Jain, you promised me that you will say something after coming to Pune. It's been weeks now. Do you remember?' I asked bringing her out of her sad mood to the mood I wanted.

She smiled and pretended as if she does not remember anything

'Umm, I have to say something?' she asked act fully

'Yes and you promised to go on a trip to Kolad with me' I said

'Hmm okay, so then I will say what you want to listen in Kolad' she replied

'Ok Cool then, we will do booking for the coming weekend, I will confirm the route once, also I will ask one of my office friend to give me his bike – thunder bird, it will be more comfortable than my pulsar and easy to tie luggage on both the sides so that you could sit free handed and hold me tight while I drive. Kolad is around 150 kilo meters that would be 3:30 hours of journey. We will cross beautiful Mulshi Lake and Tamhini ghats to reach our destination, those places are beautiful and unseasonal rain will make it even more beautiful. I will call Kolad River Rafting team too to confirm our bookings' I said all in one go

'Oh My God, you have already planned everything. Waoo I too am very excited' she said and hugged me.

We planned our day and night at Kolad. We enquired about river rafting from all the possible sources such as internet, our office friends and friends of friends. For the 1st time, she will be with me just me. I want to make this special; she did all the enquiries from her side too. Our night talks were more focused on what we will do once we reach our destination. I reminded her that she has to say something.

I made the bookings for two adults. Offer included -River rafting on Kundlika, Rafting equipment like life jackets, helmets, and paddles, a professional river-rafting guide for our support, our stay at the farmhouse (nice comfortable rooms, tents and western, Indian loos). Meals including lunch, tea with snacks, dinner and next day breakfast, barbeque, night walk and camp fire.

Arohi prepared the checklist of the things we need to carry. It included: T-shirts, shorts, floaters for rafting, extra pairs of clothes, towel, sun glass, Water proof Sun Block lotion, sleepers and snacks. She planned to make my favorite potato sandwiches for our breakfast before we leave in the morning.

Now the task was to decide what we are going to say to our parents and friends. I advised Arohi to say that she is going on a trip with her office friends. I will cook up something on the day itself.

27th September 2014/ Saturday/ 5:30 AM

I left around 5:30 while everyone at my place was sleeping. I took thunder bird from my office colleague - Ashish and parked my pulsar at his place. I got the petrol tank full, air checked and went to pick up Arohi at society's gate. She was ready with her bag pack. At 6:45 AM we headed towards our destination.

1km away from our society, we halted for tying up the bags on bike. I had small polyester rope and to tie both our bag packs using it was a little tedious task. I want her to sit comfortably without worrying about the bags. I asked her to wait for few minutes and I will bring a set of ropes. As I returned I saw my darling had applied all her brain and mechanics and have tied the bags on bike, making my work easy. I appreciated her work; she showed me her biceps pretending to be very strong. I loved her cuteness. I tied bags with the 2nd rope, confirming that it won't fall. We started with our beautiful journey.

She held me tight, sang all the possible songs she could, we played antakshari, she took few pictures of the bike mirror reflecting our images. After 1:30 hours of drive the lake came into view as we rode around a bend in the trail. It was the 1st time she saw Mulshi Lake, she was enchanted. It was a big beautiful lake, water, while calm, had so many different hues of blue, reflecting the sheds of morning sun in the sky, near the shore it was pale blue, nearly translucent, as it got deeper it changed from pale blue to deep dark blue, the trees on the far side of the lake were mirrored on the lake, lush green mountains, adds to the captivating landscape around. Lake walked with us parallel for few kilometers; our eyes tried capturing the scenic beauty. We made our way to Tamhini ghats and had beautiful romantic conversation in the arms of nature. Tamhini Ghats were no less than the Western Ghats.

My stomach growled with hunger; we decided to take a halt. I saw a small tea shop, it was a house of the villager and in front part of the house they created space for a small shop and provided sitting in patio. An old age uncle welcomed us; we washed our hands, ordered 2 teas along with Parle-G biscuits. Arohi took out potato sandwiches wrapped in an aluminum foil. We had the best breakfast ever, I loved the sandwiches, I kissed her beautiful hands that made yummy sandwiches and I thanked her for making them so early in the morning. Arohi got a picture clicked with uncle and then asked uncle to click our picture with our journey partner – our Bike. Uncle guided us the path to washroom helping us to respond to the nature's call.

We reached our destination at 11:45 AM, I called booking agent to guide us to farmhouse, small narrow muddy road covered with trees opened up in front of a beautiful farm house. Surrounded by farms on three sides, hammock tied on opposite coconut trees in the lawn, cage having beautiful love birds and parrots. Agent showed us different types of accommodations, tents and rooms with ethnic village touch. Tents had the risk of insects creeping in, I do not want those creepy things to bother my darling, we settled for a small room with attached washroom and a small verandah of its own in front of a farm. Room was normal with 2 single beds separated by a wardrobe, television placed in front of bed one, wooden and clay showpieces gave room an ethnic touch.

Farm looked green and healthy.

We took bath and got ready for the lunch, buffet was arranged for us in a small hut near lawn, we ate in one plate. Our love made us call each other by many names Shona, jaan, jaanu, My Love, baabu, baby and list goes on... Shonu was mostly used for normal conversation.

Guide advised us to take some rest and later we can go for evening walk near Kundlika River. We went to our room to grab some sleep. Arohi took out her shorts and a top, she asked me to turn around and not look at her while she is changing; she switched off the lights too. Darkness favored her to hide from me. I tried teasing her 'I can change in front of you, why can't you do that in front of me? People talk about equality, men and women are equal. Where is the equality here? Show me' I gave a little speech and pulled out my t-shirt in front of her.

She stood still, crossed her hands without giving a smile, she stared at me and said 'Ho gaya? Now can I change?'

Well her looks worked and I silently turned around. She ensured that I do not cheat.

'I am done, you can turn now' she said

'Wohoo... Someone is looking red hot in red shorts' I said. Sunlight penetrating from corner of the window helped me figuring out colors in dark room.

'You are crazy RV sir' she replied

'Stop calling me that' I said

'Stop calling you what?' she asked folding her clothes

'RV Sir, college is over long time back, I am no more your sir. Call me RV' I said

'Hehe not possible now, for me you are RV sir and will always be' she said

'Call me anything but not sir, you can call me sir in front of others but when it's just you and me. NO SIR ok?' I ordered

'Jo hukum SIR' she said and laughed

I picked her up, she shouted 'put me down else I will fall' I threw her on the bed and climbed on her. She looked at me, puzzled without blinking. My head was above hers, facing towards her, my hands stretched on the bed avoiding my body contact with her.

'Baby, my bed is that side, let me go please. I will rest there' she said nervously, wondering what could be my next move.

'You can sleep here with me, close to me' I said

'Umm, no na. Its single bed made for one person, it will not be comfortable for 2 people' she said avoiding eye contact with me. She tried to escape from the little space between my hands and her body. I blocked all the spaces left open for her, failing her each attempt to get away from me.

I could see her skin between the buttons of her top. It tempted me towards her. Feeling her quiver I decided to let her go. I stood up and lay on wall corner of the bed. She stood up as fast as she could and went towards her bed. I followed her.

She cleaned the bed, I tried troubling her, I tickled on her hands softly, played with her hairs while she was cleaning the bed, I hugged her from back, she turned and hugged me back, hiding herself in my chest. I picked her up in my arms, she grabbed the blanket. This time softly I placed her on my bed. She covered herself with the blanket, she gestured me to come inside it by lifting blanket and making space for me.

I held her tight, she hid in me again. She loves doing that. I looked down, lifted her face and kissed her on forehead; she had a calm expression on her face.

'I feel so comfortable and protected in your arms' she said in her soft voice.

'This place is just yours' I said pressing the tip of my nose against hers and rubbing softly left and right.

'I love you Arohi' I whispered coming close to her ears and kissed it.

'I love you too' she said barely audible, I could feel her fast running heartbeat. She hid in my chest, I played with her hair, she was half asleep when I went down to her level and covered ourselves with the blanket. I held her body with my right hand and her face with the left one. For the 1st time I kissed her on her lips, her hesitant lips, her warm soft lips. Kiss lasted for few seconds and then she withdrew hers from mine.

'You are such a cheater' she said gaining back her senses and hitting me like a punching bag.

'I am sorry, I tried resisting but I could not. You are tempting' I replied

She again hit me!

'I am sorry!' I said and covered her.

We fell asleep.

After half an hour, guide knocked the door and asked us to come out for snacks, we not being much hungry decided to go river side. We got ready; she wore knee length black dress with strips on shoulders and advised me to wear a white t-shirt and a knee length Cargo.

Agent guided us the path, we took our bike and followed advisors instructions, crossing the green lush farms we reached the river Kundlika. It was sunset. The water was still.

Tall trees cast their reflection on the water on the west side of the river making a dark silhouette against the blue. When the wind blows, sun's reflection makes the ripples glimmer.

We climbed the little bridge on the river, took few pictures of us with the nature and its beauty. Other side of the bridge was another village and the area looked isolated. I was a bit afraid as Arohi was with me that too in short clothes. I advised her we will not go on other side of the bridge. She insisted to at least sit on stones at the edge of the river with our feet in water. I agreed. We sat down, small fishes gathered near our legs.

Threads of light lingered in the sky, mingling with the rolling clouds, dyeing the heavens first orange, then red, then dark blue, until all that was left of the sunset was a chalky mauve.

We sat there silently with hand in hand, both lost in thoughts and in nature.

'Baabu, u know what?' she said playing with fishes in water

'What baby?' I responded to her question

'I have a very big dream' she said

'And what is that dream?' I asked

'I want to conduct my own solo painting exhibition in Mumbai; I want it to be a big success, all media covering my event. I want to see that happiness on my parents face when they will see their daughter doing something out of the box' she said

'Work for it Arohi, you have that talent in you. You can achieve your dream and for any help I am there with you' I said

'Yeah, I need to work really hard for that. I will do it. I want to spread my thoughts and messages through my paintings' she said

'That would be one of the happiest days of my life' she continued

'If you achieve your biggest dream that would be the happiest day for me too' I said kissing her hands and pressing my nose against hers.

'Acha by the way do you know what pressing nose like this is called as?' I asked

'No, tell me' She replied

'In modern Western culture it is called as "Eskimo kiss"' I said

'Hww... it's a kind of kiss' she said in surprise.

'Yes, this means I have kissed you before too, in Goa. Remember?' I teased her

'No No, we will not consider that' she said

While we discussed our dreams and had cute discussions, darkness took over the sky. Cool breeze made her shiver; I scolded her for not wearing full clothes. We drove back to the farm house. We walked in the garden, workers of the farmhouse played soft music adding romantic tint in the air. We explored all areas of the farmhouse, sat in tents, clicked pictures of beautiful wooden tables; we decided to lie on the hammock tied on coconut trees in the lawn. We both lay on a hammock, she rested on my shoulder. A group of boys (new guests of the farmhouse) enjoyed camp fire. Hammock sling was made of netting, I was worried if Arohi's legs were visible from beneath, and I tried to cover her as much as possible.

I brought blanket from the room, spread it over the hammock and then we lay on it covering ourselves, blanket made us feel cozy, we gazed the stars. The place was silvered and transformed by the light of the moon, which, at full, hung like a great luminous pearl on the radiant chest of heaven. We shared our childhood mischievous stories, she told how Priya used to get all the beating and she was safe being the little one at home. I told her about my fights in school, she told about how she followed all the mythological serials and tried doing 'tapasya' to call God on earth, she use to imitate Hanumanji flying in air by lying upside down. I laughed holding my stomach. I told her about how my elder sister punished me when I did not use to study, and we talked for hours, telling each other about our family, childhood friends and what not.

I brought our dinner plate to hammock, as my sweetheart was not in mood to move from there. We ate and decided to move in as it was cooler now in the lawn. We came in; she put on the sweet romantic music. I bend down to my knees and asked her for a dance, she smiled and gave her hand in mine. We had our best time dancing; she kept her feet on mine. Each time she looked in my eyes within a minute she use to take away her glance, on insisting to look at me she replied –I feel shy. I loved her shyness. While dancing I tried dropping strips of her dress down her shoulders, reluctantly she put those back again, I tried doing it again, this time she did not lift it up.

She in my arms, her neck in clear view, I smelled her, her fragrance made me lose my senses. I tried kissing her. She smartly took a water bottle lying behind me on bed and tried emptying it on me, water fight made both of us wet; she being wet looked more attractive. Her wet body was driving me crazy for her. I held her tightly, I forgot who I was, and I forgot all my ethics, rules, right or wrong. I forgot all the possible ways a man treats a woman. I pulled her and kissed her passionately pushing her towards the wall. I forgot about my strengths, I forgot how easily I could hurt her. She called my name as I went wild on her, Go Easy TIGER, she said.

I wanted to hear those words again. I continued kissing her this time softly and bought her to the bed. She lay down and I lay on her. My hand went back to her hair, her thick long hair, I pulled them knowing it will not hurt her much. I pulled her back relieving her neck. A tiny drop of water lay there innocently, I kissed it. My hand slipped inside her dress, she tried opposing my actions by moving in my arms. As I touched her, she too started losing her senses, she clutched me tight, scratching her nails on my back and held my head while I kissed her. I admired her curves to full extent. I unzipped her dress and unhooked her. I felt the softness of her body, there were no clothes on us by now, I kissed her neck passionately and started going down, she moaned in pleasure. I wanted to hear her moan again, I bit her below her neck. Everything was spontaneous; no one could predict the next move. She surrendered herself to me. I kissed every inch of her perfect body. I did not care about the consequences that moment. It was the moment in my life when nothing was calculated. We were sweating; her hot breath hit my ears like a blazing fire burning a forest.

I made her completely mine. I felt her nervousness and quiver I rubbed her back and helped her to calm down. She lay silently putting her head on my bare chest. 'I love you honey' I whispered and covered her, she being tired slept. I thought to myself if I would have scared her, as this was the 1st time she was out with me alone.

*   *   *

Morning ray of sunlight falling on my face woke me up. I searched for Arohi; she was not in the room. I got frightened, put on my clothes on and came out to search for her; she was not in the washroom too. I called for her; listening to me she replied 'Baabu, I am here waving her hand'.

She was standing in the middle of the farm; I caught my breath and went running to her. She was wearing my blue t-shirt with a caption on it "No Money, No Honey" My t-shirt worked like a one piece for her. I looked around to ensure that no one sees her in just a t-shirt.

'What are you doing here my baby' I asked her pulling her cheeks

'Came here to see the sunrise, you were sleeping so didn't wake you up' she replied

'And why is my Shona wearing my t-shirt?' I asked pampering her

'Coz I love this' she answered

She looked beautiful in morning fresh face. I captured her beauty in my blue t-shirt in picture with me. We got ready for our rafting experience.

Every morning Rafting operations begin at a village called as Saje, typically by 8:15 hours; water from dam gets released making the water level great for rafting. Distance of rafting would be around 11 km on water, rapids ranging from grade 2 to grade 3 and duration approx. 1hr 45 minutes. Reporting time was 8:00 AM, we reached on time. After we have been distributed the Rafting Gear – Life jackets, helmets and pedals. Guide gave us instructions and explained the associated rafting commands, he told us about the safety measures, the right way of paddling and what to do in case we fall.

'Fall...?' Arohi mumbled holding my hand. I looked at her; she was scared but acted brave.

With life jackets on and paddles in our hands, we were ready for the rendezvous with dangerous rapids. We had 11 members in the boat. Arohi being adventure freak decided to sit in between the front two positions at the deck of the raft, holding 2 ropes in both her hands. I sat at 1st position behind her.

The guide on our raft instructed us to sail forward and we started rowing our raft. Paddling looked easy until we came across the first rapid. We could see the rapid from the distance, the violent waves, the roar of water and the stones in between. It seemed that those things together were threatening us to go back but our adventurer's spirit took us right in middle of the rapid, and soon we found ourselves combating the strong current by rowing in sync and paddling as hard as we could. The spine chilling water had drenched us all. We didn't stop paddling. Before we could know, we were out of that rapid and out of breath too. It was an awesome experience. We sat on the raft looking around the beauty of river. Rafting was fun, I loved it, and Arohi loved it too. I suddenly felt I was like Bear Grylls, out in jungles for my own adventures. I felt kundlika to be amazon. Sight was beautiful. River covered with rocks and beautiful trees.

The guide patted our back for the good work and told us to jump into the water if we want to. We jumped, he taught various types of jumping styles, and we tried all. The water was cold. Life jackets helped us float on the water. It was so amazing; I was in water with my beloved. We were floating. We got one more wish from our wish list fulfilled. We celebrated. I kissed her in water; she shockingly looked around to see if anyone is watching us.

I wanted to show her my swimming skills; I bought her to a position and told her to stay there for a while.

'Look I will swim underwater from this point to that tree' I said pointing towards the tree approx. 4 mts from our position. I dived like a hero.

She laughed and laughed and laughed. My life jacket did not let me in the water.

'Ahhh to hell with this life jacket, it made a joke out of me' I said angrily

She laughed again

We floated again facing up the sky, holding hands. We enjoyed our moments in water.

We tried to swim

She was left behind me; I went to her and said

'Superman on your rescue ma'am, do not worry. I am here' I said stretching my right hand in air.

She laughed loud again.

'Come girl be my super woman' I said.

She too stretched her one hand and followed me.

'You are too cute Shonu' she said and laughed.

'This is my best trip ever' she shouted loud

'Mine too' I joined her and shouted

We tried to hug in water but again life jackets!!!! We made our life jackets hug too. ☺

Unexpected 1

29th September 2014/ Monday/ 12:00PM

'Hey Rajveer, how was your trip man?' Ashish asked

'It was cool, had a great rafting experience' I replied.

'Hope thunder bird did not trouble you and you had a safe road trip'

'Yeah! Thanks dude for the bike. It was awesome'

'And what about your bird, did she trouble you?' he laughed

'My Bird...?' I asked doubtfully

'Yes obviously, you must have gone with your girl right? Or went alone on bike?'

'I actually went with one of my school mate; he is new to the city. So old mates plan u know' I replied and turned back to work avoiding any further conversation

'Oh is it? By the way you did not inform about your trip to your roommates? I met Tarun and Prateek yesterday' he said

'Oh yeah I left early in the morning, so didn't had the chance. You had any discussion about it with them?' I enquired

'Well yes, I told them that you took thunder bird to go on a trip to Kolad. I was shocked when I got to know that your best buddies are not aware of it' he said

'Umm yeah, I forgot to tell them, what else did you tell them?'

'Nothing much it was a funny conversation, our common link is you so was talking about you. I asked about your Girlfriend, I previously thought, you are on with your girl. What man over-night trip that too with a boy? Girls here are crazy for you and you still enjoying with your schoolmates. What has happened to you dude' he said disappointingly.

'Just like that man, I don't want any Gf issues as of now in my life. What did Prateek and Tarun replied?' I was more curious to know the conversation between my roommates and him.

'They just said that something has happened to you, not sharing things these days. Prateek said he has an idea about who the girl is. Chakkar kya hai boss?' he asked with his one eyebrow up.

'Even I do not know what they are talking about, they must be joking. Well thanks man for the bike'

'You are welcome buddy, next time take it when you go with a girl. My bike will also feel the pleasure' he winked

I returned back to my work, wondering about which girl Prateek was talking about. I tried concentrating on my work. I had no idea that Ashish, Pajju and Tiddi could meet. They know each other because of me. I should have taken care of this and should have planned it properly. I hope nobody does any cross questioning to Arohi. I called her up

'Hi Shona'

'Hi baabu' she replied

'Baabu I want to tell you something' she said

'Tell me baby. Everything alright...?'

148

'I will call you in lunch break; I have a meeting and few pending tasks. I want to talk to you about something really important. I am scared babbu, something is going wrong. I will give you a call at 1. Please be available'

'Hmm finish your tasks soon and then we can discuss'

I called her up at exact 1:00PM, curious to know about the things she is concerned about.

'Now tell me Shonu, what happened?' I asked

'Priya di came home today while I was getting ready for office; she told that Jiju has an official trip so she will be staying here for a week'

'So what is the problem with that?' I asked

'Problem is, she asked me all the weird questions about the trip like how many people were there, what all places we went, she told me to show office group pictures.'

'Ohh, what did you say?'

'I was getting late for office so I left saying my cab is waiting for me. Also Neha di and Aditi di asked lots of questions regarding trip, Sunday evening when I switched on my internet I had WhatsApp messages from Tarun sir and Prateek sir asking me about the trip and when am I coming back' she said

'There is something wrong, these guys are thinking. You concentrate on work. We will figure this out after office hours'

'Hmm' she replied and disconnected the call.

She called me back,

'One more thing I forgot to tell, Priya di called me last week, saying she got the news that I spend lots of time with you and people are saying things behind our back. She told me to maintain some distance from you as she cannot tolerate any one saying anything against me. I do not believe our group members are talking about us behind our back. If they feel anything they should directly come to us na' she said

149

'Chill baby. We will talk in evening after office hours. Relax now!' I advised

I too wondered what all is happening? Priya asked Arohi to be away from me? Damn this is shocking. What are they thinking? What are they talking about us? Are these my best friends who instead of clearing things with me, discussing within themselves and making an issue out of it.

I picked up Arohi at 7:00PM and we went to CCD nearby her office.

'Now tell me what all is happening?' I questioned

She started 'I forgot to tell you this but last week dii called me', she said 'I am hearing too many things about you and RV, both of you are always caught together and you have started ignoring other group members to be with each other

I asked her who is telling her all such things.

She said this is none of my concern and instead of bothering who is talking all this about you and me, she told me to be away from you. She warned me that if she hears anything else now, she will take some action. I am scared RV sir'.

'hmm I cannot believe Priya could say all this and she considers herself to be a good friend of mine'

'It's not about being your friend, I am her younger sister na Shona, obviously she will be concerned about me and if she hears anything against me will affect her na' she explained

'Still baby, this is unexpected. She should have at least had a word with me before scolding you and if this is true, if people are talking about us behind our back and by people I mean our group, our best friends then I am really disappointed. I expected them to directly come to me and ask questions' I said in an inacceptable tone

'Let us not judge everyone by what dii is saying, she is possessive about me and cares a lot, we all are good friends, there is some misunderstanding going on' she said

I told Arohi about the conversation between Prateek, Tarun and Ashish and about Pajju's comment 'I think I know who his Gf is'

'Something is cooking up between all, I told you na our group is not same as before' I said

'Hmm, let's not jump onto any conclusion, let's wait for some time and then we will decide what to do' Arohi suggested

'I thought it will be difficult to convince your parents but Priya will support us, she knows me very well but looking at the scenarios I think it would be difficult to convince Priya too, Can I talk to Priya regarding this?' I asked

'No no no RV sir, she will kill me, you know her na, if she gets to know that I share everything with you, she will scold me a lot and I am not sure she will support us or not. I told you na inter caste marriages are considered sin in our community' She said

'Let's be away from each other in front of everyone for some time and try to figure out what's going on in their mind' she advised

'hmm, I don't feel like being a part of Gyaanis anymore' I said angrily

'No baby, it's our family, small family. We cannot live without them; they cannot live without us' she tried to convince.

'don't be in such a myth Jaan, people change with time, no one cares' I replied

She held my hand and convinced me to stay calm and observe the situations.

'I will try' I said

I dropped her near society gate. Unfortunately Aditi saw and came near us. I and Arohi pretended to be normal.

'OOho you went to pick Arohi from her office? You never came to pick me up ever'. She taunted

Her taunt made me lose my temper, I was about to give her a rude reply but before I could reply Arohi interrupted –

'No Di, he did not pick me up from office, my cab dropped me at circle, he picked me up from there' she said.

'hmm' Aditi replied. I was silently standing there

'Arohi are you coming with me or want to have chat with RV?' she asked Arohi

Things were getting on my nerves now; I did not speak a word because I knew my actions will directly affect Arohi.

Things were getting on my nerves now; I did not spoke a word because I knew my actions will directly affect Arohi.

'Di I am coming with you, he just came to drop me till society' Arohi gave clarification; I hated it when she was trying to clarify herself.

Things started changing, I felt as if everyone was against me and my love. Arohi tried convincing me to behave normal; according to her we can handle situations and bring back our old group. She loves each member of the group and she wants to hold on to the things but I moved on, I stopped talking to people, I was not doing it intentionally but they made me do so. I started avoiding group gatherings.

12th October 2014/ Sunday

Pajju asked all the boys to get ready as we need to go for Lunch at girl's place.

I refused.

I knew Arohi was not at home, she was out with Priya and it will take at least 2 hours for her to come back but this was not the only reason for me to refuse. My inner feelings did not allow me to be an active member of Gyaanis anymore.

But then I remembered my princess wish 'group to be together always, it's our small family'.

Aditi and Neha had prepared daal Bati for lunch. As Arohi and Priya were out for lunch, we did not wait for them and got our stomachs full with Daal Bati, lunch was tasty. Heavy food made us lazy, we lay on the floor at random positions. Tiddi switched on the television. I felt my mobile vibrating in my pocket, it was a message from Tiddi, and I wondered why was he messaging me sitting in the same room? I read the message:

'Arohi is not at home. This is the reason he was not willing to come': 2:20PM

I got another message from him after a minute

'Sorry wrong window, message was for someone else': 2:21 PM

I was shocked reading his messages, I read it 5 times and then replied back 'yes Arohi is not at home and who was not willing to come because of this?'

'I was sending that message to one of my school friend, his girlfriend Arohi is not coming in the school get-to-gather so he too backed out. Mistakenly I sent it to you' Tiddi replied

'Hmm, well I thought you were sending this message to someone within group and by mistake you send it to me' I messaged

'no re, why will I talk like this about our Arohi' he replied

I was not in mood of further discussion therefore I left the conversation and kept phone besides me. Arohi and Priya entered. I could make out from Arohi's face, she had been crying or she wanted to cry. She straight away entered her room without acknowledging anyone in the room. Priya sat happily with all of us.

Priya shared her experiences of being a newly wedded bride. Neha, Mini and Aditi took immense interest and enquired more about Priya's married life.

'Shona what happened? You ok?' I texted Arohi

'No I am not, you won't believe what happened today' she said

'Tell me baby what happened' I replied. As too many unexpected things were happening, believing anything else would not be too hard for me.

153

'You remember Raj? Jiju's brother'

'Yes I do, how can I forget him?'

'His parents has sent proposal for me and my parents said yes, dii is too happy, thinking we both will stay together. Raj likes me too. Shona please do something' she replied.

'What'?? I was dumbfounded

'How can your parents say yes to him? Don't they think they should ask you? You have right to choose your life partner or not?' I busted on her.

'I don't know... I don't know anything. May be after Akash's case they do not trust me on choosing a correct life partner for myself. Raj's parents and family met me at didi's wedding, they liked me. Now they want both their sons to settle in one family. Raj lives in Mumbai; today he came down Pune to meet me. It was a surprise for me rather I should say it was a shock for me. Di helped him plan things. I don't know what's happening. I do not know what to do'

'what you do not know girl? You just have to say no, Big NO' I replied

'It is not that easy Baabu. They will ask me too many questions and my 1 wrong step may create trouble for Di'

'If you do not say NO at right time Arohi, things will get worse; it will be more difficult to convince your parents later'

'Hmm I will have word with mummy' she said.

Everything is falling apart. Group- one of the best things that I had, Today everybody seem like a stranger to me. I am not able to share my biggest secret, my happiness, and my concerns with any one of them. At once we shared each and everything, today when I need their support I have no one standing with me. I decided to talk to Priya and tell her things about me and Arohi. I will let her know that we cannot live without each other and no one is capable of keeping her happy as much as I am.

Before I could say anything, Priya made an announcement:

'Guys do you all remember Raj, Rahul's brother' she asked.

'The BMW guy...?' Tiddi enquired

'Yes him' Priya replied

'Yes we remember him' people said in union.

'Well our parents are setting Arohi and him together' she announced

There was silence for few seconds, everyone looked at each other. Pajju, Nik and Tiddi looked at me. I pretended to be normal.

'Wow congratulations' Tiddi said

People started to congratulate in chorus

'How come all of a sudden? Arohi and Raj.?' Neha asked.

'Not all of a sudden, parents were planning things since November, my wedding. Raj too expressed that he likes Arohi. So green signal from all' she answered

'Did anyone ask Arohi what she wants' I interrupted.

'She will never get ready for marriage stuff, but someday she has to, Raj is a good boy and both of us will be in same family. My parents do not want to lose such a nice opportunity; Arohi will be in safe hands' Priya answered.

'What's so nice about him?' I back questioned her.

All the members of the group were silently listening to our little heated conversation. By the time everyone would have got rough idea about my intentions.

'He has a good job and a decent package. Besides this, he is setting up his own business. He is talented, smart, good looking, well behaved, belongs to an educated and sophisticated family. He likes Arohi and will keep her like a queen. What else is needed?' she answered in an offended tone

I was about to fire my next question when Pajju patted me softly understanding my intentions, he gestured me to stop.

'And I belong to the same family, I know him very well, today when he met my sister he behaved like a perfect gentleman' Priya continued

'Waoo he sounds so perfect, any pictures of Arohi and him together' Aditi enquired

'Yes I clicked few, have a look' everyone jumped in, to look at the pictures. I was least interested.

I texted Arohi and asked her to leave home saying that she has her art class.

I wanted to be with her, to support her, to convince myself that she is still by my side and figure out some solution to this new problem. I was scared to core and all these talks were frustrating me. I do not want to lose her at any cost.

She got ready and came out of her room; I could see her from the narrow passage between living room and her room, she wore sunglasses to hide her watery eyes from others. Everyone was busy looking at the pictures, they all sat on the mattress lying on floor and managing to look at Priya's mobile screen from their positions. They all behaved as if they saw an 'alien' and wanted to gather all the information about it before he takes his UFO back to his planet.

At a sudden blinking eye moment something happened, I saw her falling, her head directly hitting the floor. I ran towards her but was late, she lay on the floor. Everyone looked back hearing the bang noise of her fall, they too ran towards her. I held her in my arms, removing her glasses I pressed her head tight, I felt my hands wet. My hands were wet with her blood. My heart was in my mouth when I saw her bleeding. I had tears in my eyes. I did not care who all was there. I held her tight, her head rested on my chest and her body on the floor; she got the cut near her right eye, little above her eyebrows because of the glasses she was wearing. I placed my handkerchief on her wound, she was unconscious. I tried waking her up by patting her cheeks slowly. She responded and tried to open her eyes. I saw water near her feet, she slipped on the water lying on floor. I shouted losing control on myself 'Who the hell threw water here? Look what happened' everyone stayed quiet there.

I picked her up and placed her on bed, people were running here and there to bring essential things, Pajju bought water in a bowl, Tiddi bought cotton and Aditi bought Dettol from her room. Priya went to the kitchen and bought turmeric powder. I cleaned her blood with cotton; Tiddi dipped cotton in Dettol water and gave it to me to clean the wound. I cleaned it, blood did not stop. Priya applied turmeric powder on her wound to stop the flowing blood. We all sat beside Arohi's bed, she laid half-conscious. Priya stood and cleaned the water on floor. Arohi gaining her consciousness sat on bed.

'Why are you all sitting like this? Nothing much happened to me' Arohi said pressing lightly near her wound

'How did you fall?' Tiddi asked

'I don't remember, I think I slipped' she answered

'Is it paining?' Priya asked in a concerned tone

She nodded

'I hope it will not leave a scar on your face' Aditi said. Arohi looked at me.

I looked at Aditi giving her disgusting look; there was no need of this sentence here.

I looked at my baby in pain. I wanted to keep holding my delicate darling but I was helpless in front of everyone.

'Hey, everyone stop bothering her, things happen *"bade bade shahro main choti choti cheezen hoti rehti hain"'* Pajju said in SRK style

'And we got such a good news, you and Raj huh huh' he tried teasing Arohi

Everyone congratulated her by shaking hands. She looked at me, tears dropped down her eyes, with little fake smile on her lips she responded to the wishes.

Unexpected 2

Arohi showed good improvement, doctor advised there is no need for stiches, let the wound heal on its own; he gave a tube to apply on and a pain killer. Arohi asked innocently if there will be any scar because of the cut, doctor smiled, patted her cheeks and said 'use the tube regularly, there will be no mark.'

Arohi took Monday off from her office because of the pain; Priya gave her pain killer while leaving for office and advised her to sleep for a while. Lunch I planned to visit her secretly. I bought lunch for her and made her eat with my hands, she repeated the dialogue that once I said to her 'kisi k haath se khane ka maza hi kuch aur hai' I smiled.

I kept my hands on her cheeks and said 'You have no idea, how difficult it was for me to see you in pain. I felt so helpless.'

She came close to me and kissed on my forehead and put her head on my chest, she pulled my hands and wrapped herself. I felt as if my heart found its lost heart beat and started pumping again. Taking care of her wound I wrapped her up in me.

'It feels like it had been days that we have not hugged' I said

'hmm' she answered

'Too many things going on, I fear what will happen' she said

'Everything will be fine, let's be in this moment for now, leaving all your worries aside' I said adjusting her hairs

We enjoyed the beautiful moment we were in; we were completely lost in each other. I made her sleep and in the process of making her sleep I slept too.

'tring- tring tring- tring tring- tring'

'Ahhh what is that sound' I asked

Arohi coming back to her senses, 'someone ringing the bell, someone is home' she freaked out

'Baabu hide somewhere please hide' she panicked

'Easy baby, 1st go and check who is there' I advised

She peeped through the eye hole 'Its Aditi di, she must be here for lunch. Ohh no, she will get to know that you are here. What to do?' She asked

'I will hide. Will she come in your room?' I asked

'Yes, she might' she answered

'Trin trin trin' Aditi started banging the door too

'I will hide in Neha's room. You go open the door' I took my shoes and belongings and went inside Neha's room

Aditi and Mini shared one room, Priya and Neha another and Arohi occupied the single room of a 3 BHK, since Priya got married so Neha was left alone in her room.

'Ahhh, finally you opened the door' Aditi sighed and said

'Sorry di, I was sleeping' Arohi answered

'You home this time?' Arohi questioned

'Yes, Priya told me to get food for you and I had to pick one of my important file' She answered

She handed packed packet of daal rice to Arohi and asked her to eat; she headed towards her room to get her file.

'Arohi have you seen a blue colored file, with my name written on it' she shouted from her room

Arohi went running to her room

'No Didi, I will help you find out' Arohi answered, Aditi explored her table, drawers, and wardrobe.

'Where the hell is my file I am getting late and I need it for today's presentation' Aditi said

Arohi could you please do me a favor, please check in your books, mistakenly you must have arranged on your table, till then I will check in Neha's room.

'Neha's room...? Why Neha's room? There is nothing there' Arohi freaked out

'What has happened to you? I am just checking and I partially remember that I had given it to Neha to rectify my notes' Aditi said and stepped ahead to enter Neha's room

She was about to enter the door when Arohi stopped 'I will look in Neha di' room, you go and look in mine' Arohi said

'You are hurt bad Arohi I suppose, your mind is impacted because of that. Baby you rest I will find out' Aditi said annoyed of Arohi's disturbance and entered Neha's room. Arohi followed her too.

'Look nothing is there' Arohi said looking all around the room.

'File will not be walking na Arohi, we need to check in drawers' she said and started looking into drawers. Arohi kept looking around the room trying to find me; I waved her from washroom, confirming that I am inside. Arohi closed washroom's door.

'Ahhhhhhhhhh, finally I got it. Thank God' Aditi said kissing her file

'Ohh Waoo you found' Arohi clapped and jumped 'Let's go out now'

'Something is wrong with you girl' Aditi said looking at Arohi

'Chalo I will leave now, I have my presentation. Hold this file Arohi, I need to pee first' Aditi said stretching her hand and handing file to Arohi.

'Why you need to pee?' Another freaking question from Arohi

'What do you mean by that?' Aditi asked and stepped towards washroom

'I mean, why are you using Neha didi's washroom? She is very particular about it. You use yours na di. I like your washroom, it is more clean' Arohi gave a freaky answer

Aditi looked at her all amazed.

'Are you ok?' Aditi enquired

'Yes I am ok. You come with me and go to your washroom' she held Aditi's hand and took her to another room

Aditi used her washroom and left home advising Arohi to take rest and food.

Arohi locked the door and came running to Neha's room.

'Thank God, Thank God she left' Arohi said and asked me to come out.

I came out with my shoes in one hand and empty food plates in which we ate in another. Arohi laughed looking at me.

'You took those plates inside?' she laughed

'Yeah else your Aditi di would have seen that' I said

'You leave now babu; I almost had a small heart attack, when she entered this room'

'Yeah I know I heard what all you said' I said giving her an Eskimo kiss and left her place.

*　　*　　*

Evening Me, Pajju, Atul, Nik and Tiddi went to Arohi's place to meet her.

Priya, Neha, Aditi and Mini welcomed us. Arohi, hearing my voice she came out in the living room. She sat with us, we had normal talks and everyone teased Arohi about how she fell.

Arohi's phone rang "Raj calling". She looked at her phone and then at me. She handed the call to Priya and asked her to tell him that she is not feeling well and will call him later. Arohi went in her room to take rest.

Priya picked up the call and had conversation with Raj, She told him that Arohi is sleeping being unwell and she will call him later, Tiddi wanted to talk to Raj, he took the call from Priya. I was least interested in hearing the conversation, I left her place and came back home.

After disconnecting Raj's call Tiddi browsed Arohi's cell phone

'Oh Freak, freak' Tiddi said

'What happened' Pajju asked. Tiddi showed him Arohi's mobile.

'Look, I told you' Pajju said

Others were still clueless about what has Tiddi seen, Tiddi transferred something in his mobile and handed the phone to Priya. Priya too got shocked looking at the pictures in Arohi's cell. She had all the pictures of our beautiful moments in Kolad.

'She was on a trip with RV?' Priya said flabbergasted looking at Kolad pictures.

All the boys came back home, while Arohi was interrogated by her sister and her roommates.

'Rajveer, come out man' Atul shouted

I heard his voice and recognized him, no sir for the 1st time? He called me by my name, I felt awkward.

'What is the issue? Why are you shouting?' I asked him coming out of my room to living room.

He came close to me, held my collar and said 'Stay away from her'

I pushed him reluctantly. Pajju and Nik stopped us from fighting. All of them were on one side and I stood alone on other.

'What is there between you and Arohi?' Pajju asked cracking his knuckles

'What's there between me and Arohi?' I questioned back

Tiddi showed me the pictures. I was dumbstruck for a moment, looking at those pictures in Tiddi's cell. What the hell is happening?

'Is this not you with Arohi in these pictures?' Nik grumbled

'Yes it's me, any more doubts do you guys have or can I go now?' I confidently accepted the truth.

'Why are you doing this with her' Tiddi baffled

'What am I doing? I love her, she loves me' I answered

'Ohhh Louvvvveeeeeeee, we will not have any couples in the group, bird watching not within the group. Where the hell are your rules now?' Atul scoffed, imitated me while saying the sentences. He was getting on my nerves.

I made no rule and even if there is a rule I give a damn. Grow up buddies' I said

'Stay away from her, she is my best friend' Atul warned

'Look man, I know your situation and I understand why you are saying all this. You still feel for her and if we talk about the RULE you have also broken it.

And you talk about friendship? She is your best friend? You don't know the meaning of that word' I said pointing a finger at him

'Ohh ohh look who is talking, Mr. Rajveer, he knows the meaning of friendship' Tiddi said

'You would have shared your things RV if you call us your friends or if you knew the meaning of the word "friendship"' Nik added

'I shared almost everything with you and I am getting to know about your relationship this way? That too with our junior, Arohi...?' Pajju yelled

I showed my hand to Pajju, indicating him to stop

'You share your things with me? Think again

If yes then why haven't you told me about the back bitching, our group members were doing about me and Arohi? And you guys teaching me friendship? Then please answer me- If you all felt that there is something wrong, you could have directly come to me and clarified. I would have given you the honest answer but what you did was?' 'huh' answer me,' I said keeping my hand on Pajju's shoulder.

'I will tell you, what you all did' I continued

'You all made fun of the situation, messaged each other while sitting in the same room. Is there an Idiot written on my face that I will not understand the message sent by Tiddi that day, was about me and Arohi.

Moreover someone from my best friends went to Priya and told her all the rubbish, warned her without even thinking about Arohi. Indirectly asked Arohi to stay away from me, I should clap for my best friends' I clapped as I completed my sentence.

'Look RV, I admit I was sending that message to Pajju and mistakenly I sent that to you but all other things are not true' Tiddi admitted

'Let it be guys, you all are A**h**** and I was expecting support from you all. Let it be. I will manage things on my own'

'Screw you' Atul said

Pajju and Nik tried to stop me; I left the room without further discussion as I was done talking to them. I went to Arohi's place. I knew she would be in trouble too

I rang the bell, Priya opened the door

'Where is Arohi' I asked

'She is in her room'

'I want to meet her' I demanded

'Talk to me 1st' she capitulated

'Come in and sit' she said

I sat as per her instructions, for the 1st time I will be having formal conversation with Priya, something I had never expected.

'Why are you doing all this Rajveer, you now my family very well right? Why are you creating trouble for yourself and her too?' She questioned

'Priya few things in life are not planned; we know everything but our feelings were not in our control. We fell for each other, what to do now?' I said

'Her wedding is fixed, she is getting married within 4 months' Priya said

'Did anyone ask her what she wants?' I enquired

'She does not have any options now. Mom dad will not be able to take this insult. Dad is already a heart patient. Also, it will affect my relationship with my in-laws. Arohi is a kid; she is not able to figure out what is right at this moment. You can understand please. I request you; please give me back my family's happiness. All is in your hands' Priya pleaded

'Stop it Priya, please stop your emotional drama' I requested

'I want to meet Arohi please'

Priya took me to her room; Arohi was sitting on her bed looking out the window.

'Baabu' I called out

'Shona', she said and busted in tears. I went close to her and held her hand, wiped her tears.

'We will handle the situation together,' I assured her.

'Everyone in the group knows about us now, dii scolded me a lot. She informed mummy papa about our relation. Mummy scolded me on call, she is asking me to leave job at Pune and come back home. Priya Di convinced her to let me do the job. Papa is also very angry; they had already fixed my weeding after 4 months with Raj. No one is with us Shona, we are all alone. I cannot tell anything to Raj. If I do so I will spoil Priya di's marriage. I do not want to do that. Mom told me papa is heart patient and he will not be able to bear all this stress' she said

'We will figure out something, you trust me na?' I asked

'Yes I do' she said

'Leave it on me; I will talk to your parents. When are you going home?' I asked

'Mom called me as soon as possible, Priya di is accompanying me, may be this weekend I will leave'

'hmm, we will meet in Bhopal then' I assured

'I will tell my parents 1st, hopefully they will be happy after listening to the news and miss Arohi Rajveer Singh please promise me that you will not cry, you will take care of yourself, for me please' I said putting my right hand in front of her for promise

She nodded and promised me by holding my hand.

'You are my strength; we will not be able to talk much once you are home so you will have to support me mentally and by taking good care of yourself. Okay?'

'hmm' she replied. I kissed her on her forehead and left her room. Priya stood outside Arohi's room, waiting for me to come out.

'Had talk' she asked

'Hmm' I answered

'Could you please help me in one thing Priya?'

'Tell me'

'Can you please convince your parents to meet me once? Please just once?'

'Why are you doing this RV to yourself and to her? Please don't, I know the results. I do not want any one of you to get hurt' She said

I can feel the pressure of the situation; I had fight with my best friends, I won't be able to meet my love frequently, I cannot talk to her much. I am on the verge of losing every good thing in my life.

'Just once please' I said in my quivering voice

'Ok, I will but please be prepared for the consequences' she warned

'Hmm, take care of Arohi' I said

'You do not worry about her, she will be fine'

I picked up Arohi's picture from living room and left her place; Priya saw me from behind and didn't stop me.

Unexpected 3

21st November 2014/ Friday

I missed Arohi, I missed her very much. I could not talk to her, I cannot message her. I badly wanted to hear her voice. I needed her. I kept staring my phone, she can call me anytime. I read all our old conversations. A current of fear rolled inside me, thinking what if I lose her? What about my friendship with my roommates. I will never have my group back. How will my parents react when I will tell them about Arohi, will they support us when they will get to know about situations at her place? How will I convince Arohi's parents? What if they say NO.? Should I run with Arohi? Will she come with me? How can I ask her to do so?

Too many questions ran in my mind, little separation from her made me weak. I decided to leave for Bhopal to gain back my equilibrium, to be with people who are still mine- my parents, my family and to fight for the one whom I want to make mine, not unofficially but officially.

I reached my city – Bhopal at morning 9, I felt good as I came out of the station, too many memories in this city, I felt like I am at a place where people love me, they know me. I had spent too many years of my life here. I was positive that something good will happen. I took an auto to home, all the roads reminded me of the good time I had with my buddies, I never thought such a scenario can occur where I cannot call my friends when I miss them. In fact I never thought that I will ever miss them.

Mom saw me from balcony as I got down the auto "Rajveer" she said and came running down the stairs. 'Rajveer, beta. How come you are here? No calls nothing?' she said and hugged me

There is something about mothers; her one hug gave me strength to fight for my love with anyone in this world.

'It's my home na Maa, I can come anytime' I replied

'Yes it is your home, come! Look at you- not eating food kya? You seem weak. I will cook you your favorite food today' she said

'You go and have bath, till then I will prepare lunch for you, I will call your father too. He will join us for lunch' she said

I had my bath, Maa prepared food, and I went in the kitchen to help her in cooking

'What are you preparing Maa?'

'Daal, Rice, Roti and your favorite butter paneer Masala' She replied

Butter paneer Masala, I remembered my beautiful moments with Arohi, when she cooked food for me, butter paneer masala, how I troubled her? How she made me eat with her hands, how she slept innocently, our broken rule everything. That day was special. I had flashback of those enchanting moments I had spent with the most beautiful girl in the world.

'Kya hua? You like Butter Paneer Masala right?'

'Yes Maa, I like it' I replied coming back from my thoughts

'Maa I want to talk about something really important' I said

'Tell me Beta. Is everything Okay? Are you Okay? Is everything alright? Tujhe dekh k hi laga tha ki kuch baat zarur hai'

'Things are ok Maa, let papa come then will discuss.'

'Papa will take around an hour to reach home, till then let us sit and talk' she said

We sat in master bedroom, she sat on bed and I put my head on her lap.

'Maa, papa has always kept you like a queen na?' I asked

'Yes, he is a very good husband and a father too' She replied proudly

'Maa I want to bring a princess to our home' I said

She made me sit and asked 'Who is she?'

'Her name is Arohi, she is my college junior' I replied

'Arohi, hmm. I have seen her in your pictures on FB. People did ask me about her. She is Jain right?' she replied

I now realized that parents observe each and everything very carefully, I should have been careful while adding Maa to my Fb profile.

'Yes Maa, she is Jain. Will you and papa accept us?'

'Let your father come and then we will talk' she replied, her expression changed from motherhood to mother in law one. I could not wait any longer for this discussion. I eagerly waited for papa to come, after half an hour bell rang. I ran and opened the door. Thank god my waiting time reduced to zero. Papa is here.

'Areee my hero, how come all of a sudden you are here, what a pleasant surprise' Papa said

'Surprise to barkhurdaar ne abi tak diya kahan hai aapko' Maa said in a taunting tone

'Arey is there any other surprise waiting for me?' Papa asked

I made papa sit on sofa, I kneeled down on floor holding his hands, and I started:

'Papa, I am in love' I said. Please don't be angry. 'Her name is Arohi, she is my college junior. She is very sweet and innocent. She will keep us all very happy' I continued

'What is her full name?' he asked

'Arohi Jain'

'She stays in Pune? With you?'

'Yes she is working in a firm in Pune, we live in same society' I answered

'Do you have her pictures?' he asked

'Yes yes I have' I replied and showed him Arohi's picture in my cell. I had an album created with her name which contained all her solo pictures, there were around 140 pictures. I thought papa will only see few of them but he scrolled till he reached the last picture. I tried to figure out his verdict looking at his face but he gave no positive or negative expressions. After looking at the pictures he passed on the mobile to Maa. While Maa was looking at them I was expecting papa to say something.

'Do you have any of your pictures together?' He asked

'Yes papa' I said, puzzled with so many questions

Papa took mobile from Maa's hand and handed it over to me. This time I did not showed them the album. I just showed them one of the most sophisticated pictures of us. She stood beside me in the picture.

'hmm, Bahu kafi sundar hai aur Jodi bhi saath main achi lagti hai' Papa said and winked

I hugged papa in happiness, I was so happy, I felt like I am on cloud 9 but discussion was not yet over, Mom's turn was left.

'How can you say yes? You haven't met the girl, only looks does not matter, nature matters too and she is of other caste' Maa said to papa

'Maa she is a real sweetheart, very polite, she will accept our family happily. She will love you both just like she loves her parents. Please believe me. She will never give you any chance of complains' I interrupted

'She is from different caste' Maa said

'Does that really matters Manpreet?' papa said to Maa

171

'Rajveer loves her, she is good looking and as per our son she has all the sanskaars. What else is needed?' papa said

'What will we say to our relatives, Rajveer is getting married in other caste? What about her family? Are they ready?' Mom asked

'We are facing issues there Maa, I will have to convince her parents. I will give my best but for that I need your support' I said

'Look, now he will go there to convince them. Can't she do that? Why will my son go and beg?' mom said angrily

My cell rang, "Arohi calling". 3 of us looked at the mobile, I could not cut Maa's point in between nor could I miss Arohi's call, it had been days I had not talked to her. I looked at Maa and then my ringing phone. I was not able to decide what to do. Papa picked up the call and put it on speaker.

'Hello RV sir' A sweet voice from the phone spoke.

'She calls you RV sir? Sir? Haha, my father gestured and laughed'

'RV sir, You there?' she said again

'Yes Arohi' I replied

'Mera Shonaa, how are you? I missed you so very much' Maa-papa looked at me, I kept looking down trying not to make any eye contact, I had no other choice but to talk her this way.

She continued 'Mummy – Papa angry on me, they are not talking to me, they do not leave me alone even for few minutes. Right now both are sleeping so I got the chance to call you. Priya di has convinced them to meet you once. She will call you and will tell you to come tomorrow for lunch. You listening na? baby'

'Yes Arohi I am listening' I replied. My maa papa were listening carefully too.

'Baabu, please convince them please. I cannot live without you. I miss you so much. I want to hide in your arms and sleep' she said

172

I picked up the cell phone kept on the table and in one breath I said 'Arohi you are on speaker and maa papa listening to you'

She was silent for a minute, she would be feeling like beating me for doing this to her but I had no option.

'Arohi, you there?' I asked

'Yes RV sir' she murmured. Papa took phone from my hands

'Beta there is no problem from our side and do not worry, RV will convince your parents too' my father being my hero assured her

'Namaste Uncle, thank you so much, we are in real need of your wishes' my love spoke

'Chalo you talk to Rajveer now' papa turned off the speaker and handed the phone to me. I was so relieved; I went in balcony to talk to her.

'Jaanu meri, how are you' I asked

'Are you crazy Shona, can't you tell me you were on speaker? You scared the hell out of me' she said

'I had no other option baby, I was in conversation with them when you called, and papa switched on the speaker. Baby the good news is Papa said yes, he is with us' I announced

'Waooo, what about mumma baby?'

'Do not worry, papa will convince her, she is not against' I replied

'I wish my family also says yes'

'They will say yes, for sure and you will be mine soon' I replied

'Aacha Shona, will see you tomorrow, I think mummy woke up, miss you, and love you. Bye'

'Can't wait to see you I love you baby, take care, miss you too'

*   *   *

173

I had no idea what to wear, I decided to wear the blue shirt Arohi gifted me once, Priya asked me to reach by 1:00PM, and I do not want to be late. I got ready before time. I wrote a short speech on religion. I practiced it 10 times standing in front of a mirror and 1 last time:

"Uncle Aunty, I know the major concern is religion, what will you say to your relatives that your girl is going to marry a Punjabi boy? But uncle People say, they will talk for few days and then they will forget. As parents what should matter to you most is Arohi's happiness. We cannot live without each other. Please understand. I will give her all the happiness in the world. I will never ask her to leave her religion and follow mine. I will do whatever you say. Just shower your blessings on us, please. Any caste, culture, religion is not bigger than love, when Arohi was small you taught her the meaning of selfless love and sharing, now when she has learnt that why is she being asked to compromise on it?

When we watch a movie where hero is Muslim and heroine is Hindu, we silently pray for their love to win at the end of the movie, then why so much restrictions in real life? Please be with us, your blessing mean a lot to us"

Yippee I spoke it all in one go, I am all set ready. I reached her place at 12:45PM, I waited for 15 mins in the parking thinking to reach before time will make me look desperate; I rang the bell exactly at 1:00PM. Priya opened the door, she smiled and welcomed me.

She made me sit in the living room and went inside to call her parents, different type of silence at her place made me feel little uneasy. I looked around the room, Living room was beautifully decorated on the theme of white and purple, wall paper on the back wall added life to the room, 3 crystal chandeliers were hanging down the false ceiling; middle one was bigger. Fresh flower kept on the center glass table provided fragrance to the room. After 10 minutes Priya and her mother came out.

'Namaste Aunty' I wished her and touched her feet

'Stay blessed'

'How are you aunty?' I asked

'Little tensed beta' she answered

I had no idea what to say next, I knew I am one of the major reasons for her tension. I kept quiet; somewhere inside I wanted to see Arohi to boost up my confidence.

'When you came to Bhopal RV?' Priya asked breaking the silence

'I came yesterday morning' I replied

'Do your parents know about you and ...' Aunty asked

'Yes Aunty' I replied

'Are they ok with this?'

'hmm Yes Aunty, they are more than happy to welcome Arohi in family' I answered

Let us all talk on the lunch table Priya said and invited me to the dining table. Many containers were arranged on the table, Priya called out Arohi to help her in serving. Arohi came out from her room, I looked at her, she looked at me, and we smiled. Her mom caught our actions, she advised Arohi to go and call her father for lunch, my heart beat increased.

Her father came out; I got up and touched his feet. He patted my back without speaking a word. Arohi and Priya served us the lunch, there were variety of items, daal, raita, bhindi, chole, salad, roti, papad and rice. I ate consciously and less, we had normal conversation on the table, her father spoke very less, after lunch everyone moved to the living room.

'Look Son, your marriage with Arohi is not possible' Arohi's father said, he crushed my heart with his 1st sentence.

'But Uncle' I interrupted, I was blank for a moment

'Uncle you must have had a word with Arohi too, she would have told you that we are deeply involved and she will not be able to live happily with someone else' I gathered all the courage and replied. This was even more difficult than giving external viva's or company interviews.

'This is the problem with kids of this generation; the only thing you see is we are involved that is it. It is not enough to live happily. Marriage is not just between 2 people, it is between 2 families. You two do not share anything in common' He said

By now I have forgotten the speech I had mugged up and practiced, I tried to recall but I failed.

'Papa but...' Arohi interrupted

'You sit quietly there, I am done talking to you' He said pointing his finger towards Arohi

'Her marriage is fixed with Raj; we know the family very well. She will be happy there. Better you two forget each other' he said in his monotonous high pitched angry tone

'Sir, she is not happy with your decision' I said, this time looking into his eyes

'I know what is best for her, you tell me one quality that you have and Raj does not. He is rich, good looking, well behaved, setting up his own business, he likes Arohi'

'Sir, if you talk about quality then I would not count job, money, looks, nature, I just know one thing Arohi loves me and not him. I suppose this thing answers all your questions' I answered. This made him blank for a while but I suppose his decision will not change no matter how much we plead.

'This is not just enough for happy living. He belongs to our community; we know the family very well. Moreover Priya is in the same family, both the sisters in one family, living together happily, what else will the parents want?'

'Sir, if it is about community and following a religion! I will never force Arohi to change her religion, she can follow hers and I will help her to do so, I will not take her away from her community, she can talk, meet to whom so ever she wants whenever she wants' I replied

'Who are you to allow her or not?' he asked angrily

'I did not say allow sir, I said I will never stop her'

'You will never stop her? Have you followed your religion properly? I have heard you people do not cut your hairs and you wear a turban. Where is your turban? You are not able to handle your rituals, your religion and you will help her follow hers? Go and 1st learn your religion, then help others'

'Sir I know the main essence of Sikh teaching and it is summed up by Guru Nanak in the words: 'Realization of Truth is higher than all else. Higher still is truthful living'. I believe in what is correct and true. I do not fake around, I am true by heart and do what it says' I replied

'You eat non-veg?'

'Yes I do, if Arohi will ask I will stop' I replied

'You can stop but not your complete family right? As I said marriage is between 2 families. we do not drink water in the kitchen where people cook non-veg' he replied proudly'

Things were getting out of control now; her father was not ready to accept any of my arguments or requests. I too was losing control on myself.

'Sir, you are not ready to accept any of my request or argument, you have already made up your mind. It is just that we wanted to get married with your blessings else I would have taken Arohi with me and no one could have done anything.' I said whatever was in my mind, not thinking about the consequences this time. My each word acted like a bullet which hurt his ego and self esteem

'How dare you? How dare you? Who do you think you are? You can take my daughter and no one could have done anything? Look this is the way you talk and you Arohi you wanted to marry him?' he started to shout, losing his breath. All the ladies at home ran towards him. Priya asked me to leave as my stay will affect his health more.

'RV sir please leave, I am sorry. **I think I cannot be officially yours**' Arohi said in a breaking voice.

With a broken heart I left her place.

177

Last Meeting

My one mistake, my one sentence and everything is over, she is not with me. I am not able to talk to her; I hope she doesn't hate me for what I did. But why would she not hate me? I said those rubbish words in front of her father, though technically I said what I felt, her father was not ready to listen a word. No matter how much I convince him, it was all vague; He had already made up his mind. He just met me because his daughters forced him. What I said was true. I wanted both the families to accept us happily. I planned for their happiness else I would have taken my girl with me and no one in the world could have done anything about it but sometimes truth should not come out this way, It might hurt someone. That instant my brain was not in my control and my tongue spoke my feelings.

Will she still talk to me? Does she really mean her last sentence **"I cannot be officially yours"**, all the questions troubled me. Her condition would have been more miserable than mine. She might be crying hiding inside her blanket. I have no idea what to do. How to meet her? Should I call her? Will it create more problems for her? I want to meet her, I want to just look at her once and get satisfied that she is fine. This could be the last time. Its 1:00AM at night, Is this the right time?

Yes, if I want to meet her, this is the only time as no one will leave her alone during the day. I decided to go and meet her, she told me once her parents sleep by 10 and Priya would be busy on her calls with Rahul in another room.

Our night talks gave me lot of information and description of her home. Arohi's room is on 1ˢᵗ floor which will not be too difficult for me to climb; she keeps her room's balcony open for ventilation while sleeping. I can enter her room through balcony and meet her; the only concern is night guard. I decided to leave for her place thinking 'jo bhi hoga dekha jayega'.

I had enough courage to take this step but if I am caught, I will be called as a criminal, entering somebody's home, late night, that too from balcony in a girl's room.

'I have already spoiled all the things. Should I take this step?' I asked myself.

Her parents have not accepted our relation; she will be marrying someone else. What could be worse than this, I have already lost her. I can take this risk once to meet her for the last time. I just want to see her, her one glance and I am ready for any consequences.

I do not care if people see me and think of me as an intruder, just one hope – 'I could meet her, gave me the strength.' I took 3 rounds of her society, observing all the things and calculating how and when I can implement my plan.

Guards at the main gate were taking a nap. Main gate was locked and a small one was left open for people to walk in and out, I cannot enter along with my bike through the small gate.

Arohi's room is at the back side of the building, only issue as of now is how to enter the society. I do not want the guards to wake up. One of the options is to climb the back wall studded with sharp mirrors but climbing it without any support would be difficult. I stood outside for a while thinking how to get in, without waking up the sleepy guards.

I parked my bike outside the society, and walked in silently through the small gate, my inaudible steps did not disturb the dreamy nights of the guards.

2ⁿᵈ challenge was to climb up to her balcony, it was around 10 to 12 feet above the ground, easy for me to climb, I took support of the pipe on the

179

side wall, my athletic body helped me to climb up and I jumped in her balcony. My guess was correct; she kept her balcony panes open, Darkness of the night supported me to hide from the outer world. I entered her room and closed the balcony panes.

My heart was beating fast; the darkness that once supported me was now challenging me. I have to confirm if she is sleeping alone or with Priya. I went near her bed; it was difficult for me to figure out anything in such a dark room. I opened the curtains slightly allowing moon and street light to penetrate inside the room. There was a girl lying on the bed wrapped in a blanket, her face was on opposite side. I wanted to be sure that she is my Arohi, before I take any step. I kept my shoes near her closet and walked to the opposite side of the bed, without making any noise.

I looked at her. Yes!!!!! She is my Arohi, my sweet heart. I took a deep breath and locked the room from inside. I sat beside her; if she will see someone sitting like this on her bed she will be scared. I do not want to scare her. I woke her up softly.

'Baby, your Shona is here. I came to meet you' I whispered in her ears. She moved and opened her eyes, she looked at me. She rubbed her eyes and again stared at me. She looked around the room confirming that she is at her home. She looked at me again and touched my arm

'RV Sir?'

'RV sir...? What are you doing here?' She panicked.

'I came to meet you Baabu' I replied keeping my hands on her face

She sat on the bed and hugged me tight. 'I cannot be yours, I cannot be yours Shona. Why did you say that in front of papa' She cried

'I cannot lose you Arohi, I am sorry for what I did. I will do whatever you say but please don't say like this' I said wiping her tears

'Nothing can happen now, I said yes for the wedding' She said

'No No, baby please don't say so. We will do something' I tried convincing

'Nothing can happen now Shona, I will meet you tomorrow then we will talk, please go from here now. It is too risky, if anyone comes in, we will be in a big trouble, please go' She insisted

'Where will you meet me tomorrow?' I asked

'I will call you and will let you know' She replied

'Please go, by the way how did you manage to come here. It is not possible to reach my room hiding from everyone'

'I just knew one thing that I want to meet you, I figured out the way' I replied

'You took a very big risk, please leave as of now. I am too scared. Papa is at home please' She pleaded

I kissed her forehead and stood up to leave, I told her that I love her more than anything in this world. As I got up, someone rang the doorbell. She freaked out.

'Who could be here at this time' She asked

We looked at each other.

'Look this is why I was saying, you should have not come here' she said holding my collar

'What if they come in this room?' she panicked

'I have locked the door, do not worry. I will leave once things are normal. Till then I will hide somewhere' I said

We tried to hear the conversation and figure out who would have come so late at night. All we could hear was - 3 men talking.

I asked Arohi to empty the folded clothes so that I can hide behind the hanging ones in her closet. She arranged her folded clothes and made space for me to hide.

'Arohi open the door' her father called out.

'Ohh Nooo...Ohh God. Its papa' she freaked out.

'Wait I will get inside the closet, you go and open the door. Be calm please else they might doubt.'

Bang bang bang... 'Arohi open the door' too many voices in repetition shouted. They banged so hard that I feared just few more bangs and the door will break.

I climbed inside the closet adjusted myself, I told Arohi to behave sleepy though her sleep by now was completely vanished.

She closed the closet and gathering courage went to open the door. She opened it.

'What the hell did it took so long for you to open the door?' Her father asked angrily

'I was sleeping papa, sorry I did not hear the knock' she replied. Her mother switched on the light and confirmed looking at Arohi that she is okay.

'Haan sahib, that thief climbed through the balcony of this room' one of the guards spoke

'Thief...?' Arohi asked in astonishment

'Yes babyji, I am guard for your opposite building, I saw a thief climbing the pipe and jumped in your balcony. I came running to your society and told the incident to Sitaram (Arohi's society watchman)'

'You ok Arohi? Did anyone come here?' Priya asked

'No Dii, there is some confusion. No one came to my room. Balcony is already closed and I heard no noise.' Arohi said

I could hear all the conversation clearly; this was the only thing left, other society's watchman catching me climbing Arohi's room.

I felt little safe in the closet though it was difficult for me to breath. I smelled Arohi's clothes; they had her fragrance in them. Some pointed

182

thing beneath me was hurting me but I could not adjust myself as my one move could create a disaster, I kept sitting on it. Arohi is handling things quite well.

Guards checked balcony, bathroom and found no one.

'there is no one here' Sitaram said

'Bhaiya you must have been mistaken, we have checked the complete house. No one is here' Priya said.

'Babyji lakin hum dekhe the' other guard said in his Bihari tone

'There must be some confusion, everything is fine here. Everyone go and sleep' Arohi's father announced.

I took a breath of relief.

Everyone turned around to leave the room. Guard looked at each corner of the room, trying to be a CID agent, while leaving.

'Wait sir, look someone's shoes are kept there' guard pointed towards the male shoes near closet.

I froze inside the closet. Damn I forget to pick my shoes. Arohi froze too.

'Male shoes...? Whose shoes are these Arohi?' Her father asked

'Huh' she replied staring at the shoes.

Her father asked the guards to check bathroom, balcony and beneath the bed again.

Priya gestured Arohi to tell her if there is something that she is hiding.

Arohi moved her lips without making any sound 'RV sir' she said and pointed towards the closet

'Damn,' Priya kept her hand on her head in disappointment. Arohi gestured her to please help.

'Papa I kept those shoes there, those are Rahul's shoes' Priya said

'Yes papa, those are Rahul Jiju's shoes' Arohi repeated.

'What are Rahul's shoes doing here, when he is not here?' her father asked

'I bought it with me, I wanted to buy a new pair for him so I kept this old one to refer his size' Priya explained

'Babyji, shoes to naye lage hain aur mitti bhi lagi hai uu ma' CID guard again spoke; I felt like coming out of the closet and ask him if he is a fan of ACP Pradyuman.

'Check the entire room once again and balcony too' her father asked the guards.

They checked the room. Arohi's mom stepped towards the closet asking:

'Arohi, why are your clothes falling from the closet and she opened the door' She shouted and stepped back.

'There is someone hiding in the closet' she panicked. She saw me sitting but could not see my face hiding behind the clothes.

I came out of the closet before anyone else came near it.

'Look sir I said I saw someone, Humara akhen bahutaayi tez hain' Guard said proudly as if he will win Bharat Ratna for his bravery now.

'Rajveer?' her mom said in shock

'So if we will not agree to your thing, you will become a criminal? 'Her father shouted coming towards me

'Meri beti ko utha k le jayega?' he said and slapped me, I stayed there silently after being slapped in front of everyone.

'Come on speak up, I am talking to you? What were you doing here? Hiding in the closet, climbing pipe and entering my daughter's room?' he said and again came forward to slap me.

'Papa please stop...' Arohi stopped him.

'And you girl, you were protecting him? These are our teachings? I feel ashamed that you are my daughter' he scolded Arohi.

'Sitaram call the Police' he ordered

'No papa please, please' Priya requested. Her father did not respond to her request. Sitaram went out of the room to make a call to the police. Priya went after him to stop him.

'Papa I called him, it's not his mistake. If you are calling the police then call them for me not for him' Arohi said. I looked at her; she looked straight in her father's eyes. A daughter was blackmailing her father to save her boyfriend.

'I wanted to meet him for the last time, as I am marrying Raj. I wanted to meet RV sir once before the wedding. So I called him' she said

'Look at how this girl is answering her father; this is the first time this girl is talking like this to me' he said looking at her mother and pointing towards Arohi

'And you MR. You are lucky as I am leaving you now. Go get your bike and run. Never come in front of me again else I will shoot you' he said and left the room

Her mother gave Arohi dirty looks and left the room following her husband. Guards left too.

'Are you both crazy, are you guys out of your mind? What do you think you were doing? Meeting this way? Just one step of papa and you would be in jail Rajveer, why don't you understand? Are you both this immature?' Priya scolded

'Arohi is innocent; she had no idea that I will take such a step. I wanted to meet her so I came' I replied

'Bacho ka khel nai hai Rajveer nor this is any romantic Bollywood movie going on, this is life real life. So stop all this please and leave from here' Priya shouted

I nodded

'Arohi will you come to meet me?' I asked

'Will you come to meet me means? Where is she coming?' Priya interrupted

'Tomorrow evening 5:00pm. I will meet you at Wind and Waves' Arohi replied

'What is this going on Arohi?' Priya enquired

'I want to meet him for the last time Didi. I am doing whatever you all are saying; I am following all your instructions and compromising with my life. Please support me to get out of home and meet him, just once please' she demanded

'Ok, but make sure this is the last time' Priya wanted assurance.

Arohi nodded.

I reached exactly at 5; restaurant gave the feeling of the coastal areas, soothing breeze and the view of lake. I had an option to choose where to sit- terrace, Lawn or inside restaurant. I choose to sit in the open lawn at the corner table. The atmosphere is just awesome. Beauty of lake added charm to it. I waited for half an hour, I tried calling her but she did not pick up the call.

Waiter every now and then troubled me to place an order; I ordered a coffee for myself.

To pass the time I opened my outlook mails for checking office updates.

It showed me 126 unread mails, I scrolled up and down to see if there were any important mails.

Subject line of one of the mails was: "Relocation to Delhi". I opened it up. My manager had sent me a relocation mail. I had to move to Delhi? What the hell is going on? I called up one of my colleague to confirm. He told that our entire project has been shifted to Delhi head office and the team has to move there. I decided to deal with the situation once I am back to Pune.

It was an hour now, I called Arohi again. This time she picked up the call

'Where are you dear?' I asked

'I reached, sorry for being late where are you sitting?'

'In the lawn, corner table' I replied

She wore a simple sky blue color kurta with chicken work on it. She looked simple and pretty, she had kept her hairs open. I stood up and offered her the seat.

Weather was romantic but our talks this time will not compliment the sky, winds and the lake. I was prepared for everything.

'This is our last meeting RV sir' she said in a low tone

'Are you sure?' I asked

she nodded

'We will never meet again Arohi?'

'We can if you agree to be my friend like you were earlier; before we got involved' she said

'You seriously want to end this relationship?' I asked. She did not reply, she looked down at the table

'Look into my eyes and talk to me Arohi please' I insisted

'You want all this to end? Can you live without me?' I repeated my question

She nodded

'Look in to my eyes and then say, I will not ask you a single question after that' I said

'We have to do this RV sir. I cannot be officially yours. Being away from you kills me but I am left with no other option. I cannot run with you. I cannot cheat my parents. Papa hates you; no matter how much we try they will not agree for it now.

I have to live with some other guy. Do you even understand how difficult is it for me? My parents have promised didi's in laws. I cannot be so selfish, I cannot spoil Priya didi's terms with her in laws. I cannot see my parents fall ill in front of me that too because of me. Please understand' she spoke till her throat choked

'I know how much you love your parents; I came to meet your father because I did not want to do anything against his will. If I wanted to make you run with me then I would have done that by now but our wedding without blessings of your or my parents will be meaningless, I understand you sweetheart. Sorry I failed to convince your father' I said holding her hands

'You did not fail, papa met you because we forced him and meeting with you was just a formality, he had already made up his mind, he was not ready to hear you. No matter how hard you would have tried. He will not change his decision Shona' She replied

'I told you na earlier let's not fall for each other. We will end up hurting ourselves. Look this is what is happening' She said

'Hmm, sorry I broke the rule' I replied

'Don't be sorry, I broke it too' she said wiping my tears

'We will have to be away now? Forever...?' I asked looking at her holding her hand, praying that she will say NO

'Yes will have to be away' she said sniffling, her cheeks and nose turned pink.

'You will never be mine?' I asked

She shook her head, her tears dropping on the table

'We will not be talking or meeting but we will always be connected through heart' she said

'Is Raj a nice guy? Will he keep you happy?' I asked

'Hmm, he is a nice guy. He will keep me happy' she replied

188

'Tell him, a single tear from your eyes after wedding, he will have to face me. I will not spare him if he makes you cry' I said in a breaking voice, she smiled with her watery eyes.

'Well right now I am making you cry, I am a bad guy' I said

'You too are crying, I am a bad girl' she replied

'Something went inside my eye, these are not tears' I replied

'Liar'

'Can I get a last Hug please' I requested

She nodded. I stood up, held her hand, she stood up too. She hugged me, I held her tight. This is the last time she is so close to me, this is the last time I could feel her warmth. She broke in my arms and cried. I cried too. Pain of separation was equal for both of us. I decided to move away from her life, I decided to move to Delhi. My presence could make her life more problematic.

I did not tell her about my relocation just felt the moment with her. For the last time she hid in my chest. For the 1st time she did not care who all was looking at us, this 1st time was our last time. I wanted to tell her how much I love her, how much she will be missed. She is my life, without her I will be a body without soul. I did not speak a word as each of my word will break her more.

I decided to let her go, for her happiness, for her family......

Delhi

1st December 2014/ Monday

Life is so unpredictable, there was a time when I enjoyed life to its full extent, I had best bunch of friends. A big group with whom I can hang out. We celebrated all the festivals and birthdays together, shared happiness and sorrow. We were a small family.

Nik, Prateek, Tarun- my roommates, we had the best time together; we had been best friends since day 1 of college, 8 years of long friendship. We used to talk about gadgets and girls all night long, later Atul joined us, and he is not less than a younger brother to me.

Then a sweet angel came in my life, she filled it with more colors, she taught me the meaning of love, she was my best friend, my junior, whom I teased, taught to drive a bike, shared my dreams, for the 1st time I got to know what true feelings are, I loved her, I touched her, I played with her, I shared with her, I fought with her, I cooked with her, I did everything with her. She showed me all the brightest colors of life. My life was so perfect- satisfactory job, best friends, family and my reason to live - my love. What else does one needs to live a happy life. I had all the reasons to smile.

This moment I am sitting alone in train travelling to a new city, leaving all my relations behind. No friends, no group, no Arohi. I am left with nothing; my life took a new turn where all the colors are lost, only obscurity left. I feel like I am left alone in an isolated place and moving towards the darkness or say dark life approaching towards me, where there is no friendship, no laughs, no tickling- teasing, no love. I have lost everything.

All the memories were flashing in my mind, all my beautiful moments with Arohi, my trips with her, my last meeting with her. I could not sleep, I could not eat. All I could do was miss her. I tried not to think of her but I failed, she was there within me and to take her out of me was not possible.

Entangled in her thoughts I was about to reach Delhi, I looked out of the window, looked at different people, doing different stuff. I tried to figure out their background, if they too were facing any problems? Is life so unfair for everyone? There are few lucky people who get the chance to spend their life with their soul mates. I was lost in my thoughts when my phone rang; I secretly wished it to be Arohi. It flashed PAPA CALLING.... I smiled looking at my mobile; there is still someone who cares for me. I picked up the call

'Where are you beta' he asked

'Almost reached Delhi Papa'

'Wait at the Station, Shailesh uncle will come to pick you up' He said.

'Why are you troubling him papa, I will go on my own. I will stay in a hotel' I replied

'Beta Shailesh is my childhood friend, we both are like brother and he cares for you like his own son. When I told him about your arrival to Delhi, he decided that you will stay with him. Tanu aunty will also be happy to see you' he said

'I want to be alone Papa'

'If you stay alone it will bother us, Shailesh will take good care of you. At least your mother and I will be carefree that you are okay and having meals on time. Shailesh will pick you up from Nizamuddin Railway Station. I want no more arguments'

'Ok Papa, I will wait for him at the station' I replied

'That's like my son. Take care beta...'

'You too papa, take care of mummy too and tell her that I am fine'

I got down at Nizamuddin Railway station, I called Shailesh uncle and he told me to meet him at Comesum restaurant, outside the station. I waited for him; He arrived and bought Tanu aunty along with him. I bent down to touch their feet.

'Mera Sher Puttar, how are you' Shailesh uncle patted my back and hugged me in a typical Punjabi style.

'I am good uncle how are you?'

'We are doing great, good to see you after so long' Uncle said

'Yes last time we saw you, you were in 1st year of your engineering right?' Tanu aunty added

'Yes Aunty'

'Chal puttar ghar' Shailesh uncle said and grabbed the driver seat of his Audi Q3. Shailesh uncle looked like a complete replica of "Jaspal Bhatti" the character of one of my childhood favorite comic serial. He had turban on his head and a salt pepper shade beard covering his face. He wore simple clothes and is owner of 3 gold showrooms in Delhi. He is amongst one of the rich and respected gentlemen in the community.

Tanu Aunty looked like a typical rich show off lady; she wore Pink Saree with big flowery print of silver, along with long earrings matching her saree and applied a big bindi on her forehead. She grabbed the front seat beside Shailesh uncle. I made myself comfortable at the backseat.

'O ji puttar where is your office?' He asked

'Uncle it is in Noida Sector 16' I replied

'Ohho Noida witch haiga' Aunty said in her Punjabi

'Yes aunty' I replied

'Ohh koi gal nai puttar, driver will drop you every day, Patel Nagar to Noida sector 16 will take around 1 hour' uncle said

'Uncle I was planning to stay in Noida, travelling distance will be reduced' I replied

'Why will you stay there, you will stay with us. Rohit and Abhijeet will be happy to meet you' He said

Rohit and Abhijeet are Shailesh uncle and Tanu auntie's sons, few years younger than me. I am their best advisor. They call me whenever they need advice regarding studies, like which exams to sit in or which college to go for and other things.

'Still uncle it will be a problem for you all'

'You stay with us for some days and then if you think things are not working fine you are free to move till then no arguments, ok?' aunty said turning back

I nodded

'Is this your new car uncle?' I tried changing the topic

'Yes its Audi Q3 2.0 TDI quattro Diesel, Automatic, 11.7 kmpl' He said like a proud owner flaunting about his car.

We reached their place, Aunty showed me my room. Rohit and Abhijeet got excited to see me after long and started telling me stories about their friends and parties. Rohit showed me various parts of the house. Being tired I asked him to excuse me for some time as I wanted to lie down.

I went to my room, unpacked my bag. In between my shirts I found Arohi's framed picture that I had picked from her place. Again I went back to the memories, my sweet memories with her. Will she never be mine? How can she be mine? She is going to get married'. Can I give one more try to bring her back in my life? I questioned myself. 'My one try and more troubles for her, if I want her to have a happy life I should not contact her' I answered myself.

I pictured her with Raj, living happily with him, enjoying life, laughing, smiling. Her smile could be a reason for me to live and then I pictured her not remembering me and Raj touching her, playing with her hairs like I used to do. I felt like someone pinching hundreds of sharp pins in my heart. I cannot let this happen, it is the biggest nightmare for me but I am left with no option, the only option I have is to forget her and let her live happily.

I decided to keep myself busy in work and other stuff, being busy and occupied will help me to get rid of her memories.

*   *   *

2ⁿᵈ December 2014 / Tuesday/ 7:00 AM

I know its early morning; sunlight has turned the dark room to bright. I still lay on bed; I could not sleep whole night, still no sign of sleep in my eyes. I did not feel like standing up. I just lay on my bed with my eyes open, my mind completely blank. I heard Tanu aunty calling my name but my senses did not helped me to respond her back. She entered my room

'Good Morning Son' she said

'Good Morning Aunty' I replied and got up

'Come on get ready else you will be late to your office, breakfast is served. Go freshen up and join us' She said

I did what she said and joined them on the breakfast table.

'We are coming to drop you today' Shailesh uncle said

'Uncle I will go, just let me know the metro route' I replied

'No son we are going on the same route, we will drop you and this is your day 1 in Delhi office, allow us to accompany you' he said

I Nodded

Seating arrangement was same in his Audi Q3 like the way it was when they picked me from station. Only change was- 2 extra people, Abhijeet and Rohit, They took the window seats and sandwiched me in between. Rohit told me about the numerous ways to reach Noida; he kept showing me major spots.

I kept looking around, trying to get familiar with Delhi roads. On our way I saw a very big statue of lord Hanuman, tearing his chest with both his hands.

'Is this some famous Temple?' I asked

'Yes beta, this is Hanuman temple of Karol Bagh, one of the most popular Hindu temples in Delhi. The shrine is marked by the colossal 108ft statue of Lord Hanuman, this can be seen from the both Jhande walan and Karol Bagh metro station' uncle replied

I joined both my hands as we passed by the giant statue of lord Hanuman.

'Many people would be traveling Delhi to Noida every day right? What about the connectivity?' I asked

'Yes Noida is well connected with Delhi and over 50% of the total population travels both ways for official purposes. Connectivity to Delhi has improved with the construction of flyovers, roads and bridges. Bridge over the river Yamuna connects to Delhi in no time and the toll road would hardly take 20 minutes to reach a location in South Delhi. The city is now the most preferred destination for corporates and MNCs looking for office space or commercial buildings to set up their offices' Uncle replied.

'Some of the main reasons behind the existence of these companies in Noida is the close proximity to Delhi and good infrastructure. Another big specialty of Noida is the 'Film City', located in sector 16A where you will find offices of major news channels, film studios and other institutes' Rohit added

'Yes Noida is home to many big international as well as national companies' I agreed to their points

I reached my office and flashed my Pune office ID at reception. Lady at reception looked at it.

Are you from Pune office Sir? She asked

'Yes' I replied

'Sir your access card needs to be changed, for this location you will be given a new access card as Pune card will not work here' she said

'What is the procedure for that?' I enquired

'Nothing much sir, you just need to submit your Pune access card, fill in the entries in register and I will provide you with the new card. It will be activated within 4 hours, till then security guards will help you accessing office premises' she advised

I filled in the required details in the register and submitted my old card. Lady at the reception gave me a new access card and asked me to sign on another register for receiving the new card. I did. She asked me about my business unit, team name and guided me with the floor and location of my new desk.

My whole team has moved here, I did not find anything new other than the infrastructure and new seating arrangements. Work was same what I used to do in my last location and team members were same too. Everyone in the team talked about the pros and cons of the new location. Without speaking much, I started with my work and tried to keep myself occupied in meetings and official calls. I worked late till night. I tried to run away from my feelings but I suppose this is one thing, no matter how hard I try, will follow me.

I thought being busy and occupied will help me not to think about her but she was there in my heart, back of the mind I kept thinking about her while working, while in meeting or doing anything, she was there with me all the time.

I informed uncle aunty that I will be coming back with one of my office colleague and there is no need to send driver.

I asked Saumy (one of my team mate) about the route and timings of the metro, he guided me. I started walking towards the metro station thinking - One more day I managed without her. I started noticing couples, walking by holding hands, sitting together in metro, parks, talking with each other, getting cozy; I missed all my moments with her. I started reacting to the sad songs, I felt as if they are describing my story and I pictured me with her in all the romantic ones. I cried secretly in my bed. I missed her; I missed her in every moment. I missed her every second of my life.

*   *   *

I am shouting, calling everyone but no one could hear me. I am crying out loud. There is someone following me. I am begging for help, everything is dark around me. I am calling out all the names I know- Arohi, Tarun, Pajju, Nik but no one responding. I am down to my knees, weeping, giving bribe to my buddies 'if you come to me I will give you whatever you demand' yet no one listening. I am scared running here and there to save myself, there is a big dark dusty endless ground, with scary things on it. I am alone; I see no human race on the endless deadly ground. I have no way out to escape and beast of loneliness is after me. I beg him to let me go but it presses my neck, it's suffocating. I am not able to breathe, he swallows me and I woke up shouting 'please spare me.' I find myself sweating and breathing heavily I look around and again I find no one around me.

*   *   *

'Are you okay Rajveer?' Shailesh uncle asked at breakfast table

'Yes I am uncle' I replied

'Yesterday night I heard you murmuring something and shouting something like 'spare me', later I heard you calling someone named 'Arohi'' he said

'Must be a bad dream uncle, I am alright' I replied, finished my breakfast and left for my office. I need to have control on my feelings as it is not only troubling me but the people around me too.

Same thing repeated for many days, uncle kept asking me questions and I kept denying.

I read about - how to be balanced after breakup, how to cope up with depression and related articles. I tried following the tips mentioned.

In my absence Shailesh uncle had word with papa about my everyday dreams and the name I shout in my dreams. Papa told him the whole story about Arohi. They discussed how they can help me with this. Shailesh Uncle came up with a solution – If I marry someone else or start dating, I will forget my past life and will be stable again. They started to search a bride for me, it was difficult for me to explain them that Arohi was not just my love but she is my life, my soul. I cannot be separated from her. I will spoil the girl's life who will be my bride as I will not be able to do justice if in relationship with her.

Uncle and aunty kept showing me pictures of different girls; papa started mailing biodata of a new girl every day. I kept ignoring their calls and mails. I never felt like looking at them. Though I am not in contact with Arohi but still I feel for her and I will love her entire life even if she forgets me and make a new family, my feelings for her are selfless.

I changed my phone number; I am not in contact with anyone because I want her to be happy.

Looking at my response, my parents decided that they will choose a girl and will fix my meeting with her; I denied that I am not going to meet any one. They pressurized. Maa started with her emotional lines 'we are doing this to see you happy, looking at you like this is affecting us too, we also want our son to have a happy married life. For our happiness meet the girl we have decided once'

I tried explaining them but they did not listen to me. They fixed my meeting with a girl they chose. I have to meet her coming Saturday. They gave me all the instructions what to talk and what not to. Shailesh uncle and Tanu aunty decided the venue, they booked seat for two in a nearby multi cuisine restaurant. Shailesh uncle showed me her picture and provided her biodata.

'Girls name is Malvika, she belongs to our community and she has completed her graduation from Delhi University and now working with TCS. She is smart and well behaved. We know her family personally. You both will look great together' Tanu aunty tried to convince me.

There are too many people connected to me, my life is not just mine. I agreed to meet her for my parent's happiness.

I waited for her at the restaurant; it was kind of romantic restaurant with dim lights, soft music and privacy. If Arohi would have been with me I would have brought her here once but as she is not with me, these things rarely flatter me now

I looked at the menu thinking what I can order

'Hi Rajveer' A girl wearing designer white kurta with black sleeves stood in front of me, she looked pretty. She had long hairs and wore black framed glasses.

'Yes' I replied

'Hi I am Malvika' she introduced herself offering a handshake

'Hi Malvika, thanks for coming' I treated her formally

She ordered one mint chocolate mock-tini for her and I ordered Kiwi daiquiri for myself. We started with the normal formal conversation like how many members in the family, how long I had been living in Bhopal, how was I finding Delhi and things. She seem quite friendly

'So what are your plans? Which city are you planning to settle?' She asked

'Well say 1-2 years in Delhi, then will move back to Pune'

Waiter arrived with our drinks and placed them on our table

'Pune?' she asked and sipped her drink

'Yes I worked in Pune for more than 3 years; I had best time of my life in Pune. What are your plans?' I asked

'Well Delhi is my birth place so I love it but I am okay to move other places too' She replied

We took a pause to take a sip of our drinks.

'So why has Pune been so special for you?' she asked

'Almost all my close college friends got Pune as their job location, we had a great time together- travelling, drives, movies, gossips, games, being together made it special' I replied

'Waoo sounds good, college friends in a new city, lot many things to explore' she said

I smiled

'So just boy's gang or you have girls too in your group?' she enquired

'We have girls too in our group, we used to live in the same society' I replied

'Ohh nice, that's cool. I too have a happening group of friends here' she said

'You like pubbing?' she asked

'Not much, I like travelling and exploring new places'

'Umm hmm, nice' she said, I did not understand her expressions behind umm hmm...

I tried involving myself in her talks but I was not able to think of anything to initiate a conversation, I kept answering her questions.

'Do you have any of your group pictures?' she asked

'Yes I do' I showed her few pictures in my mobile; she took it from my hand and started browsing.

'I am allowed to browse the pictures right?' she asked

I nodded

'Generally boys do not give their mobiles as they have too much of stuff in their gallery' she said and giggled. She browsed the photographs and I was silently sipping my drink.

'Cool group yaar' she said

'By the way who is she?' she showed me a picture and asked

'Arohi' I replied

'Arohi, hmm you have too many solo pictures of her' She said with her one eyebrow up

'Yeah' I said and looked down at menu to order something to eat, ignoring eye contact with her.

'Friend or girl friend?' she asked in notorious tone and giggled.

Gathering all my courage I looked up and said 'I cannot marry you Malvika'

She gave me a shocking look

'Why? Because I am browsing your phone' She asked

'No No not that, I am so sorry but actually I am in love with someone else' I said

'You should have told this to me earlier, I would have not come here then' she said, little annoyed with what I said.

'Listen, I am so sorry, you are pretty and fun loving, any guy marrying you would be very lucky' I replied

'I am not here to hear about my looks and nature, this is quite embarrassing' she said.

'Look my parents forced me to meet you. Actually I am not in a relation any more. The girl I love is marrying someone else, they wanted me to settle down having a stable life' I explained.

I continued 'But my heart does not give me permission to marry anyone else, I still feel for her. If I say yes to the wedding I will be spoiling your life too. You are a nice girl I do not want to ruin your life.'

She calmed down and nodded, after few minutes of silence, she spoke

'So the girl is Arohi? Right?'

'Yes it's her' I replied

'She is pretty', she said looking at her picture in my mobile which was still in her hands.

'yeah, she is' I repeated

'This girl has cheated on you. Why do you still feel for her?' she asked

'No she did not cheat on me, story is little different' I answered

'So, you got a story. Niceee' she said with too many eeee's in nice.

'Would you mind sharing it with me?' she demanded

'I am sorry but I do not want to talk about her'

'Look we are not marrying that's okay, but we can be friends right?' she asked

'yes, why not? I would love to. As it is I do not have any friends here' I answered

'OK, so we are friends now. You can share your story with me' she said smiling as if I am going to narrate a fairy tale to her.

I nodded

'Wait, let's order something to eat 1st' she called waiter and ordered one Fettuccine Alfredo pasta and cheese garlic bread.

I narrated her my entire story, about my group, my friends, trips, and how I fell in love with Arohi, my moments with her, about her fairy world, being caught, bad times, family discussions and then about her wedding and my last meeting with her.

She heard my entire story patiently like a good listener. She kept quiet after I finished my story. We finished our dinner, I paid the bill and we came out of the restaurant.

*   *   *

'Are you still in touch with Arohi' she asked while we walked to parking

'NO' I replied

'What about your group? Your friends- Prateek, Nik, Tarun, Atul, Priya, Aditi, Mini and Neha?'

'I am in contact with no one, I changed my number, deactivated my Facebook' I replied

'But why did you do that?' she asked

'Even I don't know, maybe I want to be alone for a while'

'Hmm' she said thinking something.

'Don't you think so much, Go home and keep enjoying your happening life with your friends' I said

'Yeah, you can call me in case you need any help in Delhi' she said being kind.

'Sure'

She sat in her car waved me goodbye and asked her driver to move.

*   *   *

'Are you mad? Why did you tell Malvika about Arohi?'

'Mom, please don't be hyper'

'She is such a nice girl and you are ruining everything Rajveer'

'Mom I need some time, I am not ready to get married. Please understand'

'Do whatever you want, don't talk to me' she said angrily and disconnected the call.

It became very difficult for me to make my parents understand that I was not ready to get married; in fact I am not ready to think about any other girl as of now. Shailesh uncle and Tanu aunty took my wedding as their prime objective, they kept showing me pictures of different girls, their sons Abhijeet and Rohit started planning their dresses and venue for my wedding. They suggested me to marry a girl having many cousin sisters, so that they can try on them.

Every day talks related to marriage frustrated me and made me miss Arohi more, I decided to move alone in an apartment near my office. Saumy helped me finding 1HK in Noida sector 16.

*   *   *

My new home on 14th floor was simple having basic necessities of day to day life provided by the owner, hall had a Television, Almirah and a single bed. Kitchen had 2 burner gas and a refrigerator. I cooked for myself and started leading a very simple life, the way I never thought. I worked late till night to kill my loneliness, my daily routine was to wake up by 8:00AM, get ready and leave for office, work late till night, come home, cook, watch TV and sleep.

I looked at old pictures of my group. I missed them all. I kept Arohi's framed picture on the stool near my bed. Every night before sleeping I look at her picture, I weep and sleep. My decision of being alone bought me more misery. Nights I wake up shouting her name and crying. Dullness surrounded me. Once I lived a life surrounded by a bunch of friends and now I had no one around. Lonliness started killing me slowly. I got into more depression. My productivity in office reduced. I started spoiling my career too.

I badly wanted to come out of this phase. I read about articles "How to overcome depression after break up". Browsing through different web pages I found about a psychiatrist 'Dr. Ankita Shrivastava'. I called up on the number mentioned on her website and took an appointment for the coming weekend. Lady on the call asked me different questions: My name, age, city, native, job, relationships etc, before confirming my booking. She asked to come Saturday morning at 10 AM for 1st consultation.

I feared going to her clinic, not sure about the questions she will be asking me or experimentation she will perform on me but I convinced myself that this could be a step towards normal and stable life. I decided to go for consultation.

*   *   *

14th August 2015/ Saturday/ 10:15AM

I reached her clinic. I went to the receptionist and told her about my appointment with Dr. Ankita. She advised me to wait for a while.

I sat on the sofa in front of the receptionist desk. I looked around, 3 patients were waiting for their turn; they looked sad and gloomy. On the corner tables were kept few mind boggling games and motivational books. Inspiring quotes were hung on the wall. Behind the receptionist was a beautiful abstract painting, blend of many colors formed attractive and bright figures, I remembered Arohi, looking at the master piece. She loves painting.

While I was busy scanning the room, receptionist called my name and asked me to go in. She gave me my file. I entered the doctor's room. A middle aged lady smiled looking at me and asked me to take a seat. She asked for my file that receptionist has given me.

File contained all the information I had provided on call while confirming my appointment.

'So Mr. Rajveer, how are you' she asked politely

'Not so good doctor' I replied.

She asked me various questions about my past life, family, relationships, my friends, job and parents; she asked me every minute detail about my life. She advised me to answer her honestly as her series of questions will help her to speed up with my mental health and general health treatment. She formulated a treatment plan based on the severity of my symptoms, how much the depression is impacting and my ability to function at work and/or home. Her advice to cope up without medicines gave me a bit of self-confidence.

She started with the Psychotherapy treatment by providing an empathic environment which made me discuss any number of concerns and stressors in a supportive, non-judgmental and non-critical atmosphere.

She explained me various type of psychotherapy treatments including: cognitive behavioral therapy (CBT), psychodynamic psychotherapy, interpersonal psychotherapy, eye movement desensitization and reprocessing (EMDR), dialectical behavioral therapy (DBT). All was above my understanding level.

Her words that 'I do not have any serious problem, I just need to have proper nutrition, exercise and get myself involved in enjoyable activities' made me feel good. I repeated in my heart 'I do not have any serious problem'. She told me to make friends and gave me some stuff to work on and mind boggling games. She advised me to activate my Facebook again. I started meditating too.

Her twice in a week therapies made me feel better but only till the time I was in there in her clinic, as I come back to my place my past entangled me again. She asked me to remove Arohi's picture from the stool near my bed, I failed to do so. NO therapy, nothing can make me keep her away.

Tuesday morning, team did not have much work as the release was done for the month. Saumy showed me, few of his weekend trip pictures and asked me to pick the best one, so that he could set it as his profile picture. I helped him in choosing the best picture.

Within no time he changed his profile picture and asked me to like it. I remembered doctor's recommendation to activate Facebook account again. I picked up my laptop and activated the account. 1st thing Saumy made me do was to LIKE his picture, I thought of browsing through Arohi's profile but I did not have guts to see her honeymoon pictures with Raj. I typed 'Arohi' in the search box when a friend request prompted, I opened the tab, its Malvika, and I accepted the request.

'Hi, thanks for accepting the request' she pinged

'hi, how have u been?' I replied

'I am good, so finally I found you on FB'

'I just activated my account, perfect timing' I replied

'Look I was keeping eye on you ;)' she replied

'hahah how's work?'

'Going good but as of now doing online shopping'

'Ohh, nice. So buying what?'

'Speakers'

'Hey share your mail ID, I am sending you 2 models. Tell me which one to buy'

'RajveerS10@gmail.com'

'Thank you, check your mail.'

I logged in to my Gmail after 9 months, there were 8156 unread mails.

I opened the 1st one, and advised Malvika to go for JBL Flip stereo.

'Thanks buddy' she replied

I had strong desire to browse Arohi's profile, but my one click could break me more. I tried not to think about her.

I logged off.

To divert myself I started checking my mails that I had not done since I moved to Delhi, this time taking process will keep me busy. Majority of the mails were from naukri.com, job profile, times job, Dr. Batra, few girls who were interested in talking to me, I selected these mails and clicked delete.

I stopped at the mail whose subject line mentioned – "Exhibition: 'Path to Bliss' by Arohi Jain"   Sender: Priya.

I opened the mail.

Hi RV,

I would like to invite you to the 1ˢᵗ exhibition of my younger sister; it is a big day of her life. She wants her close friends to be present with her. You are one of them. She will be happy to see you.

Find attached exhibition details.

Hope to see you at the venue.

Your friend,

Priya

I read the mail twice, I opened the attached image.

"Path to Bliss": Exhibition by Artist Arohi Jain

Inauguration by Miss Shila Vilas (President Youth Art Club, India) @ 1 PM: 24ᵗʰ September 2015

Venue: Prince of whales Museum, Mumbai.

Finally she made it, it's her exhibition and she is going to fulfill her biggest dream. She is living her passion. I am so Proud. I so want to be there with her. I got goosebumps reading Priya's mail. Electrifying energy ran through me.

I browsed other mails:

Hey RV,

Sorry buddy, things happen between friends, sorry for everything. Please share your number. We had been trying to reach you but it seems you want to be away from us.

Please give me a call once you read this.

Tiddi

Few more times job mails and then it was Pajju's mail.

Brother, how are you? Sorry for the mess, I and NIK tried reaching out to Aunty but she did not share your number. We are best of best buddies. Whatever the scenario is, our friendship will never die. Group is incomplete without you. Let us unite our broken group (our life line).

Miss you

Prateek.

Tears fell down my cheeks, I was unable to understand my mixed feeling, I was happy to read the mails but tears covered my face. I wanted to shout loud with happiness and pain. I needed a hug badly but I choose a place for myself where only the walls could hear me cry.

And then I read the shortest mail

"RV Sir,

Please come back

Arohi"

"Yaadein bhi badi ajeeb si hoti hain,

Kabi wafa hoti hain to kabhi ghata hoti hain

Koi rooth jaye to khata hoti hain

Koi chod jaaye to saza hoti hain"

Exhibition

22nd September 2015/ Tuesday

I decided to leave for Mumbai, I felt giddy with excitement. I wanted to run, to shout, and to tell everyone what was going to happen...but I had to wait. I couldn't sit down, couldn't read a book and could not even watch the television. My mind was like a butterfly, whatever distraction I chose my mind kept fluttering back to the mails.

I walked in my room to and fro and counted days on my fingers

24th is her exhibition, today it is 22nd, I have only 2 days. I want to be present with her at the time of inauguration. I picked up my laptop, opened its lid, connected the net and searched for the tickets, Delhi to Mumbai. I smiled while searching the flight, I calculated the timing: I will be out of airport by 12:00 PM, 1:00 PM is inauguration for her exhibition which would start by 1:30 PM as per Indian standard delay timings. It would not take more than an hour for me to reach the venue. I imagined myself being there with Arohi witnessing her success and meeting Gyaanis.

Waooooooooooooooo!!!!! I experienced lots of butterflies flying in my stomach; my excitement tickled me from within. How will everyone react when they will see me after months? What would be Arohi's reaction? I just cannot wait anymore. I want to be there with my ones.

My thoughts took a pause when I imagined not only Arohi and my friends but everyone will be there and by everyone it means Arohi's father and RAJ too. She will be there with Raj presenting her work.

Why did she ask me to come back? Did she mail me after her wedding with Raj? Is she not happy with him? I questioned myself

I grabbed my laptop and searched for her mail,

I read it again

> *"RV Sir,*
>
> *(10th January 2015, 04:46 AM)*
>
> *Please come back*
>
> *Arohi"*

She mailed me 9 months back that means before her wedding. Damn! Damn!!! I am too late, if I would have read this on time, may be the scenario would have been different today. Damn! I banged my hand on the wall. I sat down regretting my decision. It is too late now. I was not there when she called me.

'Is it too late? Can I go back to her?' I asked myself.

'Yes it is late, she would be happily married by now' a voice within me replied.

'Why did Priya sent me an invite then?'

'She would have sent it to all her friends, also they would not fear my presence as Arohi is already married'

My excitement turned into a mental state of having contradictory desires. I was not sure what to do. I closed my laptop and lay on bed. I was not in position to take any decision, my mind went blank.

I wanted someone to help me on this, someone who can think of all pros and cons of me being there at Arohi's best day. I do not want to spoil it for her. The only person who knows my situation and with whom I can talk about this is Malvika. I logged in FB and pinged her

'Hi'

'Hey Rajveer, how are you?' she replied

'I need your help'

'Sure, tell me what happened? Is everything all right?'

'I am in dilemma; I need suggestions and honest replies from you'

'I would love to help you in any way I can, tell me what happened'

I told her about Arohi's exhibition, her mails and mails from my friends

'Waoo, that's good news. Congratulations' she said

'I am not able to decide should I go or not? It is a big day for Arohi. I do not want my presence to spoil things for her'

'Rajveer, Arohi's elder sister has sent you the invite which means she wants you to be there and they will be happy to see you after months'

'What about Raj? And her father...?'

I could see 'Malvika typing...' I waited for few minutes for her message, she replied:

'What about them? Rajveer, you have told me- how much your group matters to Arohi and you. You both were too proud to be part of Gyaanis but sad it broke. You have got the opportunity to make up for everything, to unite your scattered group. Think about Arohi, she will be so happy to see all her friends with her on her big day and if you talk about Raj, then I would like to ask you one question- do you have only one relation with Arohi? Can't she be your best friend like she was before you fell in love with her?'

214

'I don't know, I don't know how I will react when I will see her with someone else' I replied

'Malvika typing...'

'Malvika typing...'

'Look Rajveer, you have to face this someday. You cannot keep yourself quarantined for life. They are your friends; you have been with them since 8 years. Arohi is going to achieve the biggest dream of her life and you are the only person with whom she has shared it. I request you not to lose such an opportunity. Life has given you a second chance to be with your besties, go for it. Don't fear there is nothing to lose as you are not left with anything to lose. It is the time to grab things back. Even if you don't gain anything, you will not lose anything'

'hmm'

'Don't think much, go for it'

'Thanks Malvika, you are really sweet'

'I know that☺'

I liked Malvika for being honest and lively. I thanked her for her honest replies.

'I have nothing to lose now' I agreed to her point. I agreed on everything that she said except one 'to be just friends with Arohi again'. I don't know how girls do this, how can they even think to be friends with someone they loved. I remember Arohi kept the same demand on the day of our last meeting. Why can't they understand, you can never be just friends with the one you loved once.

"One can fall in love with a friend but cannot be just friend with the one you Love"

24th September 2015/ Thursday

It took 2hrs and 20 minutes for Air India to bring me from Delhi to Mumbai, Its 12:15 PM, as per my calculation I should have boarded the cab by 12:00PM. I am running 15 minutes late; I quickly booked a cab for myself.

'How much time will it take for us to reach the venue?' I asked the cab driver

'Sir, It will take around 1 hour minimum' He replied

'Can you please drive fast' I requested him impatiently.

My legs were shaking due to nervousness; I was feeling like my heart will come out of my mouth, my ears could hear my fast running heartbeat. I was experiencing quaking, shaking and all types of strange sensations. I kept moving like a pendulum on the back seat of my cab. To reduce my anxiety I hugged my bag, closed my eyes and rested my back on cushioned seat of the cab.

'We reached sir' cab driver woke me up

I looked out of the window, "Prince of Wales Museum" written in big letter on the main gate. I paid the driver and entered the big Iron Gate.

Prince of Wales Museum of Western India is one of the premier art and history museums in India. It is situated on the southern tip of Mumbai. Building is built in the Indo-Saracenic style of architecture, incorporating elements of architecture like the Mughal, Maratha and Jain. The museum building is surrounded by a garden of palm trees and formal flower beds giving a scenic look to the historical museum.

As I entered, on left was the banner approx. 6'*6' in size with Arohi's picture on it. I touched her chin, as to touch her cheeks I would have to jump. I read the text on the banner loud "Art exhibition by Arohi Jain – Path to Bliss".

Guard on the main gate handling the flowing crowd in and out, impatiently asked me to move fast. I enquired about the art gallery. He asked me to first get the security check up done and submit my bag in an irksome tone.

I submitted my luggage at the counter and collected the token; they allowed me to take my back pack in as it had my laptop and camera. I walked in, after passing through the security gate I stood straight with my arms spread, a man in black uniform touched almost all parts of my body to ensure I am not carrying any bomb to explode the museum. I asked him the way to art gallery. He turned around pointed his hand towards the crowd standing 'There is the gallery' he said

My heart beat increased with every step of mine towards the entrance of the gallery, I walked on the path constructed using big stones with small grass growing near them. I could see the bunch of people enjoying cold drink and snacks standing outside the hall. I tried to identify if I know any one of them. Most of them were people with DSLR in hand and ID card hanging down their neck, they might be media people appreciating food before start of the event.

Nervousness made me take small steps; I remembered Waheguru and practiced how I will congratulate Arohi. Suddenly I saw the crowd came running towards me, leaving their cold drinks and snacks at the stalls. Cameraman got their cameras ready to click pictures and make videos; reporters with mic in their hands came near me. I think they misunderstood me with someone else. Getting conscious I took few steps back and turned around.

Behind me was Arohi.

I froze, I could not speak anything. My bag fell down my shoulder; my hands reflexively stopped it from falling down. I bent down a little to balance my bag and myself.

I stared at her; I scanned her from top to bottom.

She looked beautiful in cap sleeves peach gown with embroidered lace detail, hem falls to floor, crystals and gleaming rhinestone details creating a stunning radiant pattern. She looked amazing, glamour queen. I looked in her eyes.

She stared at me without a smile on her face; I failed to understand was it water in her eyes or they were shining as it was the big day for her. We kept looking at each other; things around us took a pause. I was looking at her after months, my eyes expressed all my feelings but her eyes had too many questions. Behind her was her family- Her mom, dad, Priya, Rahul and Raj.

Reporters pushed me back in order to cover the star of the event. She knowingly ignored me and went ahead towards the gallery. Everyone followed her.

Chief guest Miss Shila Vilas arrived, reporters moved their focus from Arohi to the chief guest, Arohi and her family welcomed her by giving a bouquet, everyone headed for the inauguration.

Guest of honor inaugurated the exhibition by cutting the ribbon followed by lightning of lamp. Media captured every moment.

Arohi explained her paintings to the audience. She explained the purpose of her exhibition and about the theme she chose:

Arohi speaks:

"Path to Bliss" means "way to happiness, joy, pleasure and heaven". I have created 30 paintings depicting different phases of human life.

My paintings in sequence are depicting story of humans from childhood till they achieve their destination, their heaven. By the words 'destination' and 'heaven' I do not mean death, by these words I mean goals of a human life. We all want some or the other thing in life very passionately, few have the courage to fight for it till the end and some scared of failure leave their goals and run towards a satisfied normal life. People who are passionate enough can achieve their goals; the only formula is "Never Quit".

Starting with my paintings:

My first painting-'footsteps' depicts a new life on earth.

Followed by 'Mother's Love', 'Father's Care', 'Play in Nature', these paintings are portraying innocence of a new born. Child trusts his parents and thus do not have any fear of falling, he plays with nature carefree, smiles when in air because he knows his father will catch him.

As we start growing, we realize the competition and start running in the race of blind people, we believe what people say, we get worried about what will others think about us?

To show our status we want a good house, car, tabs, mobile and other things to flaunt about in society. Some fall in love but do not have courage to fight for it, believe me - pain of separation is worst. Few wants to be rich but one failure in their path breaks them up and then we take support of the astrologers, we consult them and give our life in their hands. Instead of making our own decisions, we follow what they advise us. I am not saying they are wrong but it's our life, decision should be ours. Why should we blindly follow the person who is reading our hand and predicting our future? Why can't we create our own future? What if we failed once? Stand up and walk again towards your happiness. Success without failure is nothing.

People come out of their homes in search of happiness, they search it in others and they think if they will be rich they will be happy or if someone else will love them they will be happy.

Here I would like to say, please trust yourself, all the colors, all the happiness that you are trying to search in others is actually within yourself. The thing that you actually want, work hard for it, there is no power in the world that can take it away from you. Law of attraction is what you should believe in. Universe will bring it to you, determination is required. If you see a dream, go mad to achieve it instead of asking astrologers if you will get it or not. TRUST yourself; your happiness is in your hands. All the bright colors of your life are within you, just open your arms and color your life. Be positive, live happy, remove the negativity and trust god within yourself.

When it rains, peacock comes out and dances, Instead of waiting for anyone else to join it, spreading its wings. Looking at it we feel so pleased and happy, we admire its beauty.

Similarly do not wait for any support. If you are happy you can make others happy too and if you are sad no one in the world can make you smile from your heart. So tighten your belts and go for that one thing you want desperately in your life and I am sure you will achieve it.

Her paintings showed all the phases she narrated in her speech, innocent childhood, competitive world, expectations from others, running behind success, failure, depression, consulting palmist, self-realization, meditation, finding all the colors of life within oneself, hard work, positive approach and finally achieving the goal of life. I was amazed listening to her. Confident Arohi was talking about life. I wish she would have thought of this while we were fighting for our love instead of giving up on it.

Few people covered Arohi to congratulate and appreciate her, few came out to grab snacks, few were lost in the paintings and few chit chatted in middle of the gallery. I searched for Priya; she too was busy talking to the guests. I came out of the gallery and went to the water cooler; I quenched my thirst drinking a glass of cold water.

'So finally you are here' someone said keeping hand on my shoulder. It's Pajju I recognized his voice.

'Yes, finally I am here' I replied and turned around

He slapped me and then hugged me.

Tiddi and Nik saw us, they came running towards me with a shoe in their hand, Pajju being the master of the plan held me tight, he provoked Nik and Tiddi to come fast and beat me. I applied all my strength and released myself from his grip. I ran towards the canteen which was near the entrance (main gate) of the museum, Nik ran after me and caught me in middle of the lawn, Tiddi pushed me, Nik kicked my bums. Atul joined them too, they made me lay on the ground and kicked me like a football, looking at us, guard on the main entrance came running towards us and scolded us.

NIK apologized to him and helped me to get up. Guard gave us the nauseating look and went back to his original position.

'You asshole, what do you think of yourself?' Tiddi said

'Haan tell, what do you think you are?' Nik said snapping his fingers

'I am RV' I said and winked

'Rascal' Tiddi said and hugged me, NIK, Pajju and Atul joined the hug.

'Hey, RV is back' Neha shouted and called Aditi, Priya and Mini.

'Group hug without us…?' Mini said and came running towards us

'Come join us' Nik and Tiddi invited

We had the best group hug but still one member was missing.

'Yeeeeeyupieeeee finally RV is back' Neha shouted.

Guard stared at us from the main gate, he had issues with both the things "our fight" and "our love", and this time he came along with a stick and warned us.

'Move from here, else I am going to call the police' he said

'Sorry bhaiya, we are going' Mini answered giving a sweet smile to him.

He disregarded

'Let's sit in canteen' Neha suggested

'How have you been RV sir?' Mini asked while walking to the canteen

'To alone without you all' I replied

'Thanks for calling me here, Priya'

'I should thank you for coming, RV' Priya said

'After you left, Arohi too stopped talking to all of us. Series of disputes happened between each member of the group. I am so happy we are back again' Mini said.

'I am sorry guys but things went way too bad, I was not able to judge what's right what's wrong. I did what my heart said. I am sorry to hurt you all' I apologized for my actions

'We too are sorry RV, It was our mistake too. Instead of talking with each other, we should have directly come to you. We should have helped you' Pajju said

'Areee now everything is fine, please do not bring this topic again' Priya interrupted

'Yes, finally after months we all are here back again' Tiddi added

'Yes everything is fine now, we all are here' I repeated looking down the floor.

'Except one' I added

Everyone looked at me.

'How's Arohi? She looked beautiful today. Hopefully she is happy with her married life' I said

Everyone looked at each other and then at me

'What happened? Why are you all numb?' I asked

'You don't know RV?' Nik said

'Know what?' I asked

'Is she not happy with her married life?' I enquired

'No, she is not happy with her married life' Priya replied

'Why?' I asked

All went numb again

'I am asking something guys, Is Raj not a good person?'

'Raj is gem of a person' Priya replied

'Then, what is the issue?'

'Rajveer, Arohi is not happy with her married life because she broke her marriage' Tiddi replied

I was left dumbstruck for a moment.

'She broke her marriage means?' I asked with a big question mark on my face.

'She loved you and announced that she cannot marry anyone else other than you. Everyone in the family tried to convince her but she was stubborn on her decision. She explained mom dad that she can marry Raj but she will never be able to love him. She will be spoiling his life too.

Papa failed to understand all her explanations, arguments and requests. According to him she was spoiling her life. As a responsible and concerned father, to secure Arohi's future and his position in society he forcefully fixed her wedding with Raj; date was 07ᵗʰ June 2015'

'What happened next?' I enquired

Arohi was not left with any choice but to sit in mandapam and take life vows with Raj'

I kept quiet, Priya continued

'Raj noticed change in Arohi's behavior, she stopped talking to him. In fact she stopped talking to everyone; my dad convinced Raj that it is wedding pressure on her because of which she is behaving this way, after marriage she will be alright. Raj in deep love with Arohi, tried to understand her situation, he stopped bugging her and provided her with all the time and space she needed.

7ᵗʰ June, sadness in Arohi's eyes was visible to all, guests started talking 'bride is not happy' and now this bothered Raj and his family too, Raj tried to remain calm. All the ceremonies were performed. Sangeet, mehndi, haldi, reception and now it was the time for 7 phere and sindoor ceremony which will tie both of them in life long togetherness.

Arohi sat like a living doll with no feelings inside her; Pandit ji started with the mantras, tears from Arohi's eyes fell down and did not seem to stop. Looking at her condition papa realized that he is doing something wrong to her, Raj held her hand to make her comfortable; Arohi slowly drifted her hand apart.

Losing patience Raj asked Pandit ji to stop chanting mantras, he demanded to have talk in person with Arohi. Raj stood up and waited for her in the room beside the hall where mandap was arranged. My mom helped Arohi to get up and took her inside the room. Everyone waited for bride and groom to finish their talks and complete the main wedding ceremonies.'

Raj made her sit on the chair and he himself kneeled down holding her hand, he expressed his feelings:

'Arohi, I love you but I think mine is one sided love. Something is bothering you which you are not able to share' Raj said

Arohi kept quiet.

'Look Arohi, if you will not speak today, you will lose the opportunity to do what you want. Please tell me, what is bothering you? You are not the Arohi I met at Priya Bhabhi's wedding. Don't be scared, whatever you say will remain between us unless you tell it to anyone. You can trust me on this. Your one decision can save many lives'

'Do you love someone else?' he asked

She nodded and cried

That was the end of Raj and Arohi's story. He hugged her and helped her wiping all the tears from her life. He took control of the wedding situations too.

I felt numb.

'Arohi asked us not to contact you, she said if you feel for her, you will come back on your own as it was your decision to go without informing anyone' Neha said

'She is angry on you Rajveer Sir and I think she hates you now' Mini added

'She can never hate me' I murmured to myself

'I want to meet her, I want to meet her now' I said looking at Priya

'She is too angry and occupied, meet her after she is done for the day' Priya said

'Will she talk to RV?' Tiddi asked

'I don't think so' Priya shook her head

'What to do then?' Neha asked

'What time your parents will leave for hotel' Pajju asked Priya

'They will leave by 4:00 PM I suppose' she replied

'Okay, so here is the plan' Nik said cracking his knuckles

'Uncle Aunty will leave by 4, gallery closes at 8:00 PM, once Arohi is done for the day, she will come with us back to hotel, right?'

All nodded in sync

'So, plan is we all will leave by 7:30 without informing her. I have my uncle's car, RV you can keep that. So while returning she will not have any other option other than coming with you, and you guys can talk on the way back to hotel' he concluded

'I hope this will work. Isn't it?' NIK asked

'Ek number' Tiddi replied

'I think she will be way too angry' Neha said

'Let it be, RV has to handle' Tiddi winked

After having a successful day, full of compliments, tired Arohi sat down on the chair kept at corner of the hall. It was closing time of the gallery. Gyaani's made their way to escape from her.

Arohi searched for them, she took two rounds from gallery to canteen and the way back, wondering where has everyone vanished. She handed the gallery keys to the guard and asked them to arrange the required things for the next day. She called Priya; Priya did not picked up her call. She tried to call everyone in the group but no one responded. Annoyed with everyone's behavior she collected her baggage from the counter and came out in search of taxi.

I waited for her near the main gate of the museum. As she called out for the taxi, I went and stopped my car in front of her, she bend down and tried to communicate through the window

'Bhaiya, Marine lines chaloge?' she asked without noticing me on the driver seat.

I stepped down the car, came by her side and opened the car's door for her

'Who are you' she asked indignantly

'Your Driver ma'am' I replied

'Please leave me alone'

'Arohi, I am sorry. Please listen to me once please' I insisted

'I do not talk to strangers' She replied

'OK. Don't talk to me but please come along. I will drop you hotel, please'

'I am capable of going alone. I do not need anyone's help' she replied

'I am sorry. Please don't be angry'

'Sorry for what? I am not angry on you, it's just that I don't talk to strangers' She said and called for a taxi

She sat and left for her place. I followed her ensuring she reaches safe. She got down at an entrance of the hotel I followed her till the lift.

'Arohi' I tried to stop her

'Look Mister, stop doing this else I will complain you in police' she warned and entered the lift; I stepped back and allowed her to go.

I called Nik

'Hey, lover boy. How is it going?' He asked

'She is angry dude; she is not talking to me. She took a taxi instead of coming with me' I replied

'Lol!! She came by taxi?' He announced and everyone has a great laugh on my miserable situation.

'Banta hai yaar uska gussa hona, don't worry she will come back to you just you need to try little hard this time' he said consoling me

'Hmm'

'By the way, where are you staying?' he asked

'No-where as of now' I replied

'Listen all of us are staying in the same hotel as it is nearby the gallery, you too stay with us' He advised

'Hmm, where are you all?' I enquired

'We all are at Girgaon chaupati; we will be back in half an hour, wait for us there and don't worry Arohi ko mana lenge'

I waited for them at the reception of the hotel, making myself comfortable on the white color, soft cushioned, designer sofa kept near the receptionist's table. I picked up the magazine lying on the side table beside sofa. Flapping through the magazine, I blamed myself for everything that happened. I was not there when she needed me the most, she is really angry on me and she has all the rights to do so.

A slight smile came on my face when I realized 'she is not married'. I still have the opportunity to make her mine but to make this possible I need her to forgive me. I was lost in my own thoughts when her parents walked in.

'Rajveer' Her mom called

Looking at them, I stood up in haste, striking my leg on the front table, magazine slipped out of my hands; I bent down to pick up the magazine and got my head hurt again with the same table. Couple of hurting things and then I stood straight

'Hee hello Aunty, hello uncle' I stammered

'Good to see you beta' she said and smiled, her father gave a warm smile too

Her father smiling? I cannot believe my eyes, I pinched myself secretly to confirm I was not dreaming and it is a reality. I did not know what to reply. I stared her father as if I have seen an alien.

'Are you okay RV?' her mother asked

'Yeye... yes aunty' I stammered

'Let us have a cup of tea in our room, come son' Her dad said and asked me to follow him.

'Son? He called me son?' I talked to myself, following them in the lobby

'Come sit Rajveer' her father said

Her mother prepared tea and offered me. Not knowing how to react, I kept quiet and waited for them to start the conversation. Time being I decided to concentrate on my tea; I took a sip and burnt my tongue with the hot tea. Now another reason for me to be quiet was my burnt tongue.

'So beta, where are you these days?' Aunty asked

'Delhi, Aunty' I replied

She nodded

'Met Arohi?' Uncle asked

Now how to answer this question? I simply nodded

'She is very stubborn' Uncle said

I kept quiet

'She was not like this; you know? In fact she was very obedient and sweet child, she used to do whatever we told her to do. If I compare Priya and Arohi then I would say Priya got all the scolding and beatings from me, I don't even remember if I have ever scolded Arohi, she is my innocent baby.

She used to manage everything so well, she wanted to be a designer but I told her to go for engineering, I wanted to secure her future. She respected my decision and look she topped the college and today she is a successful engineer working in top MNC but to fulfill my demands she never compromised on her dreams. She tried to balance everything; she worked for her passion too along with engineering and job. She made us proud at all stages of her life. She is dearest to me.

But then she met you!' He said and paused for a moment. He looked at me; I had no clue how to react. I looked down and stared my cup of tea.

He continued 'I do not know what magic you did on her. "She revolted!" for the 1ˢᵗ time she failed to manage both the things "our happiness" and "her dreams", may be because she cannot manage 2 husbands at a time, one of her choice and one of ours' He said the last line and laughed at his own silly joke.

I kept listening making a blank face.

'I have a position to maintain in society, people respect me and my daughter marrying any Punjabi boy will compel me to leave the community. How can I tolerate this? I searched for a very good, well settled boy for her but NO, she was not happy. She broke her wedding. I stopped talking to her but looking at her sad face I realized I had made some mistake. My princess is not happy, she has lost her smile.'

And then I got a note:

He handed me a piece of paper having many random folds. I opened it and read it

"Uncle Aunty, I know the major concern is religion, what will you say to your relatives that your girl is going to marry a Punjabi boy? But uncle People say, they will talk for few days and then they will forget. As parents what should matter to you most is Arohi's happiness. We cannot live without each other. Please understand. I will give her all the happiness in the world. I will never ask her to leave her religion and follow mine. I will do whatever you say. Just shower your blessings on us, please. Any caste, culture, religion is not bigger than love, when Arohi was small you taught her the meaning of selfless love and sharing, now when she has learnt that why is she being asked to compromise on it?

When we watch a movie where hero is Muslim and heroine is Hindu, we silently pray for their love to win at the end of the movie, then why so much restrictions in real life? Please be with us, your blessing mean a lot to us"

Damn! Damn! This was the speech that I wrote to convince Arohi's parents. How come this is with him? I was staring at the paper.

'I think you must have written this to convince me but I did not gave you a chance to speak' Uncle said

'From where did you have this paper?' I asked

'Maid found this while cleaning the house, she came and handed this to me' he said

'Must have fallen from my pocket' I murmured, hardly audible to others.

'I know Arohi is angry on you. I tried talking to her once after she broke her wedding with Raj but she told me not to talk about you with her or anyone else at home. Now it is on you, son. If you can make up things with her we are happy to accept your relationship'

His one sentence and ray of hope enlightened my heart, I repeated his words in my heart again 'we are happy to accept your relationship' but to let him accept my relationship with Arohi, I need to make up things with Arohi first, I need to apologize, I need to make her believe that I love her more than anyone else in this world and will never ever leave her.

I thanked uncle for his acceptance and took leave as I need to make preparations to meet my love.

24th September 2015/Thursday/10:00PM

Crimson Hotel/ Room no- 108

How will you make up with Arohi? Nik asked

I shrugged my shoulders

'Aane main bahut der kar di aapne Rajveer ji' Aditi said in a taunting tone

'I know it's my fault. I will make up for it' I replied

'You have to do that anyhow' Priya said

'I will do that and before I do, I have good news for all'

'What?' chorus sound in the room

'Guys the good news is – Arohi's parents agreed for my relation with Arohi'

'Waooo seriously? You had talk with them?' Priya jumped in excitement

I nodded

'when?'

'When you all were enjoying chaupati food'

'Congratulations buddy' everyone hugged me

'Now the big task is to melt Arohi's anger' I said looking at Priya

'hmmmmmmm' She said

'Priya there is some problem in your family' I said

'Problem? What?' she asked, confused

'Earlier daughter was ready; I had to convince the father. Now father is ready and I need *to* convince the daughter. Why can't all be ready at same time?' I asked Priya trying to tease her

'It's all your mistake, my family is the best' she replied

'peeen penn pa penn' I imitated her last sentence replacing the words.

'Doggy RV, stop that' Priya shouted

'Respect me you silly girl. I will be yours sister's husband soon' I said showing my one hand as if I am giving blessings to her

'Sister's husband? 1st convince my sister for that' she reminded

'Oh yes, I have to convince your sister first. Good night everyone, I am going to sleep. I need to be ready on time tomorrow as I have to drop Miss Arohi to her art gallery' I said lying down on bed and covered myself with blanket.

'oh hoo....That means again Arohi will be going by Taxi' Neha said

Everyone laughed

I peeped out of my blanket and threw my pillow on Neha

She threw it back to me; Nik jumped in and threw his pillow on me. Tiddi took revenge from my side. Priya threw her's on Tiddi. Tiddi hit Priya snatching Pajju's pillow. Pajju snatched Aditi's pillow and hit on Tiddi's head. Everyone hitting one another with the pillows and soon the hotel room was converted into the field of pillow war.

25th September/ 11:00 AM

As per the plan, everyone left for the gallery by 10:30AM, I was happy as Arohi's parents supported me in the plan. I waited for Arohi in Nik's uncle's car; I observed the surroundings, beautiful sea, and clear sky and six lane concrete roads. Beauty of the sea compelled me to come out of the car but Mumbai's humidity forced me to sit in with AC on.

A beautiful lady dressed in baby pink salwar kameez came out of the hotel, her hairs open and straight, her traditional white and pink earrings complimented her dress. Her bangles made noise as she lifted her hand to manage her hairs. She has some magic on me whenever I see her my heart starts pumping fast. I accelerated the engine and stopped my car in front of her, she ignored me again and started calling out for taxi. I came out of the car.

'Arohi, please listen to me once' I requested following her as she walked on the road chasing taxi's. She ignored me. I came and stood in front of her, without making eye contact she turned around and started chasing taxi's coming from other direction of the road. I kept talking to her; she behaved as if she does not know me. Boarding a taxi, she headed towards her destination.

Her ignorance now bothered me like anything; I was not able to bear her behavior. Is she the same Arohi who once loved me? How can she be so arrogant? Is this her ego that is not allowing her to talk to me and accept me? Or is she punishing me for not being with her when she needed me the most? Things were getting on my nerves. I waited for sundown till her exhibition to get over. Just like yesterday I waited for her today.

Just like yesterday she ignored me today when I went to pick her up, just like yesterday she behaved as if my voice is not reaching her. She called out for a taxi, losing my control I shouted on the taxi driver and asked him to go

I held her arm, bought her to the corner of the road, for the 1st time my holding her would have hurt her, my grip was tight. She applied all her energy trying to release her hand.

'What is the problem haan? I know mistake is mine but please at least give me a chance to say something' I shouted, few people passing by turned and stared us.

She got scared and tears fell down her eyes. Her tears made me feel like a local criminal, who is following a girl and forcing her to talk. I released her. I apologized for my behavior. I held her hand softly

'Please talk to me Arohi please. At least say something. Beat me, scold me but please talk'

She looked at me with her wet eyes 'Please let me go RV Sir' she said in her sweet voice. I can see love for me in her eyes, I could read them, she is hurt and I am the reason.

'Will you never talk to me?' I asked her

'What even if I talk? Someday again you will leave me alone and will never contact. I know you are here because Priya di mailed you else you would have never come' She said and left the place.

*   *   *

26th September 2015;

Last day of her exhibition, Day 3 I did not make efforts to pick or drop her to the venue or hotel; I did not attend the closing ceremony of her successful exhibition. I wished secretly that she would be missing my presence.

While everyone was there at the gallery I stood back. I went to Arohi's room. Her room was locked; I explored my pockets in search of a paper. I did not have a single piece of blank paper. I took out my business card and wrote the message on back side of it.

> *"I will be waiting for you at terrace of the hotel – 11:00 PM.*
> *Hope you will come*
>
> Yours,
> RV Sir"

Opening between door and floor helped my business card to enter her room:

*   *   *

Crimson's Terrace, 11:00 PM

I waited for her at the terrace of the hotel; I hope she would have read my message and will come to meet me. I bought a red rose for her.

Moon, the brightest star of night looked beautiful, I could see the Marine Drive also called as Queen's Necklace, from an elevated point of the hotel and street lights resemble a string of pearls in a necklace. Hotel had its roof top restaurant on other half area of the building - It's got great tunes, fake grass and a slick white canopy for shelter from inevitable downpours.

I sat down on the floor on my half of the roof, I could hear sound of footsteps climbing the stairs, and I prayed silently in my heart it to be Arohi.

She entered the terrace; she wore white sleeveless kurta, legging and blue dupatta, white silver earrings and matching bangles. She gave tough competition to the moon in terms of beauty. Flash light of her cell phone helped her to enter the terrace with no lights illuminating; she looked at me and switched off the flash light.

I stood up and gave her the rose; she crossed her hands and did not accept it.

'You wanted to talk to me? Tell me, what is it? I am listening' she said

'My Shona is so angry on me?' I said and apologized holding my ears

She stared at me, I held her hand

'Leave me' she said huffily and departed

'What do you think of yourself? You always do whatever you think is correct? Have you ever thought about me?

You wanted to meet me at night, taking all the risks you came to meet me at my place when papa was at home, then you wanted to be away from me, you shifted to Delhi, you left the group, did not call me even once and then you say you love me? Why should I believe you? Who knows, next time if I say- 'I will not be yours' instead of convincing me, you will again leave me and go away' she shouted

'What do you think? All these things you are doing now will flatter me?

No, not at all. I do not love you any more' she said folding her hands, looking away from me

'I am sorry; I know it is my mistake. I am ready for all the punishments but please come back to me. I will never ever leave you. I promise' I said bringing her close to me by holding her arms.

'Who the hell do you think you are? How could you go leaving me like this? 10 months, no contact?' she said moving her hands to get rid of my grip

I brought her closer, tried to hug her. She did not allow me; she kept her hands on my chest and applied pressure to drift away from me. I kept holding her arms

'I love you, I am sorry. You cannot even imagine how I have lived those 10 months without you. I was body without soul' I said looking in her eyes

She punched me on my chest, her thump war on my chest made me feel light. My Arohi is back.

'Thanks for coming back' I said

'I hate you, I hate you. You are bad' she said and kept beating my chest with her arms. My chest became punching bag for her. This time I managed to hug her. She melted like ice of a glacier in hot sun. She cried, I cried.

She crumbled my t-shirt, just like the way she used to do, she hid in me. I loved the feeling. I could feel her warmth.

I love you; she whispered hiding in my arms. I held her tighter.

'I am sorry; I will never be away from you. I love you my Shonpari'

Unexpected 4

Arohi's father calling....

'Good Morning Uncle'

'Good Morning Son, I wanted your father's number'

'Papa's number? What happened uncle, everything okay?'

'Nothing much son, just wanted to fix your engagement date with Arohi'

I paused for a moment, did I hear it right? He wants to what?

'Sorry uncle your voice is not audible. Could you please repeat?' I said

'I want your father's number because I want to fix your engagement with Arohi' he repeated

I did few barati steps standing in front of mirror and then sophisticatedly replied

'Sure uncle, will message you within few seconds. Thank you for everything uncle'

'You are welcome, by the way congratulations'

'Uncle one request'

'Yes'

'Please do not tell this to Arohi, let it be unexpected for her'

'OhhHooo surprise but son this might be too risky, as being a girl she will be very particular about her engagement dress, accessories and other arrangements'

'Don't worry about those things uncle. I will take care of that'

As soon as I disconnected the call, I whatsApped my father's number to my-to be father in law but before he shares this news with him, I wanted to talk to my father.

'Hello dad, how are you?'

'What is the good news son?'

'How did you got to know that I have news?'

'I am your father. I know everything. Tell me now'

I love my father, he knows me inside out. Happiness in my voice after months confirmed him, I have big news.

'Dad I am back with Arohi'

'Arohi??? she is married right?'

'No papa, I narrated him the story'

'GOD bless your love, you both deserve to be with each other. Not everyone have this much guts to live just for one person'

'But I am angry on mummy, as she did not want me and Arohi to be together, she did not share my contact details with anyone in my group. If she would have shared. We could have avoided all this mess'

'Your mother was not aware of the fact Arohi is waiting for you, according to her she ditched you and you were the one suffering alone. How can any mother tolerate this?'

'Hmm'

'She would love to hear your voice filled with happiness after long, she will accept Arohi like her own daughter'

'Hmmm, I hope'

'Wait I am getting a call from another number'

'Are do not miss that call dad, it's my father in law calling you to fix my engagement date'

Before I could complete my sentence my father put me on hold and received call from my father-in -law.

Date was decided: 29 September 2015, that is again 2 days from now. Why do I always get just 2 days to make all the arrangements?

I wanted to make this special for her, no matter what; time was just a constraint that could not stop me from doing what I want.

I thought of what all I could do to make it special for her? What is the thing that she would love? Anything from our wish list? I remember she shared one of her fantasy world dream in Matheran, 'to be the princess of the fairy world.'

YESS...She love fairy tales, she wants to be a princess of such a fairy world that does not exist in reality. I want to make her wish real. I will create the fairy world for my princess. 'The theme of the engagement would be- fairy land' I announced loud in my empty room.

All interiors, dresses and everything else will be designed keeping my princess's world in mind. I asked Gyaanis for their help. I had to arrange food, place, theme based decorations and most importantly dress for my princess.

I made the list of tasks and called out Gyaanis for the meeting, obviously only Arohi was not included. I distributed the tasks:

I asked Priya for Arohi's dress size, all the dirty minds in the room started laughing and teasing me.

'You should know her size better than Priya' Pajju scoffed, giving high five to Tiddi.

'C'mon guys, this is a serious meeting. We have just 2 days and I want to make 29th September as the best day of Arohi's life. So no masti only work. Ok?' I said staring and pointing finger at Pajju and Tiddi

They nodded

'Priya please help me with her dress size I want to gift her best possible princess dress that any bride has ever wore. Also please help me with her shoe size. She will be my Cinderella wearing beautiful glass shoes'

'Nik, your responsibility is to find the perfect place which could be decorated as per our theme. Mumbai is your uncle's native; he might help you finding one'

'Next are Aditi, Neha and Mini. I have prepared a list of decorative items. You need to make this available from where ever you can' I handed the list to Neha, she read it aloud:

1) Silver or star-patterned polyester Balloons

2) Super-shine table covers in silver as well as paper and table covers in baby pink and blue

3) Glass slippers as table centerpieces

4) Lots of Twinkle Lights

5) Few pumpkins

6) Theme based napkins, cups, plates, glasses

7) Cushiony pink and blue flip-flops

8) A big royal Clock

9) Royal Carriages

10) Crystal Castles for decorations

11) Silver curtains

12) Stuffed toys

'This is too much to arrange RV' Aditi jumped out after Neha finished reading the list

'Things will be done RV' Neha said cutting Aditi's point

'But how? 2 days and so many things' Aditi murmured to Neha

'Aditi di, this is for RV sir and Arohi, we have to do this anyhow' Mini answered

'Things will be done RV sir' Mini assured

'We will divide tasks within ourselves and will arrange whatever you need' Neha added

Aditi nodded

'Thank you so much girls' I thanked from my heart for assuring this, one of my big headache was reduced. Next are Pajju, Tiddi and Atul

'You guys will be arranging food, this is the list. Please find the caterers' I handed the list to Pajju. Tiddi snatched it from his hands and read it noticeably copying Neha

1) 3 layered Engagement cake (with a prince and princess on top of the cake)

'hunnhuhh prince and princess?' he said looking at me with his one eyebrow up. He continued reading:

2) Mini Pizzas

3) Cheese and Crackers

4) Salsa and Chips

5) Nachos and cheese

6) Stuffed garlic bread

7) Indian starters (aaloo tikki, paneer tikka, kababs, kathi roll)

8) Soups

9) Chinese salad

10) 10)Fruit Salad

11) 11)Pasta Salad

12) Indian and Italian buffet

13) fruit juice

14) Plenty of chilled bottled mineral water (sparkling and flat)

15) Lemon and lime wedges and twists, olives and other garnish

16) ice- creams, brownie for desert

17) Add whatever you feel is missing

'Add Gulab Jamun for desert' Nik raised his hand and said

'Jalebii too' Pajju added

'Wooo, nice variety. Water in my mouth' Tiddi complimented

'Thanks, you need to arrange all this' I replied

'I know few caterers here, food will be arranged' Atul said

'Good quality haan?' I reassured

'Best quality, sir. Trust me' He replied

'Cool, food is done then. Pajju and Tiddi please help girls in finding the decorative stuff. It would be difficult for them to arrange so many things in such a short notice.

And Guys, need your advice on what should I gift her on this special occasion?'

'Ring?' Aditi suggested

'Areeee...that is mandatory for engagement. What else other than that?' I said

'Art and craft material, maybe?' Tiddi suggested

'No, everyone gifts her same. She is bored of it now' Priya said

'Watch?' Pajju said

'She just bought one, few days back' Priya interrupted

'Hey hey guys, wait a minute. One of my friends told me about a site, they can help us with the gifts and also with the decorative items for the theme decorations' Nik said

'Which site?' Priya enquired

'**Amour Arts**' Nik replied

'RV you can get your gift items, also we can also get customized clocks, carriages, center pieces, paintings and other stuff too' Nik added

'If we place the order today, will they be able to deliver things within two days?' I enquired

'They have their headquarters in Pune, on special request they may ask us to pick stuff from their office. We need to call the help line number and ask them' Nik answered

'So call them, what are we waiting for?' Tiddi said

'Areeyy 1st open the website and have a look if they have anything that we need or not' Priya suggested

Pajju opened his apple laptop; everyone sat forming a semi-circle around him.

'What is the url?'

'Google it' Mini suggested

'**www.amourarts.com**'

An artistic page opened up, with news, paintings, clocks, diaries flashing on it.

'Here are different categories paintings, clocks, name plates, gift items - customized gift boxes, diaries, cards. Which one to go for 1st? 'Pajju asked

'Clocks' Aditi shouted

'Gift items' I said

'Paintings' Tiddi interrupted

'Cards' Priya said

Everyone looked at each other, Pajju got confused which one to open 1st.

'Open all the tabs one by one' Atul suggested

Pajju clicked on the paintings tab, lot many beautiful colorful paintings came up.

'Keep in mind, you are selecting a gift for an artist' Priya said

'What could be better than gifting her an art piece that resembles her' Pajju said and clicked a painting of an angel who is lost in her own thoughts

'Waooo, this is beautiful' Priya said

'Add this to cart, she looks like Arohi' I said

'Wait lover boy, let us browse some other options too, also let us check the size of the painting' Tiddi said

Numerous beautiful paintings made it difficult for us to choose the best one, we added few to the cart, and final decision will be done later.

After paintings it was turn for the clocks selection, we found one royal fairy Clock but we needed that in bigger size.

'Add this to cart for a while, we can call customer service and discuss about the size, they have mentioned about personalized clocks too, we can talk on same context' Nik suggested.

Another item was added to the cart. My most awaited thing Gift items were to be opened. Variety of artistic and creative gift items were displayed on the screen, after discussion we all agreed on the antique looking Gift box which has a message bottle, beautiful bracelet and a cute show piece of a couple dancing along with few beautiful fillers in the box.

'Write the text for message bottle here' Pajju said and pointed the text box on his screen

'I will do that later after selection of all the items' I said

Next was the card category, various creative cards were shown up for love, friends, mother, father, miss u cards, get well soon cards etc. Every card had the best possible craft work done. It made me difficult to choose.

'Which one should I pick?' I asked

'Ab sab tu hi dega kya?' Pajju said

'Yes, yours is done. We are gifting this card' Tiddi said pointing finger to one of the box card flashing on the screen

Pajju opened the tab, 'Amour arts exploding box card' Tiddi read the text

It looked like the box, on opening the cover of the box, it opened up into many beautiful sheet leaves, with different pictures and messages on each. Group decided to present this to Arohi, making her emotional by pasting all the memories in form of pictures.

'What about my gift? What will you guys gift me?' I asked

'We are doing all this for you na. This is your gift. Be happy' Nik said

'Hmm, mean people' I commented

'Aacha now on serious note, I don't think so they will be able to provide us these many things in span of 2 days' Priya said

'We can call and confirm' NIK said and dialed customer care'

'Welcome to Amour Arts. May I know your name please' A female on telephone spoke

'I am Nikunj'

'Thanks for calling Amour arts Mr. Nikunj, please help me with your contact number'

'7875445778992'

'Thank you Mr. Nikunj, How can I assist you?'

'There are few items that I have added to my cart but I need them by day after tomorrow. Will it be possible?' I enquired

'Can you please name the items?'

'Angel twinkle painting'

Royal fairy Clock (personalized)

Surprise gift box

Exploding box card (personalized)'

'Sir personalized items do take time, at least 5 days. It will not be possible for us to deliver within 2 days'

'Look it is really urgent; we can collect it from Amour arts office directly'

'I understand sir but we need time to work on your personalized items and we do not have any provision for collecting the items directly from office'

'What if I send a mail mentioning special request? Will it be addressed?'

'Yes sir, you can surely do that. Also I will talk to my manager and will let you know in case we are able to fulfil your demands by end of the day today.'

'Sure, thank you'

'Thank you for calling Amour Arts'

I requested Nik to keep me posted on these items and asked Priya to accompany me for selecting dress and accessories for Arohi.

We explored few of the famous boutiques and designer showrooms of Mumbai in search of the perfect dress for Arohi. After exploring few shops, one of the designer convinced us to buy the perfect princess dress.

I asked her the price

'Sir, price is the secondary thing, let me tell you details about this dress first-

'Dress is made of silk organza. There are six layers of skirt, corset boning and intricate beading; it is light as a feather. Off shoulder sleeves and skirt layers will give a perfect princess royal look also the beading at back seems like something out of a fairy tale. Expensive but it is absolutely the right choice' I must say.'

Material description of the dress was above my understanding level but I loved the dress.

'Also sir, as the dress is so detailed there is no need of a necklace. I will provide you with other accessories like earrings, bracelet, princess crown along with this.'

Without having more discussion I asked her to alter the dress according to Arohi's size and pack it. Half of my pocket got emptied buying the perfect dress for my princess. I hope she likes it. While I was paying the bill Nik called me and gave me the happy news that Amour arts accepted our request, they will keep our order ready and any one of us can pick up the things from their office on 28th September. Also the venue is decided just we need to convert into a palace with our decorations.

Everyone worked hard and made all the prerequisite arrangements.

*   *   *

29th September 2015/ 6:00 PM

Venue Nik selected was not less than a palace, decorations made it look majestic. Everything turned out to be beyond expectation. White colored circular tables were decorated with Silver Super as well as paper and plastic table covers in pink and blue.

Star Confetti, silver circular and star-patterned Balloons hung down the ceiling. Twinkle Lights around party room gave a romantic glow. Cloud-Patterned Gossamer was used on walls and columns.

Glass slippers filled with candy, silver confetti and flowers were kept as table centerpieces, few tables had cute small castles along with candles as the center piece.

On both the corners of the room opposite to stairs were 2 Royal Carriages. Big castle clock was hung in center of the hall. Castle Confetti was sprinkled on each table for fairy tale touch.

Angel twinkle painting was hung on the middle column with a focus light on it

To my surprise Gyaanis had painted a few pumpkins white and sprinkle some gold glitter on them for a magical touch. They pasted a few pictures of me and Arohi around the pumpkins as a reminder of how we got to this special day together. I thanked them for the beautiful surprise. Everyone in the family were happy and thankfully everyone wore dresses according to the theme, none the less all guests followed the color combinations. I forced my mother and mother in law to wear evening gowns, father and father in law wore 3 piece suits.

Now I eagerly waited for my princess to come down and have a look at her palace and her empire. Priya had already taken her to 1ˢᵗ floor's bride room, entering from backdoor. She must have got Arohi ready by now and Arohi must be troubling her by asking too many questions.

Tiddi and Pajju bought 3 tiers cake on a decorated trolley with a small prince and princess showpiece on top of it as I demanded; they placed it at center of the room. Along with the cake we placed gift box and exploding card on the decorated trolley adding charm to it. I cannot wait anymore; I called up Priya and asked her to come along with Arohi.

Meanwhile everyone enjoyed drinks and starters being served by the staff of the palace. Something went wrong and darkness surrounded the room, I got nervous as all my preparations were at stake. I switched on my mobile's flash light and asked Nik and Pajju for their help to get this rectified as soon as possible. I called and scolded the manager of the palace, his arguments 'we have 2 backups for power failure' irritated me as none of them were working.

While I was in conversation with the manager, palace got illuminated again and spot light was on Arohi, she stood at the top of the stairs; everyone gaped at her as she came down the stairs, just like everyone gaped at Cinderella when she entered the ball room. She was looking no less beautiful then Cinderella. It was Gyaanis who switched off the lights to give Arohi a perfect surprise and to give me a mini heart attack and a perfect view of Arohi in her Princess dress. I skipped my heart beat looking at her. Dress fitted her as if it was designed just for her. Six layers of skirt occupied area nearby her as she walked.

I patted myself for making absolutely the right choice. I fell in love with her princess avatar too. She strode down the stairs with her eyes shining and her inner child skipping along in her mind. If she weren't already 24 she'd skip too. She never expected something like this; I can make that out from her expressions. Excitement poured out from her like sunshine through fine white linen; she glowed from inside out. The smile that cracked her face hadn't been seen for a long time.

I went near the stairs, bowed in front of her in my Prince dress, held her hand and bought her to the center stage, she was so happy that she barely had words to express or speak.

'I hope I made your one more dream come true. You are the Princess and this is your fairy tale' I said looking in her eyes.

She nodded, with her hands on her cheeks, she turned pink with happiness, and she blushed.

'Thank you, thank you for everything. I cannot express how happy I am' she said trying to express her feelings. She noticed little things arranged for her around her.

'No need to say anything, I can make that out from your face' I said pulling her cheeks

She blushed

'And now it is the time'

'Time for what?' She asked

I bent down on my one knee, bought out the box of ring and proposed her

I held her left hand in my right hand

'When I 1st met you I thought you are a girl full of attitude, we never had much interaction in college, I thought we will never meet after college got over and then you came back in my life. I got to know you better; you are the most innocent person I have ever met in my life. You have a heart of gold; you are delicate but strong enough to tackle the difficult situations in life. All your crazy demands are like duty for me that I have to fulfill anyhow. Slowly all your dreams became mine. I never thought I can fall madly in love with anyone but then it was you, how could I resist? Thanks for coming in my life my angel. I remember once Priya told me "RV this is real life not a romantic Bollywood Masala" But I think the entire situation that occurred with us was not less than a movie. You complete me. I am ready to face all the toughs of life just the condition is 'you holding my hand'. I am the richest person in the world if you are by my side. I love you.

Will you be my forever?'

She nodded

I made her wear the engagement ring. I stood up as by now my leg started to pain.

She felt pumped, excited, more alive than she had ever thought possible. She hugged me. I held her tight. It seems all the mundane worries of our life had been muted and all there was to know about, "was this moment." No worrying about the past, no anxiety about the future. We loved the moment we were in.

We realized others were beside us when they started clapping. She made me wear my engagement ring and we celebrated by cutting the cake. She thanked all of us for beautiful decorations, gifts and cards.

We thanked all the guests for their gracious presence and took blessings from our parents.

Pajju asked everyone to hold their partners and get ready for the ball dance. I held Arohi by her waist and she kept her hands on my shoulders. We were lost in each other's eyes, we communicated through eyes, as words fell short to describe our feelings. She closed her eyes, rested on my shoulder and we tapped on slow romantic music.

Everything is perfect, my life now is perfect. I thanked God for everything.

Priya came and congratulated us, she hugged Arohi. I hugged them both. Pajju, Tiddi, Nik, Neha, Aditi, Mini and Atul joined us too.

Finally!!! A group hug, with no member missing!!

'Congratulationsssssssssssssssssssssssssssssssssssssssssssssss Guys' Tiddi shouted

'Congratulationssssssssssssssssssss' everyone shouted in sync. We hugged and laughed

I love my group, we are friends for life, I wish everyone get friends like I have and I wish everyone gets a perfect life partner for themselves just like I got my Arohi.

I think theme of our engagement was not just "Fairy World"
It was more or less a "Happily Ever After".

Arohi

Nikunj (Nik)

Tarun (Tiddi)

Neha

Mini

Rajveer (RV)

Prateek (Pajju)

Priya

Atul

Aditi

Printed in the United States
By Bookmasters